# Web of Tangled Blood

GRAHAM HAMER

Best wishes
Graham

WEB OF TANGLED BLOOD



ISBN-13: 978-1973902560

ISBN-10: 1973902567

# DEDICATION

This book is dedicated to my wife

**Marie-Danielle**

Sixteen years ago, I dedicated my first book to her. Now, I dedicate the first of my 'French Collection' books to her too.

Without her encouragement and support, neither book would ever have been written.

ACKNOWLEDGEMENTS

Thank you to the real Florence who allowed me to 'borrow' her name, and who allowed me to model aspects of the apartment in the story on her own apartment in Paris. Little did she think she would find herself in an English-language book, twenty years after we first met in a multinational corporation's offices in The Netherlands. The company has since gone bust – but that was after Florence and I moved on. You see what happens when the real talent gets up and leaves?

To my regular readers, you will already know that two other people are closely involved in these books. Nadine Sgoura sharpens her editor's pencil and points out all my typos, grammatical errors and other gremlins that could spoil an otherwise flowing script

Then Bruno Cavellec flicks his inspiration switch and comes up with original and eye-catching covers that inevitably fit the plot so well.

Thanks to all of you. It's only through your help and generosity that 'Web of Tangle Blood' got into print.

# CONTENTS

The following books by Graham Hamer are also available or will be published shortly

**THE CHARACTERS COMPILATION**
**Chasing Paper –** Characters Compilation 1
**Walking on Water –** Characters Compilation 2
**Tommy Gee –** Characters Compilation 3
**The Zone –** Characters Compilation 4

**THE ISLAND CONNECTION**
**Under the Rock -** Island Connection 1
**Out of the Window -** Island Connection 2
**On Whom the Axe Falls -** Island Connection 3
**China in Her Hand -** Island Connection 4
**Devil's Helmet -** Island Connection 5
**The Vicar's Lot -** Island Connection 6
**Chicken Rock -** Island Connection 7
**The Platinum Pirate -** Island Connection 8
**Picasso's Secret –** Island Connection 9
**Travellers –** Island Connection 10
**Flint -** Island Connection 11

**THE FRENCH COLLECTION**
**Web of Tangled Blood –** French Collection 1
**Cenotaph for the Living -** French Collection 2
**Jasmine's Journey -** French Collection 3
**Taken on Face Value -** French Collection 4

**THE ODDBALL ODYSSEY**
**A Little Bit Odd –** Oddball Odyssey 1
**Odd Gets Even –** Oddball Odyssey 2
**A Little Bit Odder –** Oddball Odyssey 3

You can find out more about the author and his books at
**http://www.graham-hamer.com**

# FOURTEEN YEARS AGO

The army patrol walked cautiously towards the centre of Khewa, a rural Pushtun village in north-eastern Afghanistan. As they had been trained, one man walked on one side of the road, the next man walked on the other side. They were spaced unevenly, so the enemy couldn't estimate when the next man would appear. They knew the dangers and the risks but they were responding to intel that a Taliban unit had occupied the far end of the village. The Taliban were not to be underestimated. They may be, as the army parlance had it, rag heads, but they were armed rag heads and they were highly motivated rag heads. Their own lives didn't matter. In fact, it was a matter of pride to be martyred for the cause.

The patrol maintained total silence. In the moonlight, if they needed to communicate, they did so using only hand signals. Each man walked slowly and with caution, scanning the side streets, windows and rooftops against the night sky. Their nerves were as taut as fiddle strings as they waited for an IED – an improvised explosive device – to detonate, each one praying it wouldn't be them whose footstep detonated it. During the day, NATO forces ruled the skies. But it was late evening, and at night the Taliban ruled the whole area, kidnapping, beating and terrorising anyone who they thought might have access to some money.

Situated at the crossroads of Central and South Asia, the area had witnessed waves of migrating peoples and conquering armies over the centuries. Alexander the Great, Genghis Khan, and even the Buddha had passed through Khewa on their way to somewhere else. Nobody ever stayed there.

The residents of Khewa still did not have electricity or running water. They depended on stoves for heat and lanterns for light. If they were fortunate, a family had a generator for a few hours of power each day, but only if they could afford the fuel. Children fetched water from streams and wells that were often far from their homes.

The residents of rural villages such as Khewa had large extended families that lived in compounds behind high walls. The average family had eight children. Grandparents, uncles, aunts, and cousins shared the same house, which might only have three or four rooms. In daylight, the damage from the previous three generations of war was still apparent. Bombed-out buildings and homes were never going to be rebuilt. The single dirt road - what little was left of it - was filled with craters and holes from landmines.

In the centre of Khewa the road was lined with small wooden stalls. This was the market. Only the most basic goods were available. On market days, there would be several fruit stands and a butcher shop with slabs of fly-covered meat hanging in the open air. A few stalls sold everything from batteries to biscuits to shampoo. Once a week, the owners would ride their donkeys the sixteen miles to the city of Jalalabad to restock their provisions. A wealthy trader might have a camel. At night, the stalls were deserted. A few candles burned in the adobe dwellings, but most were in darkness. Things had not changed much in the last 100 years.

The silence was shattered by the crackle of automatic gunfire close by. The soldiers, already tense and edgy, dived for cover behind anything close at hand. They began to return fire, not knowing what they were firing at or in which direction to fire. All they had was urgent intel that a group of Taliban fighters were hiding in the village. Now, it seemed, they were under attack. One man sheltered behind the remains of a stone wall and began shooting. A ricochet hit one of his comrades in the leg. He would live. Another soldier dived behind a large oil drum that had long been abandoned. A third, the man at the back of the patrol, was less lucky. A short, dark man dressed in perahan wa tunban with a pakul on his head, grabbed him as he dodged behind the wall of a small house.

The soldier was tall and strong, but the short man had the advantage of surprise and a vicious pointed knife. The short man, who held his knife in a thrusting grip, used the soldier's weight and momentum to swing around so he stood behind him. In a single motion, he cupped his hand over the soldier's mouth, pulled up and back, and thrust the blade hard and fast into the man's back beside the spine in an upward motion. It pierced the soldier's lung which collapsed instantly. The lung was a large target and the short man had the advantage of leverage, allowing him to control the body as it slumped to the ground. The soldier began to suffocate. He couldn't react as the short man, keeping his hand over the other man's mouth, leaned down and whispered four words in his ear. It would give the man's death some meaning.

The attacker tugged the razor sharp knife out of the soldier's back and whipped it across his throat, slicing through the trachea which prevented him from screaming. It also severed the carotid artery stopping new oxygenated blood from reaching the brain. And it cut through the jugular vein that brought deoxygenated blood from the head back to the heart. It was gruesome but humane since unconsciousness came quickly, with death following shortly after. It was a typical Taliban method of dealing with the enemy – quick, quiet, and efficient.

The attacker wiped the blade on the soldier's tunic and replaced the knife in a leather sheath. He stood and placed a foot hard on the dying man's back until he bled out into the dust. The soldier's heart continued to pump squirting blood from the carotid artery until there wasn't enough to pump. Meanwhile the dying man was taking giant, gasping breaths through his severed wind pipe gargling blood and coughing. The sound was drowned out by the noise of the gunfire in the street as the army patrol shot at a target they still hadn't identified.

When the soldier's heart stopped beating, his attacker whistled once. A moment later, he was joined by a taller man with a flat pakul hat, baggy shalwar pantaloons and kameez shirt. Shots still rang out in the street as they strode away through the opium poppy fields and into the blackness. Nobody in the village saw anything. It was just another night of bloodshed in Afghanistan.

# CHAPTER ONE

Thursday presented Ken Stafford with two problems that were to change his life. The first problem came from one of his two partners in the bodyguard training business they ran on the Isle of Man.

Like Ken, Dinger Bell was ex-SAS. Ken was tall with pale skin, fair hair and blue eyes. Those who knew his past had often wondered how he had managed to go undetected when on missions in Middle Eastern countries. Dinger, on the other hand, was short and stocky and not given to long sentences. Dinger was partially deaf after a roadside bomb explosion. Like Sparky, the third of the three partners, Dinger had also been discharged from the army on medical grounds. But now, his hearing difficulties were insignificant compared to the news he was about to impart to Ken.

"Sign here," Dinger said, laying some papers on the table.

"What am I signing?" Ken asked, looking up to face Dinger, who had become adept at lip-reading, to augment his poor hearing.

"Share transfer."

Ken studied Dinger's weather-beaten features. Recently he'd been looking out of sorts and today his complexion was like day-old porridge. There were dark circles beneath his eyes. "What share transfer?" Ken asked.

"I'm giving you and Sparky my share of the business."

Ken dropped his pen back onto his desk. "You what? What's that all about, Dinger? Where are you off to?"

"I'm off to meet a few of our old mates."

"Whereabouts?"

"In hell, I would guess," Dinger said with a poignant chuckle. "I've got cancer, Ken."

There was a long pause.

"You can shut your mouth whenever you want," Dinger said. "It's like the bloody Mersey tunnel down there."

"You've got cancer?"

"That's what I said. Sorry to drop it on you so early in the day. I wasn't going to mention it yet, but it seems it's well advanced, so you need to be ready for it."

"Shit, Dinger, after all you've been through in Iraq, Afghanistan —"

"— and that brothel in Amsterdam!"

"Yeah, that too. After all that, you go get yourself a dose of cancer. What's the prognosis?"

"Somewhere between poor and bloody awful. I've got an embarrassment of cancer, Ken. The full

English. I doubt there is a morsel of offal not included. I have a trucker's gut-buster, gimpy, malevolent, meaty malignancy of cancer."

It was the longest sentence Ken had ever heard from his friend. "Doesn't sound good," he answered with typical Special Forces understatement. "How long?"

"Between three and six weeks they say."

"And there's no treatment?"

"Far too late for that. The pain's been getting pretty bad recently and I'm told the only reason I'm still alive is because I've always kept fit. Just like you and Sparky."

"Aw fuck!"

"That's what I said too."

"That's not bloody fair."

"I said that as well. No-one ever said life was fair, Ken."

"How long have you known?"

"About a week."

"What's the plan?"

"I'm going to take a few days off to go see my family and say my goodbyes and then come back here and wait for The Grim Reaper."

"Wouldn't you be better staying with your family around you, Dinger?"

"No, mate; we've never been that close. You and Sparky are the best family I've ever known." He paused. "Will you stay with me and make up something nice about me at the crematorium?"

"Of course I will. That's a no-brainer."

"Cheers mate. Sign that share transfer form then, and I'll be off."

"Off where?"

"I don't know. Go do a bit of target practice on the range maybe. Take my mind off things."

"Have you spoken to Sparky yet?"

"About ten minutes ago."

"What was his reaction?"

"Couldn't speak because he had a lump in his throat. Big girl wanted to hug me."

Ken laughed. "In that case, I shan't bother!" He signed the share transfers then watched from under a curtain of deep sadness as Dinger's back disappeared from sight into the hallway. He, Dinger and Sparky had been through more close scrapes than a barber's shop. To think that it would be cancer that scored the winning run was bloody unjust.

And then his second problem of the day made itself known when his phone rang. He picked up and said, "Three Way Training, Ken Stafford speaking. How can I help you?"

"Ken, it's Florence—"

# CHAPTER TWO

"I miss the old bugger already," Sparky said, supping the froth off his pint.

"Me too," Ken replied, perching on the bar stool next to his friend. "He didn't say a lot, but when he did, you listened because you knew it was important."

"Like a brother, Ken. Like a brother."

"And you always knew Dinger had your back when there was a bit of grief going down."

"Do you remember that scrap we had in Lebanon when Israel was ramping up the pressure on Hezbollah?" Sparky said.

"Near the Bekka Valley and Birdbrain Bottomley went AWOL and we didn't see him till it was all over?"

"Claimed the Israelis had cut him off, and he'd done his best to get back to us."

"But we all knew that was complete and utter bollocks."

"And when he finally showed up, Dinger landed one on him, straight on the chin. Put him on the floor for about five minutes. Remember?"

"Do I ever. Bottomley was going to stick him on a charge until we all reminded him that, as Rupert in charge, it was his job to support his men, not run away and hide."

"Aye, old Dinger was a character," Sparky said in a hushed voice. "We'll miss him."

"Even though we never knew much about him, did we?"

"That's how it is in Special Forces, mate. Lots of secrets. If you think about it, you're the same."

"What do you mean?" Ken asked.

"Well, you know quite a lot about me, but I don't know much about you. And you never did tell us about that little extra curricular job. What was that all about?"

"Do you need to know?"

"No."

"Does it matter?"

"I shouldn't think so. It cost you a couple of pints - that's all that matters!" Sparky took another sup of beer. "I'm curious, Ken. Did you always know you were destined for Special Forces?"

Ken laughed. "Three days into my basic training, I wasn't even certain I would see my way to the end of the six months."

"So what changed?"

"My attitude, I guess."

"How's that?"

"A drill sergeant whose voice could blister the paint on a nuclear submarine had a few discreet words in my ear one day. He left me in no doubt that if I didn't pull my socks up, I would find my feet sticking out of my arse while they were still attached to my legs."

"So he scared you into it?"

"In a way, yes. For a few weeks, I made a real effort, and then I started to find that things came naturally to me. By making the initial effort, I got into good physical shape for the first time in my life. I discovered that I had excellent hand-eye co-ordination and that I was a natural with a sniper rifle. Hand-to-hand combat was like second nature to me. I got top grades on all the psych and intelligence tests."

"And then what?"

"I applied for Special Forces and, like you, I got through the selection process at Hereford."

"So that was it then?"

"That's as much as you need to know, except for one thing."

Sparky questioned him with a raised eyebrow.

"You need to know that I'm going to bugger off to Paris for a little while."

"What, Paris France? That place where there are lots of girls willing to take their clothes off?"

"That's the one."

"How long? I can handle everything myself until the next training group arrives."

"I don't know, Sparky. It might only be a couple of days, it might be a couple of weeks."

"Are you going to tell me why?"

"Yeah, I think I owe you that since you'll be holding the fort for a while."

Sparky waited a few beats. "Go on then."

"Did you know I was married once?"

Sparky coughed into his beer, spraying Ken in the process. Ken laughed as he wiped the front of his suit. "It's not that unusual you know. People do get married sometimes."

"Yeah but you've never even hinted at it."

"It was all over a long time ago. Her name was Florence. She was French. I was twenty-three when we got married and she was only nineteen. After a year or so, we had a baby boy called Tristan. Lovely little kid. Born one month premature, but he was a strong little lad. It sort of bound Florence and me together even tighter than before, and we were pretty tight already."

"So what happened? What went wrong?"

"What happened was that some evil shite snatched Tristan when he was three years old."

"Kidnap?"

"There were no demands for money if that's what you mean. We didn't have any anyway. Our son disappeared, end of story. There was a big manhunt round Hereford that went on for quite a while. We both appeared on TV begging for them to give Tristan back to us, but they never did. Crimewatch had a go at it, but still nothing. Not a single sighting of anything unusual. In the end the police gave up since there were no fresh clues. The final assumption was that some filthy paedophile had taken him, used him, and disposed of his body. It happens more often than you think."

"Christ, Ken, I never suspected."

"You wouldn't, would you? It's not your average family history. Anyway, I buried myself in army life and Florence yearned to be home in France near her family. So after a while, we split. There was a lot of stress and tension and both of us bottled up our feelings. We were only youngsters at the time. So Florence went back to France and reverted to her maiden name. Now, she owns and runs a business, but I don't know what it is. We seldom get in contact."

"And is that why you're going over to Paris?"

"Yes. Florence rang me a few weeks ago and wanted me to go over there straight away. I told her that I was staying here to see Dinger through to the end. But now he's gone, I feel an obligation to go and see her."

"Do you want to tell me why?"

"Since I'm going to be leaving you on your own, I guess I ought to." Ken paused a moment. "Florence thinks she has seen Tristan, our son, and she's desperate for me to check it out. She wants me to eyeball the lad and offer my opinion before she tries to trace where he's living and what happened."

"Hang on, he'd be —"

"Nineteen, Sparky, before you try doing the maths and run out of fingers."

"So what makes her think the person she has seen is your son?"

"She just has a 'maternal' feeling about it. One of

these motherly instinct things. The youth she has seen is tall with fair hair and both of us are tall with fair hair. As a child, Tristan inherited the same hair colouring. She also heard one of his friends call him Tristan. And there was some slight discoloration of the skin near his hair line where a strawberry mark had been when he was a baby."

"I thought those things stayed for life."

"Not necessarily. Its proper name is a strawberry haemangioma. They're actually small blood vessels packed tight together. Tristan didn't have one at birth. It developed during his first few weeks. They usually grow at a rapid rate, remain a fixed size, and then subside. In most cases, strawberry haemangioma disappear by the time a child is ten years old. Some slight discoloration or puckering of the skin can remain at the site of the haemangioma. And that's what Florence thinks she has seen."

"Sounds far-fetched but just inside the realms of possibility."

"She also said that his likeness to me is very obvious."

Sparky's eyes twinkled. "What? Pensioned out of the army with one leg shorter than the other and ended up on a rock in the middle of the Irish Sea?"

"Hey, you can talk. You me and Dinger— well, you and me now, are both in the same boat. Anyway, they fixed the leg with surgery. They never did get that bit of shrapnel out of your neck."

"Yeah, I know. I was just taking the piss! Poor little bugger looking like you. It must do his head in when he looks in the mirror for a shave."

Ken smiled. "Do you know, I never thought of that. My son, if he is alive, will be shaving every day by now."

"You don't think it's him then?"

"It's too coincidental and, as you know, I'm not a great believer in coincidence."

"But you're going over anyway?"

"I am, Sparky. Florence rang me the same day that Dinger told me he didn't have long to live. I told her I wasn't going until Dinger died. She got herself all wound up over it and has been ringing me almost every day since. Best I go and clear the air."

"In that case you'd better buy me another pint first."

# CHAPTER THREE

Ken's journey from Charles de Gaulle Airport in the North-East of Paris into the centre of the city was uneventful. Some of the journey was above ground, some was underground. He stepped out of the RER train underneath the mighty Arc de Triomphe and joined the hundreds of other commuters who rode the stacks of elevators to the main concourse. He knew the station well enough to take the exit marked Avenue Marceau with hardly a glance at the overhead signs. Moments later, he emerged onto the wide footpath that circumnavigated Place de l'Étoile. This was the mad, bad roundabout that circled the Arc de Triomphe with six lanes of battle-scarred vehicles joisting for position without slowing. Ken smiled. It was nice to be back.

The sun was shining, the trees were in leaf, the sky was blue and all was well with the world. Or was it? He and Florence had split up sixteen years ago and he'd not seen her for over twelve years. But, since she first rang him several weeks ago, her phone calls had become more and more persistent, with hints of anger and frustration in her voice. When Ken rang her to say he was coming over, he thought he heard her crying on the other end of the phone, but he made no comment about it.

Ken wasn't one to show emotion. You had to toughen up when you saw your mates with the tops of their heads blown off by some towel-head on a mission from God. You had to deal with it and move on. The only concessions he had ever made to his emotions were when he had a rag-head in his sights, squeezed the trigger, and watched the bloody results through the telescopic sights. Then he would think, 'That's for McGurk,' or 'That's for Stan the Man'. It didn't bring his mates back, but it moved them out of the compartment in his brain marked 'Unfinished Business' into the compartment marked 'Sorted'.

For many years, thoughts of Florence had remained locked in a compartment marked 'The Past'. Until now. Now she had poked and prodded and it wasn't a compartment he had particularly wanted to reopen.

Working clockwise, Avenue Marceau was the next road leading off Place de l'Étoile after Avenue des Champs-Élysées. Ken strolled its leafy footpath and gazed up at the six and seven storey buildings with their Belle Époque architecture. The thought crossed his mind that if Florence was now living here, she must be wealthy. These places didn't come cheap.

He paused to peer into the window of an upmarket real estate agent. He discovered that even average size apartments here were selling for between two and three million euros. Rented apartments, even small ones, cost more each year than he earned. He whistled to himself and carried on walking, glancing at the numbers as he went.

He stopped when he reached the right building and pulled a scrap of paper from his pocket. As was typical in Paris, a four metre wide pair of high wooden doors guarded the entrance to either a private courtyard behind or a parking area for the owners. Set into one of the huge doors was a small wicket door for anyone on foot. Ken tapped the code written on the paper into the vigik and the lock on the wicket door buzzed. He pushed it open and stepped inside, finding himself, as expected, in an open area underneath the first floor apartment.

Ahead of him, two cars, a big Mercedes and an even bigger Mercedes were parked in the cobbled courtyard. Four empty spaces remained. He guessed that meant there were six apartments. A quick mental calculation and he realised that these were seriously large living spaces. More often nowadays, developers split these bigger buildings into two or more apartments on each floor. Anything up to fourteen apartments for a building of this size.

Ken looked at the bell pushes on the wall to his right, which told him he was wrong about the number of apartments. The list was only five names long. He pressed the one marked 'F de Nussac' and waited. A moment later a voice asked, "Oui?"

"C'est moi, Ken."

"Oh. Ken, you made it."

"Did you have any doubts?"

Florence didn't respond other than to say "First floor." Then the lock buzzed and Ken pushed his way into a large, bright foyer with a marble floor. To his right was a window onto the street he had just left. To his left were two doors. He tried the first and found it locked. He tried the second and saw it led onto a wide spiral staircase. Next to the two doors was a lift. He opted for the lift and chose button 1.

When the lift stopped, the door glided back and Ken stepped into a hallway with an old parquet floor. Two other doors led into the same hallway. It was clear that one was the one off the stairs next to the lift. The other door was open, and the air was warm and rich with the aroma of fresh baguettes. There was no other smell like it, redolent of yeast and dough and cereal, like a farmhouse kitchen. He checked his watch as his stomach rumbled. It was 1:45pm and he'd not eaten since a hurried breakfast before leaving home in time to catch a 7:00am flight off the island.

Florence's voice called out from far away, "Come on in Ken. The door's open."

He smiled. She was still capable of stating the obvious.

Ken stepped into Florence's lounge. Here the aromas of the French bakery in the air were more delicious than any single flavour. Somehow the scents captured everything good in Ken's memories of France - a country he had visited often. And in the background, gentle hints of filter coffee and Danish pastries. The blend was perfection. The smell of cooking food, he thought, was what a serenade is to the ears of a musician - a harmony of everything that is good.

He dropped his overnight bag on the floor and cast his eyes round the room. His mouth fell open. The living room was vast, and spanned at least half of the entire frontage of the building. There were tall floor-to-ceiling windows overlooking the boulevard below. Each of them had a narrow Juliet balcony - false railings outside, reaching to the floor. When the windows were open they gave the appearance of a real balcony. Equally tall windows overlooked the interior courtyard behind. So the room was not only wide, it also occupied the full depth of the building.

Ken drew a deep breath. Large though the lounge was, a generous proportion of it was occupied by a staircase leading to the floor above. It was a wide, curving stone staircase with ornate black metal balusters and a highly polished dark mahogany handrail. A cluster of comfy chairs and sofas occupied the space near the front windows. It stopped the room from feeling vacuous or giving the impression of too much space.

Dividing the lounge was a wall with wide glazed double doors that lay open. The opening gave an uninterrupted view into the dining room beyond. Ken stepped to the doors and gasped again when he saw the long, polished dining table surrounded by a dozen or more matching chairs. Louis XIV, he thought. His brain came to a dead stop as he tried to figure it out. If her apartment was more or less the width and depth of the building and covered two storeys it had to be close to 5,000 square feet - about 550 square metres. Beyond the dining table he could make out modern kitchen units through an open door. Florence stepped out of the doorway and into a ray of sun. She carried an aura about her like the sea carries a summer haze.

Her chestnut blonde hair, although tied back in a ponytail, seemed to shimmer down her back in the light. It was like liquid sunshine against a face so fair-skinned as to be striking. Florence had been somewhat bohemian when they were first married. As a self-employed translator, she could afford not to conform. Her fair hair had been long and sinuous with streaks of electric indigo running through it. Amethyst was her birthstone and purple was her colour of choice. She often wore a purple flowing skirt that touched the ground. Open-toed sandals, even in the harshest weather, would kick out from under the fabric when she walked. With her mad hair and nose piercing, some people half expected her to get out a guitar and start singing 'Kumbaya'. Not that she ever did.

Now, as she was approaching forty, her hair was its natural blonde with no hints of false colours. She had a wide, generous face, a chiselled chin, and long dimples in both cheeks. Her smile was attractive; her laugh, contagious. Gone was the flowing skirt. Now, she wore a tailored blazer and skirt in a matching blue fabric. Her white silk shirt neither exaggerated nor hid her curvaceous breasts, small waist, and wide hips. It just said 'style' with a capital 'S'.

She smiled in welcome and strode across the dining room to greet Ken. And then she stopped, uncertain whether to hug him, kiss him or shake hands. They'd bathed together, slept together, and made love together at one time. She looked into his eyes that were blue but had flecks of grey which caught the light like quartz shot through with granite. In the end, she air-kissed him on both cheeks, closed the apartment door that he had left open, and invited him to sit down.

"I don't suppose you've eaten, Ken, have you?"

He shook his head.

"Tu veux une assiette de charcuterie?" she asked.

"Cold meats and baguette will do me just fine. Any Rocamadour going begging?"

"I got some in for you. You always did have a soft spot for that Cabecou cheese. And I suppose a nice red wine would help?"

Ken laughed. "You've not forgotten, have you?"

A look of regret flashed across Florence's face but she regained her smile and said, "No, Ken, I've not forgotten. Sit down."

"Visit to le petit coin first if it's okay."

Florence pointed to a door adjacent to the one he had entered by. "There's a toilet there, to save you going upstairs." She left for the kitchen and came back a moment later, with two glasses of red wine.

Ken reappeared in the living room and Florence offered him his glass. "It's a 1986 Chateau Chauvin," she said.

Ken sat down, took the wine from her, and held it under his nose for a moment, savouring its rich bouquet.

"It's quite nice actually," Florence added, taking the armchair opposite him.

"Bloody well should be if its over thirty years old. Expensive too, I imagine."

"Pffft. Doesn't matter."

Ken looked up at her but said nothing.

"Santé," Florence said, leaning forward so they could touch glasses.

"Santé," Ken replied taking a sip of the wine. "Oh man," he said after an appreciative pause, "That's nectar, Florence. Where did you get it?"

"I bought one hundred bottles seven or eight years ago. They're at their prime right now. Another few years and they will begin to Maderise."

Ken knew enough about wines to know that Maderisation was when a wine became too old, turned tawny and developed an acetic smell. It gave even a good wine a dull, flabby, and generally unpleasant palate. But just before it began to turn, the wine was at its best; rich and fruity with a heady aroma. And this wine was at its best.

He took another sip and allowed it to wash round his palate. "That is amazing, Florence. And you say you bought one hundred bottles? How long's it going to take you to get through a hundred bottles?"

Florence laughed. "It's what I do, Ken. My main business is dealing in top end French wines. I provide quality aged wines to the best restaurants in France. I'm just breaking into the London market too."

"Jeez, you never told me you were doing this sort of stuff."

The look of regret flashed again across her face again. "You never asked, Ken. We've only spoken half a dozen times in the past sixteen years."

He glanced at her, unable and unwilling to keep his eyes off her body. It was more full and mature than when they were together sixteen years earlier. A delicate gold chain holding a solitaire diamond protected her neck. The vision of Florence wearing just the diamond and nothing else jumped into his head unbidden. He pushed it aside. It wasn't why he was here. "I didn't call you because I wasn't sure there was much to say. We went our own separate ways and now we've become two different people than we were then."

"You still compartmentalize, don't you." Florence said. It was a statement, not a question.

"Yes, I guess I do. I find it's easier that way. I try not to let emotions get in the way."

"I know."

Ken glanced at her, but without reproach. He cast his eyes round the room. "Tell me about this apartment," he said, happy to change the subject. "There's trickery afoot here because it was never built like this."

Florence laughed and her body relaxed. "You're right, it wasn't. I had all the internal walls removed."

"But it doesn't look as though anyone has disturbed those big ornate cornices or that gorgeous ceiling. And no wall has ever broken up those ceiling mouldings. The mouldings and insets are exactly as you see them in the châteaux and fine houses of the same period. Same for the cornices. Combination dogtooth and cast crown I think they call them." Ken looked further, craning his neck. "And I don't suppose that bloody great stone staircase was there to begin with. Yet it's exactly as you'd expect for a building of this style and this age. The whole apartment is an optical illusion. It looks like you've opened it up into an enormous living space. Is the upstairs the same size?"

"Too many questions all at once," Florence said. "I bought the whole building, gutted it and started again."

"The whole building? That must have cost a bomb."

"Straight to the point as always, Ken. Yes, it cost quite a lot and the renovations cost even more. But I sold the other apartments at a good price, so this one didn't actually cost me that much. Those big cornices are new. We took wax moulds of the originals and recast them. Same for the ceiling mouldings. And before you ask, we exactly copied all the doors and frames from what had been here when I bought the building. The staircase is an original. I just had it rebuild where I wanted it. We even salvaged the parquet floors from the building, cleaned and sanded them piece by piece, and re-laid them in their original herringbone pattern. Or à bâtons rompus as we say over here."

"I'm impressed," Ken said.

Florence gave a small nod of her head. "Thank you. But in fact, it's also what I do nowadays. As well as the wine, I have another business in real estate. We buy older buildings, give them a complete make-over and sell them on for a profit."

"Jeez, Florence, anything else I should know about your business activities?"

She chuckled. "Just a little one. We're in the throes of setting up retail outlets in Britain called "Just France". We sell cheeses, wine, regional speciality foods, foie gras and so on. We've got over twenty retail outlets set up in the bigger cities. We'll see how it goes for a year or two before we make a decision whether we expand into the smaller towns."

Ken shook his head. "My, my, you have been a busy

lady haven't you?"

"I had nothing better to do with my life Ken. Shall we eat?"

"In a moment, let me just take this room in first. It's huge, yet it's intimate. How did you do that?"

"By creating small spaces within a larger one. It's a regular interior designer's trick. Arranging the chairs in squares or, over there, in a semi-circle round the fireplace."

Ken half-turned in his seat. "Oh bloody hell, I'd not even noticed that fireplace. It's beautiful. That mirror over is gorgeous."

Florence beamed.

"I'm amazed, Florence," Ken said, gazing around the room. "And I won't insult you by suggesting the furniture is reproduction. I suspect most of it is Louis XIV. Nothing but the best, eh?"

"It's not like that at all. It's a question of leaving something behind for a future generation. We were lucky that, four or five generations ago, the builders of these homes had a free hand to use only the best quality craftsmanship and materials. I believe I owe it to a future generation to hand them something the same or better. Meanwhile, I get huge enjoyment from my surroundings. Come on, let's eat."

Ken stood and, as they passed through the wide double doors into the dining room, he couldn't resist diverting to the windows that overlooked the boulevard below. After looking out at the vista for a moment, he was about to turn back but stopped to touch a bow-fronted chest of drawers that shone in the sunlight. "Louis XIV?" he asked.

"No, a bit later," Florence said. "It's actually Louis XV."

Ken stood back and admired the exceptional deep yellow ochre of the wood and patina. The top was coloured marble and the six drawers retained their original period gilt bronze mounts. The corners of the chest each had matching gilt bronze mounts leading down to the short legs. "Go on then," he said. "Shock me. That must be €15,000 if it's a penny."

Florence chuckled. "It's not a question of money, Ken. It's a question of what pleases me."

"Humour me, Florence. Was it more than €15,000 or less?"

"No comment."

"So come on, stop being so secretive."

Florence sighed. "If you must know, I paid €49,500 for it."

"How much? €49,500 for a chest of drawers? What's wrong with Ikea?"

"It's an investment, Ken.

"And the table and chairs over there?"

"Louis XIV and don't ask the price. But they're not just for looking at, Ken. They get used, you know. Come on, let's eat."

"On your Louis XIV table?"

"No, follow me. You can finish exploring the apartment later."

Florence led Ken through the dining room to the kitchen and again Ken stood in the doorway with mouth wide open. The room was about half the size of the dining space, which made it a big kitchen by any standards. Ken had seen many restaurant kitchens much smaller than this.

"Close your mouth," Florence said. "It's a handmade kitchen built to commercial standards. For business reasons, I often entertain and then I hand the kitchen over to a hired chef or a hired caterer for the evening and we eat on the big dining table out there. It can seat up to twenty at a push." She led him past the polished kitchen units to the far end of the room where she had laid a regular kitchen table for two. Ken was still staring at the kitchen layout.

Florence said, "There's a smaller separate kitchen at this end of the room. Americans call them butler's pantries. People use them when catering large events as a secondary kitchen, to help handle the load of a large party. But also people like me use them as a small kitchen for themselves. It's handy when there are just two or three people and I don't want to dirty the larger kitchen."

Ken looked where Florence was waving her hand. "But even the butler's pantry is so well equipped. I can't imagine you install to these standards in the apartments you rebuild to sell?"

"I do. When potential buyers see a kitchen that has expensive products, they assume that the rest of the house or apartment is to equal standards. They are correct. At the prices the company sells for, our clients are selecting exotic-looking stone for their countertops and choosing special flooring. Carrera marble is still beautiful, but people see it everywhere, so they're looking for more exquisite marbles. Marbles that have a little more colour and a little more drama and are a bit more daring. Our clients are more interested in quality materials than cappuccino makers. As people re-do their kitchens, they learn that sometimes gadgets are just gadgets."

She clicked her fingers twice and a hanging globe light over the table illuminated. "But even I like the occasional gadget!"

Ken smiled. "I thought France was in the grip of a long term recession."

"It is, but there is always money in a city like Paris. If I can't attract local buyers, the Chinese are buying everything of quality they can get their hands on at the moment."

Ken pulled back a dining chair for her and then sat in front of the other table setting. "Florence, I am astounded at what you've achieved. My admiration knows no bounds. It must have all come at a hell of a price though. I mean a price in your time and social life."

Florence regarded him with deep sadness in her eyes. "Look, Ken, I'm not going to keep saying it, and I know it was sixteen years ago, but Tristan's disappearance, then us splitting up, hurt. It hurt both of us." She took a deep breath and withheld the sigh that threatened to escape. It was clear in her face and her mannerisms that the anxiety that had lain dormant all those years, having now been stirred again, stretched its hand, and gripped her stomach.

She continued, "The counsellor I started seeing

when Tristan disappeared told me that the pain would lessen over time. She told me that I would never feel his loss as much as I did during those first dark days. She lied to me. Then, when I came back to France another shrink told me that I would get over our break-up in time. He lied too." She paused, took a deep breath and said, "Okay, now that I've killed the elephant in the room do you want butter. I never think to use it myself."

"Not with fresh baguette, charcuterie and Cabecou. I'm good thanks." Ken offered her the selection of deli meats and she took some rillettes, a form of pâté that Ken's father had always referred to as pork cheese. Ken helped himself to saucisson, a slice of Jambon de Bayonne, and he too took some rillettes to load onto his baguette. He saved the Cabecou cheese until the end.

Florence nodded towards the wine bottle. Ken reached out and replenished their glasses. They were already falling back into the non-verbal communication shared by many married couples.

Ken munched his food for a moment then said, "Since you have killed the elephant and we are free to talk about Tristan and our break-up, what I was trying to say a moment ago was that I admire what you have achieved. You have an inner strength I never knew was there."

Florence grunted. "You never know how strong you are until being strong is your only choice. Let's get off me. Let's get onto Tristan." She checked her watch. "By the time we've eaten, it's going to be too late to try and see him today. I've had a private detective keeping an eye on him since I first spotted him. When we've eaten, I'll show you the photos, though there is no substitute for actually seeing him in the flesh. He has regular habits regarding his lessons."

"You say he's studying languages at Paris-Sorbonne University?"

"Like mother like son, eh?"

"And you said on the phone that he doesn't use the regular student accommodation though."

"Finding accommodation in Paris and the surrounding areas is not simple, Ken. But it is not impossible. The Sorbonne has agreements and partnerships with several institutions in Paris but Tristan— "

"The young man you think is Tristan— "

"Yes, okay, the young man I think is Tristan, lives in a poor area in the east of Paris."

"Why do you think that is?"

"Money, I would guess. Even student accommodation has a price. So maybe he's obliged to share somewhere less agreeable."

"And where was it where you first saw him?"

"In the Latin Quarter, not far from The Sorbonne. I'd gone there to look over a property that had come on the market. I blinked, and there he was with a group of friends."

"What did you do?"

"I made a real fool of myself."

"Go on."

"When I saw him, I lost the plot completely. I was

so sure it was him. I ran across the road shouting, 'Tristan, Tristan, wait!'. I almost launched myself at him and his friends had to pull me away. Tristan looked at me like I was something out of a horror movie and backed away, leaving me looking like the village idiot. Then just as they turned to go round the corner, still looking back at me, I heard one of his friends ask him how the crazy woman knew his name. I couldn't move. It was like the earth had just tilted on its axis. It's the only way I can explain how I felt."

Ken nodded and added a little more wine to both glasses.

"I felt a bit like I did when Tristan disappeared," Florence whispered.

"How do you mean?"

"I felt impotent. When we lost Tristan, my life became one long wait. I've never felt more inadequate in my life. You and the police wouldn't let me help in the search. You said I needed to stay at home in case anybody rang after the television appeals. But I knew all along the real reason was that you were worried in case I broke down if you found something awful."

"And would you?"

"Of course I would, but I hated just sitting there waiting and not being able to do anything. That's how I've been feeling ever since I saw Tristan a few weeks ago. It's why I was so adamant that you needed to come over and see him for yourself."

Ken touched the back of her hand. "It's okay. I understand."

"Do you, Ken? Do you really understand? Years ago, when they stopped looking for our beautiful little boy and more or less gave up, you processed what had happened, put it into one of those boxes in your head, then shut the door and got on with your life in the army. I wasn't able to do that. I had no life to get on with. That's why I came back to France and constructed a new life. But it's a life without the son I loved and the husband I loved."

Ken rested his cutlery on the plate and took a deep breath. Florence may have killed one elephant in the room, but it was only a baby compared to the big bad beast that still stood in the corner. He calmed his impetuosity and decided that now was not the best time. He'd only been here a little over half an hour. But he knew they would have to discuss the subject soon. He had it in his 'Unfinished Business' box for the moment, but he needed to move it into 'Sorted' along with all the other issues in his life that he had squared away.

# CHAPTER FOUR

The heat of the sun had died a little as Florence and Ken set off for Montmartre, the highest point in Paris. Florence had suggested they get out of the apartment for an hour for some fresh air. "Clear the fug of wine," she had said as she put the empty bottle into the bin for glass recycling.

Montmartre was like a village within a city and, at the beginning of the twentieth century, many well-known artists had studios or worked in or around the village. People like Salvador Dalí, Modigliani, Monet, Toulouse-Lautrec, Mondrian, Picasso, and Vincent van Gogh. Little wonder that it had become a magnet for today's 'bobos' - bourgeois bohemians. These were the caviar socialists who wanted to be seen to 'feel' the hardships of the working classes. They could never pull it off, of course, because everybody knew they were today's affluent yuppies. You had to be, to be able to afford to live in the Montmartre 'village'.

Despite it being a tourist trap, there was a certain welcoming atmosphere to Montmartre. It didn't take long to get there in Florence's red Mini

Cabriolet. She found a parking spot at the foot of the hill and dived into it before anybody else could grab it. Then they took the funiculaire, the little cable railway, up the steep slope to the top. Facing them was the white basilica of the Sacré Cœur. It was an ornate building which, in style, would have been more suited to Red Square in Moscow. It was a building that Florence disliked, nicknaming it 'The Wedding Cake'. So she turned her back to it and stood at the top of the steps, staring out over Paris.

"I love the view from up here," she said. "It's like you can see Paris with its pants down."

"You like seeing things with their pants down don't you?" Ken said, smiling.

Florence huffed and shielded her eyes from the sun, which was just beginning its long downward trajectory in the West. The water on the river Seine looked as though it was stationary from up here. The late afternoon sun stretched its sparkly fingers across the long, twisting ribbon of water with promises of more good weather to come. A good day for friends, wine and lunches on the terraces of the brasseries.

Standing behind her, Ken rested his hands on her shoulders. He lowered his head so his line of sight was level with hers. Their cheeks touched. Florence was aware of their closeness and found it difficult to concentrate. She pointed to the Eiffel Tower but was thinking that, if she leaned back, her head would be in the crook of his shoulder.

Ken continued to point out various landmarks, seemingly oblivious to the intimacy of their bodies. "If you look this way," he said, leaning in and turning her body, "you can see that bloody awful

Pompidou Centre. And over there, there's Montparnasse Tower; another monstrosity that blights Paris. But when you block those out of your mind and take in the whole vista, you've got to admit that Baron Haussmann made a damn good job of redesigning and rebuilding the city."

For several minutes, they stood together admiring the view, saying nothing. Florence was enjoying being in such close proximity to Ken, who had one hand raised to shield his eyes from the startling reflection of the sun. The last time they had been so intimately connected was the day before Tristan had disappeared.

As Florence turned to face him, Ken took a small step back as if to distance himself from her. "Shall we grab a coffee?" he asked, as if realising that he had broken his own self-defined personal space. "As I remember there are loads of cafes in the streets behind the church."

She nodded and followed as Ken marched off without her.

In less than five minutes, they were sitting outside a small café that bordered Place du Tertre. It was a small square that most Parisians felt was the single most touristic spot in the capital. Artists' easels choked the street and pavements. Most displayed prints of the city. Here and there were a few genuine artists, painting scenes they had painted a hundred times before for tourists who had more money than sense.

Florence ordered un café, an espresso in any other country, and Ken ordered une noisette, an espresso with just a tiny splash of milk. As they waited for the coffee, they enjoyed the sunshine and watching the tourists flow past. After a while, Florence asked, "What was the appeal of The Isle of Man, Ken? How did you end up over there?"

"You ask a lot of questions, don't you?" he said.

"I've hardly asked you anything yet. Anyway, I was just curious."

"I needed a change from Hereford, I suppose. And I had a past that needed to stay in the past."

"Like what?"

Ken held her gaze for a moment before speaking. "Like what happened to us."

"You mean us splitting up?"

"Yes, I mean us splitting up. We had some good times, Florence, and I er— I thought a lot of you."

Florence touched the back of his hand with her finger. "You're right. It was good to begin with, but when Tristan disappeared, you found some sort of support from the banter of the guys in the regiment and by getting engrossed in your work."

Ken sighed. "I can see that now. It just wasn't obvious then. But there was other stuff too, as you know."

The big elephant was back.

"I still want to go back to how it was," Florence said. "I want things to be exactly the same as they were before Tristan disappeared."

Ken took a deep breath. He looked around at the tourists and for a moment it didn't seem as though he planned answering. Finally he settled his eyes on Florence and said, "I don't get the impression that you've had your life on hold for the last sixteen years, Florence. You seem to have done well for yourself. I'm pleased for you."

"I have, but remember Ken, I was seventeen when I met you, nineteen when we got married, twenty-one when Tristan was born, twenty-four when he disappeared, and twenty-five when I came back to France. It's only in the last fifteen years that I've had a chance to find out what else I can do apart from being a housewife and a mother.

When we were together with Tristan, though I did some part-time translation work, my life revolved around my duties of husband care and child care. I used to dream what it would be like to have a career where people respected me instead of taking me for granted. To have some space of my own where I could retreat when I'd had enough of the world. Don't get me wrong, those thoughts didn't define me. They were always fleeting and I would dismiss them. I used to tuck them away deep in my mind where they wouldn't bother me.

I knew how lucky I was to have a husband who loved me, even though he wasn't always there. And I had a healthy, beautiful little boy who filled those gaps. I'm thirty-nine now, fast approaching forty, and I have three successful businesses. It doesn't mean that I don't miss what we once had."

"What we had until Jean-Luc." Ken said. He couldn't help himself. He knew that saying it would hurt her, but maybe that's what he needed to do after all this time. It was out in the open at last. The elephant that they had avoided talking about for so long.

Razor sharp weasel teeth took up residence in

Florence's stomach and there was no room for anything else. "As usual, you've got straight to the point in your no-nonsense fashion."

"I don't know any other way," Ken said. "I am who I am and I know I can be blunt, but at least you know that you'll always get the truth from me."

"I guess I deserved that," Florence said. She gulped, took a deep breath, and carried on. "I've never told you, but I actually married Jean-Luc before I met you."

"You what?"

Florence snorted. "I was six at the time and we got married in the school playground. Little Louis Lasne officiated. He had bottle glass spectacles and suffered from a debilitating stammer. It took the whole of playtime and we didn't even get to the 'I do' part."

"So why did you choose him as your celebrant?" Ken asked with a short-lived smile.

"Because he was an altar boy in the local church, so he was the closest thing we had to a priest."

Ken turned serious again. "The playground antics didn't have to follow into adult life, Florence. I was sure I was in love with a girl called Celia Corris when I was eleven. But I've never seen her since and, though I often wonder what became of her, I've never felt the need to follow up on those thoughts."

"Neither of us went looking for each other, Ken. Jean-Luc was in Britain as part of an elite liaison team between the French and British Special Forces. I wasn't looking for anybody. I bumped into him in the Tesco supermarket in Hereford."

"And had an affair."

"Yes, Ken, we had a bloody affair." Florence wiped at her eye. "For what it's worth, guilt was beginning to eat me up well before Jean-Luc went back to France. The affair had ended a long time before that, but the guilt stayed with me. Starting that affair and imagining that you wouldn't get hurt was the worst decision of my life. I shall regret it to the day I die. But I can't turn back the clock."

Ken nodded. "You and I could still have been together if it wasn't for Jean-Luc."

"It takes two to tango, Ken. I was just as guilty as him. More so, because he wasn't married and I was." A large tear rolled down one cheek. She wiped it away with the back of her hand. "God, I hate it that my default emotional reaction is crying. I wish I could just shout or scream or punch something to get it out of my system."

Ken said, "You know I compartmentalize to deal with stressful situations. When I found out about Jean-Luc, I shut it away and buried myself in my job. To this day, I try not to think too much about the fact that the woman I loved had had an affair. We'd only been married a year, God damn it."

Florence looked down at the cobbles between her feet and didn't speak for awhile. When the silence became oppressive, Ken asked, "Do you want another coffee?"

Florence was grateful for the opportunity to lower the old tensions and she beckoned to the waiter.

She watched Ken's features as the waiter bustled

around them, collecting their empty cups. Ken's fair hair had darkened a little over the years. It was still thick but grey was beginning to creep in at the sides, and the lines around his eyes seemed more pronounced. She could imagine his friends referring to him as 'distinguished' but Florence knew that was just a fancy word for 'getting older'. She reached across the table and took his hand in hers, questioning with her eyes whether they could at least be friends. Ken responded by gripping her hand in a gesture of solidarity. She welcomed his reassurance. But she knew it would be a long time before they could consign the matter to the dustbin of history. If ever.

While Florence was gaining assurance from Ken, she would have been less pleased had she seen the three men who were crouching in front of the door to the wine cellar below her apartment. As two of them poked and prodded at the lock, one kept watch at the glass entrance door, to warn of anyone coming in from the street.

# CHAPTER FIVE

The following morning, Ken rose early to go for a run. He usually tried to fit in one or two runs a week to maintain his fitness levels. It was even earlier than he thought since France was one hour ahead of Britain. There were few people on the sidewalks as he ran up the hill to the Arc de Triomphe. He swung left down Avenue Foch, one of France's most expensive and prestigious chunks of real estate. Halfway along, he turned left again and descended on the diagonal towards Trocadéro. He stopped when he reached the stone balcony of the Esplanade du Trocadéro. It overlooked Gustave Eiffel's famous tower; a structure he never tired of seeing. Ken paused a moment, jogging on the spot, to take in the vista of the tower and the River Seine below.

As he jogged, half thoughts chased around his mind like leaves caught in an eddy of wind. The past. The love. The disappointment. The hate. The revenge. The loss. Then he closed his eyes and it was like he had blocked out the wind. His thoughts began to settle again as he put everything back into its allocated compartment.

Traffic was beginning to build and Ken was sure that, before long, the exhaust fumes would make running almost impossible. One by one, various mayors of Paris had tried to limit the traffic, but whenever there was a high pressure system over the city, the smog would build and confine asthma sufferers to their homes. Ken turned and began his run back up the hill onto Avenue Marceau and towards Florence's apartment.

As his feet hit the pavement with rhythmic thuds, his mind was free to wander and he smiled at the thought of his 'gypsy' wife having become a successful business woman. He was glad that they had shot the big elephant in the room, but he knew that it was only wounded and that if they were ever going to kill it dead, there was more that they needed to discuss about Florence's affair. Things she knew. Things she didn't know.

He let himself in through the wicket door and used the magnetic pad that Florence had given him to access the building. Ignoring the lift, he ran up the stairs and let himself into the apartment. He glanced at his watch. It was not quite eight o'clock.

Stood in the kitchen doorway was Florence in a long multi-coloured kaftan robe. "Shower first, then bacon and scrambled eggs?"

Ken nodded, still drawing deep breaths into his lungs.

"Don't you have to do cooling down exercises or something after you've been running?" Florence asked.

"Should do — get bored — don't always bother."

Florence smiled. “Grab your shower then and I’ll get the coffee on the go.”

“Did you know — you can see— through that kaftan when— when the light’s behind you?” He laughed and ran up the wide marble staircase as Florence scampered back into the kitchen.

Half an hour later, dressed in jeans and sweatshirt, Ken sat at the table in the kitchen. Florence placed a glass of juice and a plate of scrambled eggs and bacon in front of him. “You not having any?” he asked.

“Sure I am; I’m not going to let you eat a cooked breakfast if I can’t join you.”

Ken smiled. When he had first met her, he had mistaken her for a New Age Vegan Hippy, but nothing was further from the truth. Mind you, Florence once admitted to him that if it wasn't for bacon she could have envisaged being a vegetarian. Even it's greasiness was perfection to her. Ken recalled, when they had been together, those rashers sizzling in their own fat under the grill, filling the kitchen with a smell that had her salivating in seconds. She used to butter the bread and wait with hungry eyes on the grill for the bacon to be crispy. It had to be crispy for Florence.

Ken admired her figure as she returned to the kitchen counter where she had prepared her own plate. He noticed that she had done nothing about the semi-transparent kaftan. As she passed by the window, the outline of her body was quite clear. Was that intentional, or did she not consider it important? Either way, he couldn’t help but admire her rounded form. She had a fuller figure than in her youth. It was a figure that showed maturity but few signs of ageing. For a woman approaching forty, she was in great shape.

"Where did you run?" Florence asked, breaking into his thoughts.

"Halfway down Avenue Foch then down to Trocadéro. It's nice to see the city again. It's been a few years since I was last here." Ken bit into the crispy bacon, cut thin French style. "Mmmmm that's good," he said as the bacon broke over his tongue, crisp to perfection and salty. After his run, the flavour was like a bomb in his mouth, exploding in all the right ways. It was the way Florence had always used to start their weekends, a sort of edible party to celebrate two days together. "So what are the plans today?" Ken asked.

"I have some work to do this morning, so I'll have to leave you to keep yourself amused. After lunch, we can go to The Sorbonne and see if we can spot Tristan. It seems he's a creature of habit and he leaves the university between 2:00pm and 2:30pm. He uses the same entrance each day. Unfortunately there are no convenient cafés in view of the entrance, so I have to hope I can find a place to park and we can sit in the car while we wait."

Ken nodded.

"What do you fancy for lunch?" Florence asked.

Ken laughed. "God, that is so French. Here we are just having breakfast and you want to know what we are going to eat for lunch."

Florence giggled, and Ken thought it sounded like the gentle clamour of a distant wind chime.

"I'm happy with what we had yesterday," he said.

"It's a long time since I had a plate of cold meats like that."

"You know what we call that in French, don't you?"

"I've forgotten. Go on—"

"We call it une assiette anglaise - an English plate. I'll add a slice or two of fresh melon with it. Anything else?"

Ken smiled. "Any of that Chateau Chauvin left?"

"Not up here, but I've two or three more bottles in the cave." She pronounced it 'kav' which Ken knew to be the French word for a wine cellar. "I'll take you down there later and you can choose the wine you want."

"No way, Florence. We can just have a little vin de table."

"I don't have any of that. I decided a long time ago that if I was going to sell the best French wines available, then I would enjoy them myself too. The tax man can't get his hands on the ones I drink!"

"So you have a buyer or buyers who go round the vineyards?"

"Yes. There are a few vineyards where I have a personal relationship with the owners like Château Yon Figeac in Rochefort sur Loire. I've known Alain Château - yes that really is his name - for several years and he understands how we work. Same with the de Montille family near Beune, who produce the Corton Clos du Roi which is outstanding in good years. They always offer me a case when I place a large order, so quite often my own wine costs me nothing anyway."

Ken knew that Florence was using the word 'offer' to mean 'give'. It was one of the many false language friends he and Florence had understood during their time together. "But where did you learn all this stuff on wines?" he asked. "I don't recall you being a wine aficionado when we were married."

"I got it all from my father, Ken. He was very knowledgeable and, as we do in France, he passed that love of good wines on to his children. Or on to me, anyway. I never discussed it much when you and I were together. We never had the sort of money needed to splash out on luxuries like this."

"And how is your father?" Ken asked.

"He's dead, Ken. He and my mother were on Air France flight 447 travelling from Rio de Janeiro to Paris. It crashed into the Atlantic."

Ken dropped his knife and fork on the plate with a clatter. Her parents had been good, genuine people. "Ah, Jeez, Florence, I'm so sorry. I never knew."

"Well no. We didn't keep in touch did we?"

"That was the Airbus A330 wasn't it? Took them months to find the wreckage?"

"Yes, that's the one. The crash killed all 228 passengers, aircrew and cabin crew aboard. It left our family devastated. My grandparents were particularly hard hit by the news. At the time they were both in good health and active but after my parents' death, they just faded into sedentary old age. My grandmother died two years ago and my grandfather died two months later."

Ken took her hand. "I'm sorry Florence. I really am."

She stroked the back of his hand. "It's all done bar the shouting now. My parents weren't wealthy but my grandparents had a reasonable sum stashed away. I'm afraid that, as a family, their deaths have caused us to just break apart. My brother doesn't even give me the time of day and my sister, Geneviève, is a nervous wreck."

"I don't get it. Why is that?"

"Well we never were very close-knit but my grandparent's estate has become a problem."

"Why?"

"You probably don't know about French inheritance laws. And why should you? The central point to grasp is that French law protects your children or, in this case, your children's children. You can't disenfranchise them from your estate. They can't be disinherited. With three children, you split your estate into three equal portions. That is called la réserve. But you are free to create another part of your estate that you can dispose of any way you wish. That is called the quotité disponible.

If my grandparents had wished to split their estate other than in three equal parts, they would have seen a notary and written what is in effect a will. They could have created a quotité disponible and divided their wealth into four equal parts instead of three. Three of the parts would go to the three children and they could have given the fourth part to anyone they wanted."

"So what's gone wrong with your grandparents' inheritance?"

Florence stood up from the table and collected both plates. She placed them on the worktop and brought the coffee pot back with her. After filling both cups she answered, "The problem, Ken, is my brother, Yves-Marie. He is, as I believe you might be inclined to say, a complete asshole."

Ken smiled at her pronunciation. Florence had no strong accent – by no means the stereotypical 'allo 'allo. But there was a gentle lilt to her voice nonetheless, and asshole came out almost as azzole.

Florence continued, "My grandfather was a successful businessman. After my parents' death he slipped into dementia. He was still in his seventies at the time and it was distressing to see his mind go as it did. However, the dementia was not enough to have him placed under curatelle."

Ken raised his eyebrows in question.

"It's a legal curatorship or guardianship. It puts somebody, often an accountant or a notary, in charge of that person's affairs. Particularly their financial affairs. Anyway, after his death, I discovered that my brother, Yves-Marie, had talked my grandfather into transferring a total of over €400,000 into his business.

At first, Yves-Marie claimed it was from the quotité disponible. But my grandparents never made any legal declaration to that effect. If they had done it officially, they could have divided their estate into four instead of three. They could have even given the fourth part to my brother if they so wished. But it was never intended to be like that."

"Couldn't you make a legal challenge?"

"Oh I did, believe me, and after a while he backed down. He changed his story and said that my grandfather had invested the money in his company."

"In which case, you and your sister now own part of his business."

"I'm not sure we want to. Yves-Marie claims the money was a long-term investment and if he has to repay it now, the business will fail so the money will be lost. My argument is that the administrator should include the €400,000 as part of Yves-Marie's one third share of the estate, paid in advance. My grandfather left almost two million euros."

"And?"

"And Yves-Marie won't agree to this. He is sticking to his story that it was a long term investment in his business and that in time it will be repaid. I'm betting that, if we let it go, once they finalise the inheritance, he intends to let the business crash. So the €400,000 will be lost. Before doing so, he will have transferred many of the assets, plus all his best clients to a new business that he has already set up."

"Do you have any proof of that?"

"None whatsoever, and that's the real problem. It's only speculation at the moment."

"What business is he in?" Ken asked. "I only met him a couple of times, and he didn't seem too bright, to be honest."

"He's not. About ten years ago, he set up an insurance and investment agency. A few years ago, it seemed to suddenly grow rapidly. Now, he tells us it's struggling. I wish I could find out more. If I had the full story, I might be able to lean on him and make him change his mind."

Ken closed his eyes and thought for a moment.

Florence could see his mind working. She'd seen him go like this many times before, so she stood from the table and loaded the dishwasher. When she came back, Ken said," How much is it worth to you to find out the full details of Yves-Marie's business?"

"I'm not sure what you mean, Ken."

"Well I know a young lady who can access computer networks and seems to be rather good at copying complete computer drives onto portable storage. She then dissects the information and comes back with answers. She's very, very good, but she doesn't come cheap."

"How much is 'not cheap'?"

"It depends on the complexity of the problem. Last year she dredged up information for me and charged me over £20,000 - in cash. It took her about ten days, but what she produced at the end was gold dust."

"£20,000 wouldn't be a problem if it helps to recoup €400,000."

"There are no guarantees, Florence. All I can say is that she's the best I've ever met. I knew some blokes in The Regiment who could access government networks without anyone knowing they'd been there. One of them even gave himself a medal, just for the fun of it. But she beats them hands down."

"So will you see if you can get her over here?"

"Sure I will. I should warn you though, that she is strange. Very strange."

"What do you mean?"

"If I can get her over here, you'll find out." Ken said with a broad smile. "Prepare to meet Harry."

"Harry? I thought you said she was a woman?"

"She is. People who have met her speculate that she's called Harriet, but few people know for sure. Due to the nature of her work, she is actually quite a wealthy young lady, but she never flaunts her wealth. She's someone who keeps herself to herself."

The corners of Florence's eyes wrinkled. "You always did know some weird folk, didn't you?"

"Like you, you mean?"

She smacked his shoulder in fun, and then became serious. "Thanks for your help, Ken. It's appreciated."

"So it should be," he joked. "If you want, I'll go and kick the shit out of your brother for you. I'm not sure I'd recognise him after all these years though."

"Oh, you can soon put that right if you choose to. Monique, his wife, is a nice lady and she makes big efforts for Yves-Marie. I'm not sure he appreciates what she does. Anyway she's holding a cocktail party for him tonight and he's invited his so-called business associates. Monique has met them all before and can't stand them. Reckons they're a bunch of bobos. She asked if I would go in solidarity with her and I said yes. You can come with me if you want."

"Sounds like a bundle of fun."

"Solidarity, Ken."

"Yeah, I know. Solidarity, Florence. Looks like

that's my day sorted. I'll give Harry a ring now, then we go looking for Tristan this afternoon, and a bundle of laughs cocktail party this evening."

"I'll make it up to you," Florence said.

"How?"

"I'll wear this kaftan again tomorrow morning so you can keep staring at my boobs."

"Oh bugger. Was I that obvious?"

"Yes, Ken Stafford, you were that obvious."

# CHAPTER SIX

Ken passed the rest of the morning with a walk to the massive Arc de Triomphe. He climbed the 284 steps up its internal winding staircase to the viewing platform 50m above the relentless traffic below. He'd always held Paris to be his favourite city in the world, and he'd visited lots of other capital cities. One of the joys of Paris was that, apart from a few odd structures, there was a consistent height to the buildings. From his vantage point, he had a view right across the capital.

The Arc de Triomphe was in the centre of Place de l'Étoile. Many people referred to it as 'Charles de Gaulle Étoile' after the train station deep beneath the street. And Étoile, or Star, was one of those perfect descriptions that one seldom finds when checking out place names. In this instance, twelve major roads radiated out from the massive roundabout. To the South East was the well known Avenue des Champs-Élysées which led in a straight line to Place de la Concorde. And if you allowed your eye to continue straight ahead through Jardin des Tuileries, the impressive former palace of The Louvre was sitting there in the distance to welcome you to it's world famous museum.

A 180° turn and Ken was looking North West, where the straight line of the Champs-Élysées continued down Avenue de la Grande Armée. After Porte Maillot, the road system ran true and straight, all the way to Grande Arche de la Défense which dominated the commercial hub over four kilometres away.

From where he stood, Ken could see the whole vista of Paris laid out before him. The river Seine winding past Notre Dame in the direction of Versailles before meandering its way back and snaking its way towards the sea. The golden dome of Les Invalides which, amongst other things was the burial site of Napoléon Bonaparte. The twin towers of Notre Dame. And, of course, the ever present Eiffel Tower, built for the 1889 World's Fair, but now the global cultural icon of France. It had become one of the most recognisable structures in the world.

Funny to think that they planned to knock it down after 20 years. But the French government put a stay on the process as the Tower proved to be a fantastic platform for radio broadcasts. Now, over one hundred years later, the 10,000 tons of wrought iron that Gustave Eiffel brought into being had become France's showpiece tourist attraction. It had even been listed as a historical monument. How the world turned, Ken mused.

After a while, he checked his watch and made his way back to ground level and towards Florence's apartment. On the way, his phone sounded. Ken listened as Harry, in about ten words, instructed him to pick her up at Charles de Gaulle Airport at 16:40hrs. She was already in Manchester, she said. Ken agreed and chuckled as she cut the call without waiting to say goodbye. Harry was already on her way and Florence was about to get a culture shock.

As he entered the apartment, Florence was coming down from the first floor where she had spent the morning working in a bedroom that she had converted into an office. There were still four other bedrooms to choose from, all with their own bathrooms. Ken laughed. "You look just like Elizabeth Taylor in 'Gone with the wind'. Wrong colour hair, of course, but descending that sweeping staircase is just—"

Florence chuckled. "Back for some lunch?" she asked.

"Do you want me to do it?"

"No. I know where everything is. Shall we go and choose a wine? It can be breathing while I prepare lunch."

"Sure. Where's the cave?"

"Downstairs. Come on."

Florence picked up a set of keys and led Ken down the staircase adjacent to the lift until they arrived in the entrance vestibule. She turned to the door that Ken had found locked when he arrived the day before. As she slid the key into the lock she paused.

"What's up?" Ken asked.

Florence bent her head towards the lock plate. "It's scratched," she said. "Like somebody's been trying to open the lock with a screwdriver or something."

Ken took a look over her shoulder. "Sure it wasn't like this before?"

"Certain. I'd better add a second lock just to be

sure." Florence turned the key, opened the door, and reached inside to flick a light switch. Ahead was a narrow stone staircase. "Careful as you go, Ken, it's quite steep." She stepped through the door and down the old, worn stairs. Ken followed, a few steps behind. Being under ground level, the cave had an unusual smell; musty like a charity shop or a dusty attic. And somewhere far away was a vegetative smell, but nothing that jumped out at you. When Florence reached the bottom, she turned and waited for Ken to catch up.

As he set foot on the cold stone floor he gasped and held the wall for support."What the bloody hell?"

Florence smiled. "It's my own private store, Ken. Some wines are new and they'll lay here until I'm in my retirement before they get used. Others are ready to drink now."

Ken just stared open mouthed at the racks of wine that seemed to go as far as he could see; right up to where the light from the dim overhead bulbs got absorbed. "How many bottles do you reckon you have?"

"I'm not sure of the exact number, but I guess it's getting close to five thousand."

"And all this," he waved his arm to signify the entire cave, "is yours?"

"Yes. It goes under the whole building. We fitted all the other apartments with two rows of built-in wine fridges that keep everything at 14C. That's the optimum temperature for wine storage. Down here it's a natural 13C which is fine."

"It's —"

"— It's a long time since I saw you lost for words, Ken."

"I've only been here 24 hours, Florence, and I'm still not sure if I've come to the right place."

"What do you mean?"

"You're a different Florence Stafford to the one I married in Britain."

"That's because I'm Florence de Nussac. I reverted to my maiden name — sorry."

"You don't have to apologise. I'm seeing a successful, independent woman. But the woman I knew sixteen years ago was just a housewife. A competent and beautiful housewife, but a housewife nonetheless."

Florence looked him in the eyes. "Was I Ken? Was I just a housewife, or is that just the way you saw me?"

Ken struggled to find an answer. He just shrugged and walked to the nearest wine rack. "How do you know where everything is?" he asked.

"When it comes to wine, I have an almost photographic memory. The Château Chauvin is over on the left with the Bordeaux wines. The Burgundies are on the right. If you go to the fifth rack on the left, about six rows from the top, you'll see the 1986 vintage. If you prefer to try something different I can make a few suggestions. The Château Guibot is a nice light St Emilion, or the Château Tronquoy-Lalande is a rather pleasant St Estephe. Either of them would go well with une assiette anglaise"

"I'm fine with that Château Chauvin, Florence, if

it's okay with you. It's rich and deep, but not too heady."

"Go get it, Tiger," Florence said, smiling.

As they climbed back up the stone steps, Ken clutching his prize, he said, "Oh by the way, I had a call from Harry. She'll be at the airport at twenty-to-five. After we've been to the Sorbonne, you can drop me at Gare du Nord and I'll go and meet her. It'll be five o'clock before she's off the plane and through customs."

Florence locked the cellar door and, when she turned, Ken could see she was frowning. "That makes it difficult for you to come with me to Yves-Marie's so-called cocktail evening. You can't leave her alone on her first night here."

Ken smiled. "You don't know Harry. She's a born loner. Sometimes I've walked past her in the street and she's completely blanked me out. Don't worry about her; she'll be fine."

"If you say so."

# CHAPTER SEVEN

Florence wound down the car window and breathed in the warm air. "The weather was like this the first time we went out together," she said. "Do you remember it?"

Ken smiled. "Of course I do. It took me a week to pick up the nerve to ask you out. Me, a top sniper for Special Services, afraid of a little bitty woman."

"But you did, Ken, and I'm glad you did. Do you remember when we first saw each other?"

"I'll never forget it. There was this bit of posh totty in one of the heavy drinking bars in Hereford and I couldn't work out why you were there."

"I was there because I had just arrived in Hereford and didn't realise that half the bars were more or less owned by Special Forces. So is that what caught your attention? Posh totty, as you call it?"

"More than anything, it was your eyes. After I first spotted you sitting on your own at the bar, I got to staring at those eyes. You could lose yourself forever in eyes like those."

"What's with my eyes?"

"Has no-one ever told you about your eyes?"

“Well no, not that I recall. What’s wrong with them?”

“Nothing’s wrong with them Florence, nothing at all. They’re like deep pools. Like mossy green orbs with rings of silver that are magical. There isn't a thing that I could hide from those eyes, and they always had the ability to capture me. Stupid, I know.”

“Why is it stupid?”

Ken ignored her, “And if I'm being honest, I guess I was curious to meet the owner of those eyes. I wondered what she would be like to talk to. I could tell just from your poise that you were a bit cultured - not at all coarse like some of the women who frequent the bars in Hereford. All very obvious with bright red lipstick and big tits.”

Florence held a breast in each hand, like holding a pair of melons. “Actually, Ken, mine are a bit bigger than they used to be.”

“I noticed.”

“Does that make me coarse?”

“Don’t be daft. You’ve always been class, even when you were younger.”

“What, even with my hippy hair?”

“Oh you weren't pretty in a common way. You were pretty in a refined way with those green and silver eyes and yes, even with your indigo streaks and open-toed sandals.”

Florence laughed. “I spotted you out of the corner of my eye. It was obvious to me that you liked me."

"How was that?"

"The way your eyes avoided me until you thought I couldn't see you, and then they followed me around the room. I felt flattered. It was harmless, and a nice boost to my ego."

“Well actually I fell in love that evening. And it hadn't occurred to me that everyone must know that I fancied you. But one of my mates had this simple, plain-speaking way of seeing the world and you couldn't argue with it. He said, ‘You're going to marry her, aren't you?’

I laughed at him. ‘Yeah sure,’ I croaked, ‘She's alright, I think. She's like pretty hot.’ I remember reaching out to grab my mate's newspaper off him, as if the conversation bored me. There was a picture of some celebrity or other on a Caribbean island and I realised I wanted to be there on that island with you. Then when someone put some music on the juke box, all I could see were your high cheekbones and mischievous eyes. And the fact that you danced like no-one was watching. But of course we all did. You just hadn't cared.”

Florence smiled at Ken with a warmth and fondness from the past. “You know,” she said, “I fell for you harder than a fall on black ice. You were funny, always cracking jokes. You had me in stitches on every date. Friends flocked to you like you were the only light in the room, hanging on your words, buying you drinks and slapping you on the back. But after only a short time I wanted more than just the ‘Mister Happy’ persona. I already loved you and I wanted to get to know the man behind the punch lines. One day a friend asked me some things about you: where you grew up, what your parents were like, who your best friends were, and I froze. After six months I knew nothing about you other than your alcohol and bed preferences."

"That's what Special Forces does to you. You do stuff that you never, ever talk about, except with the other guys who were there. Everyone in Special Forces takes secrets with them to the grave."

"But I spent time with you, Ken. I reached out with my open heart and invited you to reciprocate and to make that connection. I knew I loved you, but I missed you so much because I only knew the part of you that you wanted to show me."

Florence ended the conversation and looked away. Ken followed her gaze as student after student began to file out of the imposing building opposite. None of them paid any attention to the red Mini Cabriolet parked a little way up the narrow road. Florence tapped a continuous rhythm on the steering wheel and Ken glanced at his watch. It would take about quarter of an hour to get from The Latin Quarter to Gare du Nord. It was half an hour from Gare du Nord to Charles de Gaulle Airport. It would take another quarter of an hour to get from the airport station to the right terminal where he would meet Harry. He didn't dare leave Harry waiting on her own; there was no knowing what she would do. He had given her Florence's address and phone number just in case, but that didn't mean she would use the information. Harry was the most unpredictable person he had ever met - and one of the most intelligent.

Ken glanced at Florence sitting beside him. As the crowd of departing students started to thin, it was clear that so did Florence's hopes of seeing Tristan. "What if he's decided to stay in the lecture hall to finish a project?" she asked.

A large white van drove alongside them and stopped as the driver checked his street map. It blocked their view for a few precious seconds and then as it moved on again, Florence dug her elbow into Ken's ribs. "There he is. That's him. It's Tristan, isn't it?"

"Hold on," Ken said. "Let me see him for more than a split second." But as he said it, the youth had jogged a few steps to catch up with some friends and then turned the corner.

"What do we do now?" Florence asked.

"We follow him."

She made to pull the door handle but Ken put his hand over hers and stopped her. "Not on foot. If he turns round for any reason and sees that 'the crazy lady' is behind him, he's going to know something is going on. Just take your time and drive round the corner. When you get close, stop, just like that van did, and pretend to be looking for a house number or something. Just keep moving forwards in small steps and keep him in sight."

Florence did as Ken had said and found it was quite easy. A few minutes later, the group started to run and Florence said, "What the—" but Ken smiled.

"Look," he said, "They're just running to grab that table that's become vacant outside the café."

Sure enough, the group pulled a couple of spare chairs from other tables and formed a tight circle round their table.

"Now what?" Florence asked. "We can't sit here for long, we stick out like a sore thumb. As she said it, a car horn sounded immediately behind them.

Ken turned and said, "The gods are smiling on us. It's the guy who's parked at your rear wheel. He wants out of his parking space, but you're blocking him."

Florence reversed the car, let the driver go, and then dived into his space. It wasn't perfect, but it would have to do. "What do you think?" she asked. "It's Tristan isn't it?"

"Calm down, Florence. Give me a moment or two to take a proper look. Let me just watch him for a couple of minutes."

There wasn't a single empty table outside the café. Everywhere Ken looked there were young men and women in torn T-shirts or shorts or vest tops or frocks. Like all in their age group, they were drinking, smoking and chatting and enjoying the warmth of the summer.

Florence took hold of Ken's arm. She shivered in her thin summer dress and sandals, but she knew it had little to do with the temperature. Her right foot juddered up and down on the accelerator. Shake-shake-shake. Shake-shake-shake. She focused on it, willing it to stop, and it did just for a couple of seconds before starting up again.

Ken stared at the fair-haired young man who had ordered nothing more than a pitcher of water. He blanked out everything in his peripheral vision, just as he had trained to do. He felt as though he was looking at him through a rifle scope that had zoomed in on his features. He watched as the lad chatted with his friends. He tried to morph the young man's face into the face of the three year old who he hadn't seen for sixteen years. It was easy. It was a perfect fit.

The young man's appearance was stern, even a little melancholy, but he was transformed when he smiled. Here was the same fine-boned face, tapering to a chiselled chin. The same eyes; spaced wide. The same steady gaze as his mother, with just a hint of irony. He had a mouth that was precise with small, firm, full lips. His attitude was full of humour when he smiled. And to top it all, he had the same long dimples in his cheeks.

Ken's mind went back to the moment that Tristan was born. When he picked him up and held him in his arms for the first time. When he didn't want to let the little baby out of his sight, not even for a second. Nestled deep in his arms where the child was safe. And now he was sitting with students from The Sorbonne, chatting and joking. And the intervening sixteen years were forever lost. Not just between Ken and Tristan, but between Ken and Florence. What a bloody waste.

He turned to Florence and offered her a crinkle-eyed smile. "90% certainty, I'd say."

Florence flung herself at Ken and buried her head on his shoulder. Large sobs wracked her whole body. Ken held her tight, and wondered what the future held now. He was going to have to deal with the big elephant sooner rather than later.

When Florence had taken hold of her emotions again and she had wiped away the tears with a tissue from her handbag, she said, "There I go again. I'm strong at work where I handle all sorts of situations. But with anything emotional outside of my control my default reaction is tears."

Ken smiled. "Better than no reaction, Florence. The thing is, what do we do now?" He checked his watch again. "I need to get going shortly to meet Harry, so there's not much we can do today. You tell me that your private detective knows where Tristan lives, so we're not likely to lose him."

"He only knows his address here in Paris. We still don't know what last name he is using so he was unable to come up with a home address."

"I think Harry may be able to resolve that for us. Why don't you run me up to Gare du Nord. If the traffic's okay, I'll have a few minutes in hand, so we can grab a quick coffee and discuss tactics."

Florence was still sniffing. "Best if you drive. My legs are shaking."

Ken chuckled and jumped out of the car as Florence slid over to the passenger side. He eased out of the parking space and drove past the café, watching the table where the group of students talked and joked together. The lad had grown and matured but now Ken understood Florence's claim to have a parental instinct about him. He felt the same way now.

They continued the journey in silence until they pulled up one hundred metres from Gare du Nord in the only space Ken could find. He glanced again at his watch. "Okay, I'm in good time, let's swap thoughts."

With un café and une noisette in front of them, Florence said, "What's the best way forward, Ken?"

"I've been thinking about that as I drove here. The only thing we can do now is get a DNA sample."

"I don't understand. What would you do with his DNA?"

"When Tristan disappeared the police took some of his hair from his brush, do you remember?" Florence nodded. "They never tested it against you and me: they only needed it in case they found a body. That hair sample and the DNA result will still be on record in Hereford. I have a good friend on the Isle of Man who is a Detective Chief Inspector. As a favour, he would be able to check if the two DNA samples match."

"But how are you going to get Tristan's DNA now?"

"Leave that to me," Ken said. "That won't be a problem. So what do you think?"

"I'm not sure, Ken. Can't we just find out where he goes at weekends and check him out there. There must be someone who he calls his parents."

"And suppose that they were somehow responsible or partly responsible for his disappearance. How do you think they would react? And if they weren't involved in his disappearance, how would you react?"

"What do you mean?"

"If that boy is Tristan, we don't know the circumstances surrounding his appearance in France. He has people who he has always known as his parents. What if they are good people and have brought him up well? Are we going to break that up and drop a bomb on his life?"

"Oh God, I never thought of all that. But what if they had something to do with his disappearance?"

"We'll have to deal with that when we know whether the boy is Tristan. First of all, we have to be sure, and we can only do that through a DNA check."

"Yes but—" Florence left the sentence unfinished and it hung there between them.

"But what?" Ken said. "There are no other options. Why are you holding back?"

Florence looked at her watch. "You'd better go and get Harry. We'll talk about it when you get back."

Ken nodded, stood and headed towards the station. He thought he knew why Florence was hesitant, but they had to cross that bridge or call off the search. Now he'd seen Tristan for himself, he wasn't prepared to give up without knowing for sure.

Forty minutes later, at Charles de Gaulle airport, he glanced at his watch again. Five o'clock. He was just on time. It was Tuesday, Harry's favourite day of the week, or so she had once told him. Ken approached the tall glass partition that separated the public area of the airport terminal from the baggage reclaim.

He spotted her straight away as she came down the escalator from immigration control. In fact, he didn't spot her so much as he had spotted the vivid red hair that she had piled on top of her head. She had secured it with two wooden sticks that could have come from the last Chinese restaurant she had visited. When she approached the baggage carousel, Ken could see chunky beaded earrings swinging from her ears. She wore her trademark old lace glove on her right hand and was tapping on an iPad, oblivious to everybody around her.

Ken knocked on the glass and she looked up with her broad, high-cheekboned face. He pointed to a day-glo green suitcase with coloured tape and ribbons attached to it. She looked at him as if he were a stranger but then nodded her thanks and picked up the case. Ken had been sure that it had to be hers. Nobody else would dress a suitcase like a red indian chief.

As she took her case from the carousel, Ken allowed himself a smile. Harry, the eternal enigma. She wasn't beautiful in the classical way. She had no flowing golden curls or ivory skin. There were no piercing eyes of green. She was a little shorter than average and a little larger than a catwalk model. But in her ordinariness she was stunning. She had a kind of understated beauty. Perhaps it was because she was so unaware of her prettiness. That lack of awareness could be very disarming.

Something radiated from within Harry that rendered her irresistible to both genders. Men desired her and women courted her friendship. But only when she behaved herself. Otherwise Harry was like a barbed tornado, and she didn't give a damn about normal polite conversation. She didn't even understand about normal polite conversation. A moment later she walked through the 'Nothing to Declare' customs position. Ken approached her, "Hi Harry, how are you?"

She stared at him. "And you are?" she asked in a low, clear voice.

Ken exhaled. He'd been through this before with her. "I'm Ken Stafford. It was me who asked you to come to Paris to help me sort out some stuff. You've done work for me before."

"What sort of work?"

"The last job was checking out a man who claimed he had been in Delta Force in USA."

"Wait." Harry tapped on her iPad with her gloved hand and paused a moment. "Nothing here about that."

"Okay, try either 1st Special Forces Operational Detachment-Delta or Raymond Herold. That was the guy's name."

Harry went back to her iPad. Ken waited. He knew Harriet Lewis almost as well as she knew herself - maybe even better. He knew that she was Obsessive Compulsive and had been born with the need to have everything symmetrical and in a perfect order. She also counted things. Anything. Maybe she should have been an accountant. She had an amazing memory - an incredible memory even. But, to create some moments of discomfort, she suffered from repetitive confabulation. Complete loss of memory. The doctors said that her continual note-taking was a form of autism. But Ken knew her well and knew that, for her, taking notes was a necessary survival strategy.

Harry had told Ken that, at school, they had laughed at her for always taking notes but without notes she was lost. Bit by bit, what few friends she had at school had all deserted her when she walked past them in the street. They never knew that on certain days she hadn't even recognised them in the sea of faces that presented themselves to her. Note-taking was a strategy that Harry had developed as a young girl. Because from time to time there were days when she woke up with memories that stretched back no further than the moment of going to bed the night before. It didn't happen often, but when it did, it scared her. And her notes helped her to get back on track quicker.

In the days and weeks after a memory wipe-out, her memories came back in sporadic bursts and knitted themselves together like building a jigsaw. The medical term that doctors and psychiatrists gave it was confabulation. It was like reformatting a laptop: the basic operating system was still in place, but all the files were lost. So each time her memory wiped itself clean, it left her confused and uncertain. Her notes acted like a data backup and helped her re-establish her life and who she was quicker than nature could.

The doctors suggested it was triggered by some form of epilepsy but offered no answers to her problems. The psychiatrists said she was disassociating herself from a world she didn't want to be part of. But nobody ever actually understood why she was like she was. Nobody but Ken, who had had a short-lived relationship with her before finding out what her problems were.

Their relationship had been brief, not because of her confabulation, but because Ken found it a strain living with her OCD. Whilst he understood her memory issues, he couldn't cope with her obsessive compulsive disorder on a daily basis. It was even worse when she was in her own home. They had arguments because the salt cellar wasn't in exactly the right place on the dinner table. It had to be millimetre perfect. They had arguments because Ken didn't fold his socks when he took them off. They had arguments if the stamps weren't aligned and equidistant from the corners of envelopes. They had arguments about most things during the few months they were together. Harry was a loving, happy lady when things were going right, but she could be a royal pain in the arse otherwise."

Harry looked up from her iPad. Ken could see that she had been looking at a photograph of him. "You're Ken Stafford," Harry said. "You live in Church Street, Peel."

"That's me."

"Former SAS. You run Three Way Training on the Isle of Man. Your son disappeared when he was three."

Ken smiled to himself. She had obviously done her research on him too because he'd never mentioned Tristan to her. "That's me, Harry."

"Three years ago, we had sexual relations fifty-four times over a period of one hundred and twenty three days. That's an average of 0.439 times a day. Or 3.073 times a week. And according to my notes, you don't treat women like they have an expiry date."

"Well I'm glad we got that cleared up," Ken laughed. "Are we good to go now?"

"Hang on."

"Tap, tap. Yes, you paid me last time."

"What? Last time we had sex?"

"Don't be silly. Last time I worked for you."

"Why would I not?"

"Some people think I'm stupid and will forget them. But my tablet never forgets."

"I know, Harry, so let's get moving. Give me your case. Jeez, that weighs a ton. What have you got in there?"

"If you had sex with me fifty-four times, you must know the sorts of things I carry."

"Apart from clothes, I would guess, laptop, backup iPad, a couple of king-size storage disks, and assorted computer stuff that nobody else understands."

"Okay, you're Ken. Where are we going?"

"Avenue Marceau near the Arc de Triomphe."

Tap, tap, tap. "Number forty. Florence de Nussac."

"Correct. Now can we go?"

"How many times have you had sex with her?"

# CHAPTER EIGHT

Florence came back down the stairs and into the kitchen with a huge grin on her face. "You were right about her being strange, Ken. Are you sure she's the right person to find out about my brother?"

Ken smiled. "She's very much the right person, Florence. She has no boundaries. Others might stop if they thought that they were compromising personal information, but Harry has no such limits. It's not that she doesn't respect people; it's just that she doesn't understand that there actually are limits. If there is information available, it belongs to her - simple as that. Did you have any problems when you were showing her round her room?"

"Not problems, just a complete disconnect. When she stepped into the room, I was pointing out where things were and trying to show her the en-suite bathroom but she stood looking round the bedroom as if she was in a daze."

"Aha! In a little while, she will appear with a smile on her face. Meanwhile, she'll be busy rearranging the room."

"Rearranging what?"

"Everything! She'll lie on the bed, look to her left and move the alarm clock, then look to her right and move the telephone so that they are aligned in her line of sight. Then she'll get round to the pictures and ornaments. Meanwhile, she'll be busy taking photos of everything."

"You didn't say she was this strange. How do you come to know all this about her?"

"Because, a couple of years ago, we lived together for a little while. One hundred and twenty three days, I'm told."

"But Ken, she's —"

"Different. She's different, Florence."

"She's as nervous as a grasshopper. And the hair—"

"Oh that will change as the days move on."

"It's a wig?"

"She has several. I have no idea how many she brought with her. Her natural hair is rather nice. It's a long, curly, caramel-coloured mane."

"So why does she cover it up? And what's with the lace glove on one hand?"

"You ask too many questions."

"Meaning what?"

"Meaning I don't have the faintest idea why she covers her hair or wears a lace glove on one hand. Under the glove, there's an anchor that she had tattooed years ago. I've asked her about it but she always said she didn't know why it was there."

"And you believe her?"

"Yes. She's too honest to lie. She doesn't even know how to lie."

"Unusual."

"She has another tattoo in a place that most people never get to see."

"Too much information, Ken."

"It's a Dara Knot."

"What's that?"

"It's a Celtic Knot. The word Dara comes from the Irish word 'doire', which means oak tree. It's considered to be the king of the trees, and the Dara Knot means internal fortitude. To remain strong regardless of the circumstances around you."

"And she can hack computers and networks?"

"She's the best."

"I'll have to take your word for that."

"You can take my word for it as well," Harry said, stepping through the open doorway. "What time is this cocktail party?"

Florence looked shocked and wondered how much of the conversation her guest had overheard. Ken just smiled and said, "Florence and I are expected at eight o'clock."

"I'm coming with you."

"Er, it's cocktail, Harry. You know; long dresses and frilly bits and posh people."

"And small talk. I can't do that small talk thing."

"I know," Ken said, "So why would you want to go to a cocktail party?"

"I'm not going to the party. I'm just going with you. I'll sit in the car?"

"But why?" Florence asked. "There are English language channels on the television and you'll be quite comfortable here."

"I speak French," Harry said. "And German."

"Well, okay, there are French channels on TV too, if you prefer."

"I don't watch television. It bores me. I'll just sit in the car while you do small talk."

"But—"

Ken now stood behind Harry, He winked at Florence and he put his finger to his lips. "No problem Harry. Are you going to see what you can find at Florence's brother's?"

"I'll do some research on it."

"Would that research involve hacking into his home computer?"

"That would be illegal," she said, "and impossible from this location. But I might be able to manage it from outside his place."

"Do you want to take some sandwiches and a flask, or do you want to eat here before we go."

"I'll eat when we get back."

"It might be quite late."

"Yes, it might."

"Why not eat now?"

"Because I've not finished sorting out the room yet. I just wondered if you have a tape measure? Those armchairs and table are so out of balance."

"Out of balance?"

"Not equidistant. They should be equidistant."

Florence glanced at Ken who was smiling behind Harry's back. Harry didn't look round, but she said, "Take no notice of him. He's always been rude. And do you mind if I nudge that commode in the dining room a few centimetres to the right?"

Ken laughed. "I hope you're not talking about Florence's Louis XV chest of drawers? It's worth more than I earn in a year, that."

"Yeah, well maybe you're not worth much," Harry said.

Ken spotted the twitch on her lips that told him she was joking. With Harry, it was sometimes difficult to know because, if nothing else, she could hold a poker face. "I'm deadly serious," Ken said. "€49,500 for that chest of drawers. If you feel the need to 'nudge it' I'd best come with you so it doesn't get damaged."

All three stepped into the dining room, Florence looking apprehensive and biting her tongue. Ken had said that Harry was unusual, but this was pushing her luck a bit. "What's the problem with it?" she asked.

"Well, I presume it's meant to be halfway between the windows," Harry said. "But it's not, is it?"

Florence looked and squinted and after checking and rechecking had to agree that maybe it was a centimetre or two to the left. She held her breath as

Ken and Harry moved it until Harry was satisfied.

Harry stopped and stroked the deep yellow ochre wood and the gilt bronze mounts. "It's beautiful, isn't it?"

"Well I'm glad someone appreciates it," Florence said. "Ken thought I would have saved some money if I'd bought something from Ikea."

"Ken's a heathen." Harry looked around. "Do you have the matching commode?"

"It's a one-off," Ken said, somewhat smugly.

"Wrong!" Harry said

Florence smiled. "Harry is right, Ken. For your continued education, in France it's called a bombé commode. Bombé meaning it's bowed at the front. The commode started to appear in about 1700 and it meant a low cabinet, or chest of drawers at the height of the dado rail."

"You do know what that is, don't you?" Harry asked.

Ken smiled and nodded.

Florence continued, "Commodes like that occupied a prominent position in the room. A single commode would stand against the pier between the windows, in which case it would often be surmounted by a mirror glass, exactly like you see it here. However, in wealthy homes – and this piece comes from a wealthy home - a pair of identical commodes would flank the chimneypiece or occupy the centre of each end wall. Bombé commodes like this were a feature of the rococo style called 'Louis Quinze'. In this condition, they are very rare indeed, hence the price."

"That's me told," Ken said.

"You're learning," Harry muttered, taking multiple photos of the piece with her iPad.

A little while later, after Florence had freshened up and changed, the three of them stepped into her Mini Cabriolet. While Florence drove, Harry sat at the back clutching a collection of wires and hardware.

Avenue Marceau was a wide boulevard with cobbles laid in fan shapes. Either side of the main boulevard was a line of trees and then a narrow traffic lane to allow local people to access their homes and park where available. Florence manoeuvred past a large white van and turned onto the main boulevard.

As the car pulled away into the early evening traffic, a small dirty-looking man in a shiny suit stepped out from behind a nearby Morris Column, the tall cylindrical sidewalk structures used for advertising. He called to the driver of the van that Florence had just passed.

"Back it up here. There's space now."

The white van reversed and squeezed into the space in front of Florence's building. Two men stepped out and slid open the rear door. Two more men stepped out of the back. All of them wore long brown lab coats with no markings to indicate the company name.

"How long have we got?" one asked

"At least two hours," the small man said. "If my information is correct, they are heading out to St Germain which is a good half-hour drive. They'll be at some cocktail do for most of the evening. If we're quick, we can be in and out in an hour. Grab some of those packing boxes and we'll get moving."

Half an hour later, Florence pulled her Mini Cabriolet to a halt in front of a square building five storeys high in the centre of Saint-Germain-en-Laye.

"Is this it?" Harry asked from the back?

"This is it," Florence said. "The entrance to my brother's apartment is on the fourth floor but it's a duplex, so the bedrooms are on the fifth floor.

"How many apartments are there?"

"Eight. Each apartment is roughly half the width of the building. The first three floors are flats and the top levels are, as I say, bigger duplexes."

Ken turned to look behind him. "You sure you're okay out here, Harry?"

"No problem. I've got my iPad and laptop and I'll have a WiFi connection within two minutes. See you later."

Ken looked at Florence and chuckled. "Come on Florence, I think we've just been dismissed."

They stepped out of the car and crossed the road to the shared entrance of the building. Harry watched them walk away, holding her arms across her body, one elbow in each hand. Florence keyed a number into the vigik and, as they disappeared inside the building, Harry smiled to herself. Now she could have some peace while she explored what networks were available to her dancing fingers. She plugged her laptop into the lighter socket to keep it charged in case Ken and the woman were a long time. She tapped her iPad and checked. Florence, that was her name. She seemed okay.

Inside, Yves-Marie's wife, Monique, welcomed them at the door to the apartment. She kissed Florence on both cheeks then looked at Ken and did a double take. "It's Ken, isn't it?"

Florence answered, "Hope you don't mind, Monique. Ken's over on business for a few days and I didn't think you'd mind if I brought him along tonight."

"Of course not." She air-kissed Ken. "It's been years. Hey, are you two er—"

"Don't go jumping to conclusions," Florence said, smiling. "Ken's just helping me out on some business matters."

Monique half closed here eyes. "Hmmm, if you say so."

"I do. Come on, let us in so we can see who's here."

"Usual bunch," Monique replied, taking the bottle of Champagne that Ken offered her. "Oooo that's nice and chilled. I'll pop it in the fridge till later. How's your French, Ken? Not that you need worry too much. With this bunch of poseurs, as soon as they discover you're English, they'll be clamouring to talk to you in English. They like to show everybody how smart they are."

"Florence has promised to stay close," Ken said. "I'm okay with spoken French until everybody starts talking at once at full speed, then I can get a bit lost."

Monique placed a palm flat on his chest. "If you get fed up sticking to Florence, you can stick to me. I could do with a bit of excitement in my life."

Florence raised her eyebrows. "That's not like you,

Monique. Unless there's a Monique that I've not met yet."

"Yes, well, I don't usually have a big hulk standing right next to me." She let her hand fall away and winked at Ken. "It's either her or me, Ken. I know she's a couple of years younger, but sometimes experience makes up for age."

Ken laughed. "I'll assume you're pulling my leg, Monique. If not, I'll see you in your boudoir later. Meanwhile, lead me to the cocktails and let's see who is the first guest to drop into English."

As they stepped into the lounge, it was clear to Ken within seconds that the men were there to talk business and that they had brought their wives along as trophies. The atmosphere wasn't strained, but it could have been a lot more jovial. The patio doors were open onto the long balcony and most of the men stood outside smoking and posturing amongst themselves. The wives were sat on the sofa and chairs, chatting and making themselves small.

Ken did a quick head-count and thought there were five couples already there. At the centre of the group on the balcony was Yves-Marie de Nussac, Florence's older brother. Ken eyed him up from a distance. He'd not changed much over the years. Short, but trying to look important by waving his finger at somebody to emphasis that he had the right answer.

His hair was thin on top, almost non-existent, but Ken stifled a smirk when he saw the ponytail at the back. That was new since the last time he'd seen him. New also was the designer stubble but it did no more than emphasise his pudgy face and double chin. His nose was like a little potato, the size of a baby's closed fist. Ken felt, as he had at his wedding to Florence, that Yves-Marie was the sort of person you wouldn't invite into your home unless you had to.

Yves-Marie looked in Ken's direction then did a double take, just as his wife had. In English he said in a loud voice, "Well, well, the prodigal son. Good evening Kenneth. Welcome to our humble abode." He spotted Florence and added, "Nothing like my little sister's palace, of course, but it's the best we can do with what income we have."

"Good evening, Yves. Glad to know that some things don't change."

"The name's Yves-Marie."

"And my name is Ken. Glad we got that sorted out."

Yves-Marie glanced at Florence and reverted back to French. "Didn't realize I'd invited you," he snarled, with ill-disguised contempt.

"You didn't. Monique thought it would be nice to have a little company in the kitchen."

"Glad you know your place then."

The telephone rang and Monique rushed to answer it. Ken heard, "D'accord— oui d'accord— OK— merci— à bientôt." She put the phone down, crossed the room to the balcony, and whispered in Yves-Marie's ear. She stood back as his face turned red and he fiddled with his glass.

Florence whispered, "I bet he was expecting more people than this and they've been ringing up with excuses and saying they can't make it."

"Then they'll have enough petit fours and finger snacks to see them through, won't they?" Ken said.

Monique passed by them and, with an almost imperceptible flicker of her eyes, indicated that they should follow her into the kitchen. Florence sauntered away and Ken followed a moment later. From his peripheral vision he could see that Yves-Marie was watching him.

In the kitchen, Monique said, "He knew you were coming, Florence. He was just being unpleasant."

"I'm well used to that," Florence said. The kitchen window was small and the ceiling light was almost always lit. Under the harsh fluorescent on the kitchen ceiling, Florence looked at her sister-in-law and touched her cheek. "Even makeup won't cover that bruise, Monique. How long has this been going on?"

Monique stared at the floor.

"Come on, Monique. How long has Yves-Marie been hitting you?"

"It was an accident."

"Must have been an open door you walked into," Ken said.

"He didn't mean to do it."

"Like he didn't mean to do it last time," Florence said.

"Things are not easy at the moment, Florence. He tells me that the business is struggling and this argument over your grandparents' inheritance is not helping."

"I don't know what Yves-Marie tells you, Monique,

but he could settle the issue over our grandparent's inheritance in five minutes."

"You leave her out of this," shouted Yves-Marie from the doorway.

"Shhh," from Monique.

Her husband made no attempt to moderate the level of his voice. Still addressing himself to Florence, he shouted, "It has nothing to do with her; it's between you and me."

He attempted to shoulder Ken out of the way, but Ken stood firm. He turned to face the shorter man. "Whatever business you have with Florence regarding your inheritance is none of my concern. But when I see a bruised woman, I get a little hot under the collar. So let me say this to you just once, Yves-Marie. If I ever find that you have hit Monique again, I will make a very personal visit and show you what a bad idea it was."

"I'm not afraid of you, big man," Yves-Marie shouted, pushing his square, gunmetal spectacles up his nose.

"You should be, if you know what's good for you," Ken replied in a low, quiet voice. "It doesn't pay to underestimate me."

"Oh yes, big man, special forces, shoot a few Arabs in the back when they're not looking."

Ken took hold of Yves-Marie's shirt with slow, calculated calmness. He pulled him close. Then he looked down into his eyes and said, "Don't push it, little man. And don't let me find out you've harmed your wife again." He let go, looked towards Florence and added, "I feel we might have outstayed our welcome already. Best we leave your brother to his guests although judging by the queue at the front door, there may not be many left."

Yves-Marie looked over his shoulder at the entrance to the apartment. Three couples were pulling on their coats and looking embarrassed. "Got to rush, Yves-Marie," one man said. "We forgot to let the babysitter know we'd be late back."

The others all mumbled something and left together.

"Have a wonderful evening," Ken said to Yves-Marie. "Best go look after the ones who are still here or they'll be leaving too."

Florence's brother turned on his heel and strode out of the kitchen. Florence kissed her sister-in-law on both cheeks and said, "Sorry, Monique. That wasn't intentional."

"I know, but he's going to be like a bear with a sore head now."

"I meant what I said," Ken said. "If he lays a hand on you, call Florence and I'll come and straighten him out."

"And don't be afraid to come round to mine if it gets hard," Florence added. "There are spare bedrooms and I've plenty of space."

Monique nodded. Her face was grey with fear but she held back the tears. "Don't worry. I think Ken's message got through to him. I'll just have to suffer his unpleasantness, that's all. Best you get going, I think."

Ken air-kissed Monique and they headed out of the door. From the lounge, Yves-Marie called out "Au revoir Flo. Don't rush back."

Ken looked at Florence and raised his eyebrows. Flo was a tender nickname he had used for her at intimate moments when they were married, and he knew Florence didn't appreciate anyone else using it. Least of all Yves-Marie. "You okay?" he asked.

"Oh, I'm not bothered about him," she lied, forcing a laugh. "But it gets a bit boring after all these years. You'd think when he reached his forties, he'd have grown out of all that stupid nickname business."

"Sounds like he's still got some growing up to do," Ken said, picking up the poorly-suppressed irritation in her voice. "Come on, let's grab something to eat."

When they reached the car and slid into their seats, Harry looked up from tapping on her laptop. "I've not finished yet."

"Yeah, we were booted out by the bouncer," Ken said. "Do you need a long time? We can come back tomorrow if you want."

"That might be better. The connection is patchy anyway. I guess a lot of people log on to the network in the evenings. Can you hire me a car?"

Ken looked at Florence and she nodded.

"With GPS," Harry added.

Florence nodded again. "We'll get it sorted first thing in the morning. Do you want to eat now?"

"Yes. Food would be good."

# CHAPTER NINE

Florence drove back to the apartment and tutted as she saw a large white van parked in front of the building. Behind the van, two men in movers' overalls were loading boxes. "Strange that someone is moving at this time in the evening," she muttered to no-one in particular.

She drove on and found a space one hundred metres higher up the slope. On their right was the five star Intercontinental Hotel. "Hey, what about dinner here?" she said. "They have a top chef and an excellent restaurant called Le M64."

"Strange name," Ken said.

"It's the number of the building," from the back seat.

"They don't just have good food; they're also one of my best customers." Without waiting for an answer, Florence jumped from the car and waited as Ken and Harry unloaded themselves.

"I can't do the small talk thing." Harry said to Ken. "Can I take my iPad?"

Ken nodded and slid her laptop under the passenger seat out of sight. “No problem, Harry. You can talk when you want and hack the hotel’s network when you want to do something else!”

As they entered the hotel, a tall concierge greeted them. He asked, “Would you like to dine this evening Madame de Nussac, or would you prefer seats in the cocktail bar?”

“We’d like to dine if possible, Roger. Are there any free tables?”

“For you, Madame, I’m sure that the maître d'hôtel will be pleased to see you.”

Florence nodded and beckoned Ken and Harry to follow her through the cocktail bar towards the restaurant. Norbert, the young maître d'hôtel, welcomed Florence like a lost sister. “If you and your guests would like to take an aperitif in the bar, Madame, we’ll have a table ready for you in minutes. I’ll bring the menus through to you so you can select your meal as you relax.”

Again, it seemed that Florence was well used to the routine and she turned and indicated to three club armchairs in the bar. “They are famous for their cocktails here. There’s quite a long list to choose from.”

After scanning the list, Florence ordered an Americano - Campari, Red Vermouth and Soda - for herself. Ken went for a Talisker whisky on ice. Harry, having studied each item on the list with great care decided on a Glam64 cocktail. It consisted of vodka, lime juice, raspberry coulis and a bewildering cocktail mixture called Hpnotiq. When asked about it, the waiter informed her it was a combination of premium vodka, natural tropical fruit juices and a smidgin of Cognac. Harry was sold on the idea when the waiter brought her the bottle to inspect. The alcohol inside was a pale cloudy blue and pleased her. Not many things pleased her as much as a cloudy blue liqueur, so she noted the name on her iPad.

While the barman prepared the drinks, Norbert, the maître d'hôtel, brought them the food menus. Both Ken and Florence chose a starter of smoked salmon with horseradish cream, saffron potatoes and Savora sauce. Harry took delight in ordering the most complicated starter on the menu: poached foie gras, quinoa, snow-peas and radish, perfumed with jasmine tangerine juice.

"Are you having fun?" Ken asked her.

"Is it okay?"

"Of course it is," Florence said. "Choose away to your heart's content."

For a moment, Harry seemed to forget her iPad as she sipped her Glam64 cocktail and ran her finger down the list of main courses. She recited each one to herself as she read. Ken and Florence said nothing, respecting her concentration. When she was done, she chose Mallard duck in two different cooking styles, bucatini pasta, beetroot and chicory. Florence went for Japanese beef tartare with bonito broth and seaweed. Ken was happy to settle on thirty days matured beef with sweet potatoes and pummelos.

"Hope it's good," Ken said. "I'm starving."

Florence replied, "The chef is Edward Hiroaki. He grew up in Montreal in a family of Japanese restaurateurs but is now a big supporter of French gastronomic tradition. He was a student of the famous Joel Robuchon. He has two Michelin stars and is aiming for a third. He buys only the best of everything, and that includes my wines."

"Oh, so that's why all the bowing and curtseying, is it?"

Florence laughed. "When we sell wines to them, it's our representatives who have to bow and curtsey. We all scratch each other's backs." She turned to Harry, "And you seem to be having fun with the menu, young lady."

"Yeah, well it pleases me. Maybe I could get to know you. Then I could do the small talk thing."

"You've been doing pretty well so far," Florence answered, not troubling to hide a smile.

Harry blushed and picked up her iPad.

The sommelier approached. "Would Madame like to choose the wine?" he asked. Then he explained in near perfect English to Ken, "Usually we ask the gentleman first but since Madame de Nussac is our most respected wine supplier, I felt it only right to ask her."

"No problem," Ken said. "She has forgotten more about wines than I will ever know."

Florence checked with the other two, "We're all on red meat, so okay with a red wine?"

Ken nodded. Harry tapped on her iPad.

"I think the 1989 Château Chasse-Spleen should work well, don't you?"

The sommelier nodded his approval and left to

fetch the wine from the cellar.

"I take it that's one that you supply?" Ken asked.

"Of course. I'm hardly likely to support another supplier, am I?"

"How do you spell Chasse-Spleen?" Harry asked, looking up from her iPad.

Florence told her and Harry tapped on her screen.

"And what made you choose it?"

"It's been ripe for drinking for a few years and has reached a stage where anyone with a nose for wine would say it was sensational. It's graded as a Cru Bourgeois Exceptionnel. Dark bright red wine, meniscus slightly orangey, unclouded. Nose of fresh plum and cocoa. Neat and straightforward attack. Flavours: cocoa beans, leather and black berries. Tight and unctuous structure, mellow tannins. Balance and power. Great persistence."

"Bloody hell," Harry said, tapping away. "You sound like a wine encyclopaedia."

Ken snorted and covered his smile with his hand. Florence wasn't quite sure whether it was a compliment or an insult. She said, "I write all the descriptions for our catalogues, Harry, so I not only get to know the wines, I get to describe them too."

After their cocktails, Norbert seated them in the dining room. Harry checked out the table. "That cutlery is immense," she said, looking at her reflection on the back of a spoon. "I'd like these at home."

"Well don't go stealing them," Ken laughed. "And no taking photos of your meal as soon as it arrives.

Or selfies with Norbert in the background. I saw you looking at his bum as we came in"

"You're childish." Harry said, laying the spoon back on the table and rearranging her cutlery so that it was symmetrical.

Ken smiled at her and laid a hand on her shoulder. "Only joking, Harry. You relax and do what you're comfortable doing."

"I shall."

"But leave Norbert's bum alone."

"Shut up."

During the meal, Florence came to the conclusion that Harry was doing her best to make small talk. She asked about everything and made copious notes on her iPad. At the end, when she excused herself to make space for coffee, Ken explained to Florence about Harry's memory problem. He pointed out that taking notes was a necessary survival strategy in case she woke up in the morning with all her mental directories wiped clean.

"My God, the poor girl," Florence gasped. "And she's Obsessive Compulsive too. Life must be a nightmare for her."

"That's why she often shrinks into her shell. Tonight is the most I've ever heard her say in the space of two hours."

"Why do you think that is?"

"I guess it's because she has decided to trust you. She will have judged early on whether you were a perceived threat to her or whether you fell into the 'friends' category. Seeing the two of us together, she will have judged you to be okay."

"So she'll not have judged me by the way I react to her?"

"Not to begin with. That part of her character and her bluntness are a form of mild autism. I did warn you she was strange. But don't let all that fool you. She is a smart cookie when it comes to figures and computers, and her memory is prodigious. If she took an IQ test she'd ace it."

"I did," Harry said, sliding back into her chair. "They're too easy."

Florence reached across and held Harry's hand in hers. She noticed that, while she'd been in the toilets, Harry had removed the old lace glove from her right hand and not replaced it. "Harry, we're delighted to have you over here. Thank you for agreeing to help."

"Oh it's alright. You're paying anyway."

Ken chuckled. After coffee, as the waiter presented the bill, he reached for his bank card, but Florence passed it back to him. "You're my guests," she said. "It's my treat." She laid her card into the leather folder with the bill then looked at Harry. "So, how was the duck?"

"Not very good?"

"Not good? Why what was wrong with it?"

"Don't ever play poker with her," Ken said. "She may not do small talk, but she does straight face better than anyone I know."

"I did small talk this evening."

"You did, Harry, and you were a pleasure to be

with," Florence said.

She blushed and went back to tapping on her iPad.

As they left the hotel, Florence looked up. Night had fallen and the sky was as clear as it got in a big city. Ken said, "Are you leaving your car here?"

Florence confirmed with a nod. "It's only a hundred metres to the apartment and I won't find a parking place any closer. I can't be bothered manoeuvring into the courtyard tonight."

"Can I retrieve my laptop then?" Harry asked.

They strolled down the boulevard in companionable silence until arriving at Florence's. "I see the big van's gone," she said. They stepped through the wicket door and Florence opened the door into the main entrance foyer. As she turned to watch Ken and Harry follow her, she did a double take. "Oh bloody hell, what's happened?"

Ken followed her line of sight and saw the door of the wine cellar was closed, but somebody had forced it. There was obvious damage to the lock area and the surrounding wood had been splintered. He stepped in front of Florence and approached the door. She followed him. "Don't touch anything," he said, "there may be fingerprints." He took a clean handkerchief from his pocket, pushed the door open and reached in for the light switch. Together, with Harry close behind, they descended the staircase.

"Oh no!" Florence wailed as she saw the rows of empty and part-empty wine racks. "Someone's helped themselves to all the best wines." She approached the nearest racks. "The 1989 Château Terrey-Gros-Cailoux was there. There was a 1997

Château Notton here. This was where I kept the 1998 Château Yon Figeac." She continued to list the missing wines on her fingers. To Ken, they all sounded the wrong end of expensive.

"Are you insured?" he asked.

"I have some cover. But it's not just the money, Ken; it's the fact that someone has invaded my home. And I was looking forward to trying some of those wines. I've had the 1975 Château Margaux for years and was planning serving it at a dinner party for my best customers. It's worth about €300 a bottle, but that's not the point. Presenting quality wines is my livelihood, and I can't afford to serve buyers a wine that I don't know."

"Well talking of invading your home, hadn't we better go up and check on the apartment?"

Florence nodded. "It should be okay. There's a top of the range security system on all these apartments."

"The code's 8430," Harry said. "A child of three with a simple laptop could crack that in ten seconds. I did, anyway."

"Oh Jesus," Florence said. "I didn't realise we were vulnerable there."

"Stay here and call the police," Ken said. "I will go up and check the apartment. I take it Harry had the right code."

Florence nodded.

When Ken had left, Harry stood a little to one side looking awkward. "Is there any way to trace them, or prove the wines are yours if the police find the thieves?" she asked.

"Yes, but the chances are remote that we'll ever find them now. I put a tiny mark on the label of all my bottles. Take a look if you like."

Harry stepped to the nearest occupied rack and removed a bottle. She searched the label until seeing the initials 'FdN' in tiny script in one corner. "Why not write it in large letters right across the label?" she asked.

"It would devalue the wine, particularly if I ever decided to sell it for some reason."

"But nobody is ever going to notice this."

"I know, but in fact every bottle in here has my telephone number written across it with an ultraviolet marker pen. Invisible to the human eye, but visible under UV light."

"Not many places use UV light though," Harry said.

"It's a security method that many wine amateurs use nowadays. Wine theft is becoming more and more prevalent and if you are suspicious about someone offering you wines on the cheap, you can use an ultraviolet blacklight torch to check if they have been marked."

"So your only chance of having these found is if they are offered to someone as knock-off and that person is honest?"

"That's more or less it, yes."

"Most unlikely, I would have thought. Anyone buying stolen goods is hardly going to worry as long as the marking isn't obvious."

"Thanks for cheering me up, Harry."

"I'm just stating the obvious," she said. "Hadn't you

better call the police?"

# CHAPTER TEN

It was almost one o'clock by the time the police and the scene of crime technicians had left. It seemed that the thieves had worn gloves since only two sets of prints were found and the most common one was the small hand of a woman. The police technician speculated that the prints were those of Florence and one other, most likely Ken. They'd taken their fingerprints to cross-check.

Florence sat nursing a glass of Calvados. Ken had another Talisker whisky with ice. Florence had called out an all-night locksmith who had replaced the broken lock. At her request he was now downstairs adding a high security second lock and a steel keep to the door. He'd given Florence the name of a security company who did work for banks and security vaults. Florence planned to call them in the morning and have the cellar alarmed and her apartment redone. It might have been closing the door after the horse had bolted, but at least the door would be closed.

"Where's Harry?" Florence asked.

"I think she went to bed an hour ago. She muttered

something about that white van then disappeared up the stairs."

"Do you reckon that van had anything to do with it?" Ken asked.

"It's possible. I told the police about it and they said they will take a walk up and down outside and see if there are any security cameras that would give a clue. Maybe I should get this security firm to add a camera to our entrance too."

Ken nodded. "Get to bed, Florence. I'll wait up till the locksmith has finished."

She shook her head. "I don't think I shall sleep, I'm so damn annoyed. Like I say, it's not just the financial loss, it's the feeling of having been violated. If I knew who planned it, I'd be happy to waste a good bottle of wine by smashing it over their head."

"What's the financial loss?"

Florence picked up a notepad from the arm of the chair where, for the police, she had earlier listed the wines that she knew to have been taken. "I've not got them all, but at the moment it looks like somewhere between €175,000 and €190,000. That's cost price of course, not retail. Retail would be double that, and restaurant prices about four or five times that."

Ken whistled. "Will the insurance cover it?"

"About half of it, maybe. I was given many of those wines by the vignerons, so there are no invoices. On the other hand, I use the same insurance company for all the company business, so maybe they will take a kindly view of things."

Harry came down the big staircase. "Can you help me with some French?" she asked.

"Go ahead," Florence said.

Harry sat down opposite her, iPad in hand. "Well, I'm just downloading all the emails off your company's server. Once they're—"

"You're what?" Florence screeched, her body going rigid with shock.

"I'm downloading all the emails off your company's server. Is that a problem?"

"Of course it is. Why are you doing that and how did you get access?"

Harry stopped and dropped her eyes to her lap, picking at the arm of the chair with her nails. She put the end of a curl of hair into her mouth, making her next few words indistinct. "I logged in on the computer in your office upstairs. You've got a network connection up there."

"But you don't know the— Oh never mind. So tell me why you are downloading private emails from my business?"

Harry looked up. "I'm sorry."

"It's okay," Ken said. "Tell us why you need those emails though."

"Because you weren't just chosen at random. Even the wines they took weren't chosen at random. You said they had taken all the best wines."

Florence's body relaxed back into the chair as she pondered what Harry had said for a moment. "Okay, let's assume someone targeted me."

"They did. That white van was parked just down the road when we left tonight. When you got back it was parked outside your apartment. If you hadn't come back early, you wouldn't have seen it: they would have loaded and gone. If we'd not gone to the restaurant, you would have caught them in the act. So somebody had a pretty good idea you wouldn't be here this evening."

Ken nodded. "Makes sense so far."

"It also has to be someone who knows what wines you have here," Harry said. "Or at least knows what sorts of wines they are likely to find. I bet you that if you think about it long enough you'll come to the same conclusion as me. That it was someone who works for you or who knows your business well."

"Er—"

"Don't worry, you'll get there in the end. So anyway, I'm at the moment downloading all the emails off your company's server onto a 30 terabyte storage drive that I brought with me. It shouldn't need anything like that amount of memory unless there are lots of attachments. The download will take at least overnight because the download speed isn't brilliant here. Meanwhile, though, I need to know what keywords to start looking for once I've downloaded all the emails."

"But looking through every email will take—"

"I'm not going to look at any emails until I've narrowed the field. That's why I came down to ask you to help me with some French"

"What do you need to know?" Florence asked.

"I'm going to set a bot to run—"

“A what?”

“A bot - a robot. An automated search programme looking for phrases that might pick up emails to or from someone targeting this building. For example, the word ‘Marceau’ is a keyword, because of the location. The number 40 on its own might be worth looking for. 40, Avenue Marceau is an obvious one.”

“You should try 40 ave Marceau too, since that’s how the French would write it.” Ken said.

“See, now you’re thinking.”

“I have a list here of the wines that they took,” Florence said, waving her notepad. “There are going to be others but I can recall most of them now. You could use those as search terms.”

“I’ll keep it as backup if I find nothing,” Harry said.

“But these are well-known good wines.”

“Exactly. There could be thousands of innocent references in people’s emails. Yours is, after all, a business that deals in wine.”

“Of course. Do you think someone planned the robbery to that extent?”

“It had to be. Unless one of them tonight was a wine expert, the people who broke into your cellar would need to know what to look for. You say you had about 5,000 bottles and they stole the best 2,500. That means someone would have made a list.”

“The vigik,” Ken said. They must have known the vigik too.”

“What’s that?” Harry asked.

"It's the security pad outside. Each resident has a badge that you press to the vigik and it springs the electronic catch."

"Oh, one of those. We've known the weaknesses in those for about ten years. With the right reader, you can check the contents of the badge and you can manually key it in on the touch pad. You can also duplicate the badges if you want."

"Well, ignoring that for a moment, the code here is 14C78 so you might want to key that into your search terms." Ken scrutinised Harry for a moment. "You seem certain it was someone linked to Florence's business," he said. "But what if it was a resident of this building who's seen Florence entering or leaving her wine cellar?"

"No way," Harry said. "It's too close to home. In any case, there are now in the region of 2,500 bottles of fine wine to dispose of. It's going to be obvious to the police if someone tries to put them on eBay or something. There's a limited market for those wines so it's almost certain that there's a dealer involved somewhere. The obvious place to start looking is in Florence's own business."

Ken looked at Florence. "She has a point."

"Of course I do. Now then, how heavy is a bottle of wine?"

"A standard case of wine contains twelve 750ml bottles and has a total weight of roughly 18 kilos or 40 pounds," Florence said.

"So if they took 2,500 bottles, that's just over 200 cases, so a total weight of just over three-and-a-half metric tonnes. They must have had someone loading wine into empty cartons while others carried them to the vans."

"We only saw one van," Florence said.

"You only saw one, but they must have run a relay of at least two, and maybe three. When we got back, the van outside was a long wheelbase Mercedes-Benz. I just looked it up on the net and the maximum payload is a fraction over two tonnes. I don't know what the van was that was here when we left, but I didn't have the impression it was a long wheelbase. So they must have had four or five people chasing up and down your cellar steps for at least an hour, maybe an hour and a half. And, at a minimum, they had two vans that they fully loaded. I'm more inclined to think there would have been three vans that they loaded to safe limits."

"Makes you wonder if anyone else in the building saw anything," Ken said.

"I'll go and ask them tomorrow. I guess the police will as well."

"I also checked your accountancy department records, Florence—"

"Is nothing sacred?"

"Do you want me to help or not?"

"Yes, I'm sorry Harry. Go on."

"I checked your accountancy department records. Your company runs two long wheelbase Mercedes-Benz 311cdi Sprinter Box 2.2. You also have an assortment of smaller short wheelbase panel vans. They're all white and, as far as I can tell, they're not sign-written. Can you make some discrete calls in the morning and see if anyone is aware of them being where they shouldn't have been?"

"Why discrete?"

"Because for the moment we don't want to scare anyone into trying to cover their tracks."

After a moment's silence, Florence said, "Thank you, Harry. Sorry I jumped when you said you'd hacked my own company network. I was just surprised, that was all."

"I didn't hack it," Harry said. "I used your password."

"But where did you get that?"

"You allowed the computer to remember it so you didn't have to key it in every time you logged onto the company network."

"And you looked in the file where the computer stores the information?"

"I didn't need to. Because you'd asked for it to be remembered, your computer offered it to me as soon as I went to the log-in screen. I just had to hit Tab."

"But how did you log onto my computer in the first place. It's password protected."

"What? Your birthday backwards? That's no protection."

Florence's jaw fell open.

"How did you know her birthday?" Ken asked, smiling.

Harry tapped her iPad and said, "I looked it up when you asked me to come over here. I wanted to know if she was someone you might be having sex with, or whether she was too old."

Ken roared laughing. "What difference would it make?"

"None. I just like to know these things. I like information. I have stored everything I know about each of you and I used that information to log on to Florence's computer."

"But it could have been anything. You could have been there all night."

"I used a bit of software that creates a brute force attack. Using what I already know about you, it calculates every possible combination that could make up a password and tests it to see if it is correct. It can test up to one thousand different combinations per second. It found yours straight away."

"So how do you protect your own laptop?" Florence asked.

"I've added a one-time pad cryptograph, where every cleartext bit has a corresponding key from a random sequence of key bits." Harry stood, turned, and headed back up the stairs.

When she was out of earshot, Florence looked at Ken and chuckled. "I know you said she was strange, but I think you maybe could have expanded on that a little."

"If I'd told you the truth would you have been happy to have had her in your home?"

Florence thought for a moment. "Yes, I believe I would. People are what they are, Ken. They don't design themselves that way."

"At least with Harry, what you see is what you get. She's incapable of lying, because she doesn't see the truth as a problem."

"But how does she do what she does with computers?"

"I have no idea. I did actually ask her that question once and she muttered about WPA and weak passwords. She said she captures the authentication handshake and cracks it in the 'cloud' using a brute force algorithm, whatever that means. Oh, and she tells me she spoofs her own IP so as not to get caught. Are you any the wiser?"

"Yeah much!"

"All I know, Florence, is that she charges a lot, but always gets good information."

Upstairs, Harry fumbled with the bedroom door handle. If her appearance matched her emotions she cringed at how all over the place she must look. She hadn't spoken so much in a long while, and now she played back the conversations to check that she hadn't said anything wrong. She had a habit of saying things wrong according to one child psychiatrist from the past.

She was too blunt and should learn to be more diplomatic, he had said. At the time, she didn't know what diplomatic meant. She still wasn't sure that she grasped the concept. You had to say something you didn't mean so that people would understand what you really meant without being angry with you. Sounded like a stupid idea.

Once inside the bedroom, she could feel herself relaxing. There was no-one in here watching out for her faults. She threw her iPad onto the bed and then threw herself next to it and rolled onto her back, staring up at the ceiling. At least up there, everything was symmetrical.

After a moment, she closed her eyes and breathed in through her nose. She counted to ten then let the breath escape through her mouth as slowly as she could. She felt the panic inside her begin to subside and flow outwards. She pictured it as a physical entity that she could expel and watch float away towards the mouldings on the ceiling.

Repeating the exercise twice more, she began to relax, her thoughts organizing themselves into a list in her mind. She liked lists. She could manage lists. She could organise them and control them. How anyone got through their lives without numbered bullet-pointed tasks to guide them was beyond her comprehension.

Harry sat up, pulled off her wig and shook her head. She fingered her curly, caramel-coloured hair that sat on her shoulders in waves. Maybe tomorrow she'd go without a wig. She cast a quick glance into the gilt mirror screwed to the wall. It was going to annoy her until she went home because it was a couple of millimetres out of upright. Her dark brown eyes glistened with good humour. It was a sentiment she only gave way to when she felt secure.

She knew that many people thought she had attitude. Of course she had fucking attitude. In this disorganised world, anyone who was born with the need to have everything symmetrical and in a perfect order was at a disadvantage right from the get-go. She knew she did things differently to other people but she'd long ago stopped worrying about that. She'd done well for a twenty-six-year-old. Her home was large, comfortable and paid for, and she had more money in the bank than she knew what to do with. Unless, of course, they found a cure for her confabulation. She'd spend every penny she had, if someone could sort that out for her.

She thought back to her long day. It had been demanding but exciting. Travel was always a challenge in case she had a memory wipe-out on the way. Not that it had ever happened. But once she had established at the airport that Ken Stafford was a former lover - there had been few of those in her life - she felt more anchored to his world. The outline information on her iPad had triggered the filling of a confabulation memory gap, and the details had all come flooding back of their own accord. Her time with him had been good. He was a nice guy and a good-looking guy and if he was at a loose end any time, she'd be glad to have him back in her life - and her bed. It wasn't a boyfriend she needed, it was a good old-fashioned shag. She didn't miss him; she just missed the idea of him, and sex always made things better. It was a long time since she'd had sex.

Florence had been nice enough too. When they had met, she had held out her hand for Harry to shake. Harry didn't do handshakes but she had registered the well maintained nails and had relented and taken the offered hand. Florence had a grip as strong and genuine as the smile she offered.

And Harry liked Florence's kitchen as well. The lounge was too big and there were too many items of old furniture, but the kitchen was modern with sleek lines and chrome appliances. Not cosy. Nobody should have a cosy kitchen. Everything was in there for a purpose but was so shiny that it was a stain or hand-print hazard. Not that that mattered to Florence, who had a woman come to clean twice a week, it seemed.

Harry opened the cover on her iPad and tapped the screen a few times. She already knew that Florence de Nussac and Ken Stafford were married once and had had a child who had disappeared. All that information was available on the internet and Harry stored information because - well, because she could.

Tomorrow with a rental car, she would go back to Florence's brother's apartment block and see what she could learn from his home computer. Then she would sit outside his office address and see what she could get there too. There was bound to be something that they could use as leverage against him.

Maybe tomorrow evening they could go back to Le M64 restaurant and see if Norbert was there. She'd not spotted a wedding ring, but perhaps she would ask him if he was married, just to be sure.

# CHAPTER ELEVEN

As Florence placed scrambled egg on toast in front of Ken, Harry stepped through the doorway. "The download is still going from your company emails," she said. "It's a slow connection here."

"And good morning to you," Florence said.

"Oh yes. Good morning. What's Ken got?"

"Scrambled egg on toast. Would you like some?"

"Yes please. I don't care if eggs are white, brown, or speckled; I just plan to eat them. Fried, boiled or scrambled, I don't care."

Florence shook her head but, as soon as Harry sat down, she placed her breakfast in front of her.

"That was quick," Ken said, between mouthfuls.

Harry placed her iPad next to her plate and moved her plate until she was satisfied with its position. "Florence gave me hers," she said, "because it was already made and it would go cold while she was making mine. So it was easier to give me hers and make a fresh one for herself."

Ken looked at Florence, who was smiling. "That's me told," he said. "Juice Harry?"

"No thanks."

"Your hair looks nice," Florence said. "I like it better than the wig."

"That's me told," Harry said, looking at Ken with a straight face.

"Oh I didn't mean— "

"She's joking, Florence. She's got the poker face on."

"I can do small talk and jokes now," Harry said with a slight blush. "Can you get me that car when we've had breakfast? With a GPS. And can you give me the address of your brother's main office; the one he uses as his base to work from?"

"No problem," Florence said, with her back to them as she beat her eggs and placed them in the microwave.

Harry glanced at Florence. "Do you know you can see through that kaftan when the light's behind you? Is that for Ken's benefit?" Without waiting for a response, she bit into a piece of buttered toast. "Du pain, du vin, du Boursin," she continued. "Strap line for a French cheese advert years ago. What are you two doing today?"

"We have a little problem we're working on," Ken replied. "Florence is going to make a couple of calls and arrange for them to upgrade the security system here. And then we shall be going to the east of Paris near Parc Buttes-Chaumont."

"What's that?"

"It's a park in the 9th arrondissement."

"Why are you going there?"

"Someone we know lives there and we want to try and find out a bit more about him."

Harry looked at Ken and said, "You don't want to tell me what it is, do you?"

"Not at the moment, Harry."

"You know I could find out if I wanted to."

"I'm sure you could. But if Florence and I asked you not to, you wouldn't, would you?"

"No."

"Okay, well we're asking you not to."

"Fine. Let me know if you need any help."

"We will."

"So tell me instead how you and Florence met."

Florence laughed, though she had her back to them. "Ken played the hero," she said, and her voice was smiling. "I went to Hereford to do some translation work for a French company who were setting up there. Ken and I had actually seen each other in a pub a few nights earlier, but hadn't spoken. One night, I went to the same pub with a girl I was working with. A couple of loud-mouthed men came in and started pestering Jill, that was my friend's name, and me. They were making some unpleasant remarks about the pair of us."

"So Ken came in and hit them?" Harry asked.

"More or less. Ken came in and bet them that the two of them together couldn't beat his mate Billy in a fair fight."

"The idiots were up for it," Ken added. "So we went outside and Big Billy laid them both flat."

"And who was this Big Billy?" Harry asked.

That would be me," Ken said. "If you are going to pick a fight in a bar, best not to do it in an army town. Particularly Hereford which is the headquarters of Special Services."

"So then you hit on Florence?"

"I whispered in her friend's ear."

"What did you say?"

"I asked her to tell her friend that I'd like to meet her later."

"And?"

"And her friend, Jill, shouted, 'Oy, Florence, this guy fancies you'. So now I knew her name, I considered we had been formally introduced, and asked her out."

Harry smiled and she and Ken continued to eat in companionable silence. Florence joined them moments later when her scrambled eggs were ready.

When Harry had finished eating, she laid her knife and fork down on her plate, adjusted them into the vertical, and said, "Do you want to tell me now?"

Ken said, "What? Tell you what?"

"Tell me who it is you're trying to find out more about."

"For goodness sake, Harry, is nothing sacred? Do you deem every bit of information yours?"

"Of course I do. It's how I earn a living."

"Yes, but normally people ask you to look for information; like we've asked you to look into

Florence's brother. Just because you hear us talking about finding out a bit more about someone else, you don't need to be involved."

"Unless you ask me?"

"Yes, unless we ask you."

"Okay, well ask me then. What do you need to know about Tristan?"

Florence dropped her knife and fork. The knife bounced off the plate and scuttled across the floor.

Ken said, "Harry, what have you been up to?"

"Nothing."

"You must have been, otherwise you wouldn't have known about Tristan."

"Don't be silly. You phoned me and asked me to come over to France. My memory wiped out a week ago, so when you phoned I didn't know who you were. But I had you in my iPad and that filled in the blanks. And you told me it was to help Madame Florence de Nussac. I looked up the de Nussac family on the web so I know who I'm dealing with. I find that the two of you were married and you had a little boy called Tristan who disappeared when he was three. The papers were full of it sixteen years ago."

Florence took a clean knife from the drawer, dumping the dropped one into the sink. "But how did you know we were looking for information on Tristan?"

"Because nobody who has lost a child ever gives up looking. And I knew you hadn't stayed married because you've reverted to your maiden name. And

Ken and I had sexual relations fifty-four times over a period of one hundred and twenty three days. It was on my iPad."

Florence's eyes half closed and she said, "Are you trying to shock me?"

Harry looked surprised. "Why would I? I'm just stating a fact. If Ken lived with me for one hundred and twenty three days, and he lives on the Isle of Man, it's obvious you and he are no longer together. Did I get it wrong? I get things wrong sometimes."

Florence pushed her unfinished breakfast away. "No, Harry, you didn't get it wrong. Maybe it was just the way you described it."

Harry looked down at her plate. "Oh, it's —" and her foot began to jiggle on the tiles.

"It's okay," Ken said, taking hold of her hand. "We're good, Harry. It's no problem, honest." He looked at Florence with an unspoken message that she understood. She hadn't realised just how fragile Harry was when challenged about her careless attitude. She, too, leaned across the table and touched the back of Harry's hand with her fingers.

Harry mumbled. "I didn't mean anything by it. I don't know which bit of what I said was wrong, but I meant no harm."

"Sorry, Harry, you and I don't know each other as well as you and Ken know each other. I'm sure that I'll get used to you and you'll get used to me very quickly." Harry looked up. Her foot stopped jiggling and Florence could see an unshed sliver of a tear in the corner of her eye. She kicked herself for being so stupid. Of course the girl meant nothing by it. It was just her way. It was who she was, and she was doing an amazing job coping with her problems. "Cup of coffee?" she asked.

Harry nodded. "It's just that to me it was obvious that Ken was over here because you were looking for information on Tristan. In fact, I thought that's why you'd asked me over. It was also the most logic conclusion out of a total of three."

"What were the other two conclusions?"

"There were two other possibilities. One was that you had news and that Tristan was dead. If that was the case the newspapers would be full of it. The other was that you'd found Tristan. But again, if that was true, it would be all over the news, 'Missing boy found after 16 years'."

"We think we may have found him," Florence said, getting up to fetch the coffee pot. "There's a young man who matches him. The person we believe is Tristan is fair like Ken with the same wide eyes, prominent nose and generous lips. He has a masculine face; strong and angular with a wide expanse of forehead where there's a slight discoloration of the skin at the site of a childhood haemangioma. His friends even call him Tristan."

"So it's all over then?"

"Our ordeal isn't over, Harry. It isn't even close. The lad may look like the person we imagine Tristan to be, and we may both believe that's who he is, but proving it is going to be a bit harder. To begin with, we have to find out his full name and where his home is. I had a private detective onto it a few weeks ago. Tristan is studying languages at The Sorbonne and we have an address near Buttes-Chaumont where he lodges. But we need to know more about him, particularly the family name he's using. The private detective wasn't able to get that information."

"He wasn't very good then," Harry said. "It shouldn't be too difficult; just ask at the university."

"They would never give that sort of information," Ken said. "You know how particular official establishments are nowadays about privacy and data protection."

"Well I can ask in my own way," Harry said, blowing across her coffee. "If you don't find out today, let me know and I'll go and log into the university's student register and find out."

"You reckon that's feasible?"

"Of course it is. Walk in there with a load of other students, head for the IT lab or the library. Borrow someone's login and get onto the server, then do a bit of straightforward hacking to get to the student records. There can't be too many people called Tristan, and the university should have their home addresses. It doesn't sound like the most challenging of tasks."

Ken looked at Florence and raised his eyebrows.

"You do what you can regarding my brother today, please," Florence said. "And you've already said that you're also still downloading all my company's emails at the moment looking for the wine thief."

Harry nodded.

"Well it sounds like you're pretty well occupied I would say. If Ken and I can't discover more today, we'll ask you to take a look tomorrow. How does that sound?"

"Yeah, fine by me." She turned to Ken. "See, some people can be nice. You should try harder."

Ken smiled. "Poker face."

# CHAPTER TWELVE

It was late morning before Ken and Florence arrived on the street where the private detective had told them Tristan was lodging. Rue Compans was a dull street of bland buildings that would improve only if somebody demolished them. It was a mish-mash of styles, shapes and sizes. The only thing the buildings had in common was the fact that none of them looked as though anyone cared.

They walked up the slope from where they had parked, looking for number 87. When it came into view, Florence shuddered. It was a square concrete structure which, when built, had been a cheap Art Deco copy. It was difficult to estimate the building's age, but Florence guessed early 1920's as France was rebuilding after the First World War.

The entrance door was up three concrete steps. What was left of the paintwork was red and there was a square glass pane at eye level. Behind the glass were metal bars. Across the front of the building at street level were three windows with external metal shutters. It didn't appear that anyone had opened them for many years, the rust having taken hold of the hinges and welded them together.

Directly above those, on first floor level, were three

more windows of equal width. There were no shutters to draw but all three had grey net curtains clinging to grey wet windows, making sure that no superfluous light would enter there. It was unlikely that the nets would even survive ten minutes in a washing machine. The concrete exterior displayed running rust in places where reinforcing rods had blasted off a poor mix of concrete. At low level, tags and graffiti were the dominant architectural styling.

Opposite the house was a tall infants school, and it was clear that sunlight never reached the street or, indeed, the house that Tristan shared with others. Ken tried the door but it was locked. He pressed the bell push but heard no noise from the inside. The only sounds were the white noise of Parisian traffic mixed in with muffled music pulsing from a building to their right.

"No mail boxes," he said, "so I guess it's one house with everybody sharing."

"That's more or less what the detective said," Florence answered. She looked at the buildings on either side. Though constructed of brick rather than concrete, their condition did nothing to lift her spirits. If Tristan was her son, she owed it to him to find him somewhere better than this. "Bloody depressing, isn't it," she said.

Ken nodded. "Either we wait for someone to turn up and ask them if they know Tristan or we get Harry on the job tomorrow."

"Even if someone shows up, they're unlikely to give any information to a pair of strangers. The only other thing to do would be to wait for Tristan to arrive home."

"And what? Ask him what his name is?" Ken said. "Come on, let's get out of here. Let's go back to The Sorbonne. If we see Tristan, I'll get us something for a DNA test."

"How are you going to do that?"

"Watch and see!"

Three hours later, after a light lunch at Le Procope, one of the city's oldest restaurants, founded in 1686 and still going strong, Ken and Florence sat waiting for the student exodus. When it began, Florence's right foot began to judder up and down on the accelerator, just as it had the day before. Shake-shake-shake. Shake-shake-shake.

"Calm down," Ken said. "It won't be long." The words weren't yet out of his mouth when the tall fair-haired youth they assumed to be Tristan appeared with his friends. "Stay here," Ken said, and slid from the car. He strode across the road and disappeared from view round the corner towards the cafe where they had seen them go before.

Florence's foot started again, Shake-shake-shake. Shake-shake-shake.

And then Ken was back and smiling. He opened the door with his left hand and slid into the car. "Put your hand in my jacket pocket will you, Florence. You'll find a small plastic food bag in there that I took from the kitchen." Florence pulled out the bag. "Be very careful. Open it, so you don't contaminate the inside." She did so and Ken placed his right hand over the top and sprinkled a few light hairs into the bag. He took it off her and sealed it. "Done job."

"Those are Tristan's hairs?"

He nodded.

"How did you get them?"

"I apologised for speaking to him in English but told him he had a wasp in his hair. Then, without waiting, I pretended to get it out and wave it away. He wasn't even aware I had a few of his hairs. He thanked me and went on his way."

Florence smiled. "And now that you've been close up to him, do you still think it could be Tristan?"

"I would say I'm about 90% certain. There's just something about him that is just - well - right."

"I don't suppose you asked him his family name while you were at it, did you?"

Ken laughed. "Of course I did. He told me to mind my own business."

"So how do you get that hair tested?"

"I have a friend back on the Isle of Man who is a Detective Chief Inspector. His name's Angus Slooth."

"You're kidding me?"

"No honest. He often has to explain that he's Slooth by name and sleuth by nature. If we courier these hairs to him today, he'll get them tested as soon as he can and have a comparison made. We'll also need to send some samples of our own."

Florence turned her head. "Why? Why do they need our DNA if they already have Tristan's from the original searches?"

"Because DNA sampling is now very refined. Much more so than it was sixteen years ago. Now they check for familial matches and so on. The more information they have, the more accurate their results. Does it trouble you?"

Florence hesitated a beat, then said "No," in a small, quiet voice.

"So anyway, Angus is not without some considerable influence. I rang him yesterday and explained the nature of what we were doing. He said he would talk to a senior officer in Hereford and see if they would release a copy of the DNA results to him from sixteen years ago."

"He won't get into trouble will he?"

"Not Angus. He'll clear it with David Pownall, the chief constable, first. We've done the police lots of favours since we set up on the Isle of Man seven years ago. Sparky, who's holding the fort at work at the moment, almost got himself killed two years back when we had a crazy man with a chemical agent running loose on the island. I don't suppose David will worry too much about a few quid to get a DNA test done."

"So now we get hold of a courier?"

"Let's go."

# CHAPTER THIRTEEN

To the West of Paris, not far from the Château de Saint-Germain-en-Laye, Harry shuffled around in the car seat. She willed the WiFi connection to speed up. The French might be good at baguettes and foie gras, but they were lousy at public toilets. And it was a toilet that Harry needed more than anything else right now.

She was as fidgety as an old maid as the data continued to download. She knew she could walk to the brasserie at the end of the street and use their loo. But she also knew that if she cut the connection to Yves-Marie's house, she would have to start all over again. And she dared not leave her laptop in the car while she relieved herself.

At long last, the download completed. She bundled her laptop into a hessian bag as fast as she could, jumped from the car and strode to the brasserie on the corner. She darted in, ordered a Diet Coke, or Coke Light as it was known in France, and a 'Croque-Monsieur' - melted cheese and ham on toast. Without waiting to draw breath, she disappeared down the steps to les toilettes below.

When she emerged, she felt better than she had for the last hour and slid onto a long leather banquette with her back to the wall. She felt tempted to take out her laptop and her 30 terabyte storage drive, to see what she had downloaded from Yves-Marie's hard disk. But she knew there was a lot there, particularly in the 'Pictures' directory, so she went to her iPad instead. She spent a few moments entering the details of the day's activities so far, and indexed the entry under the date and several different keywords.

It had been the child psychologist's idea that she kept a diary. The psychologist thought it would be therapeutic. In fact, it turned out to be more than that. It had kept Harry sane because if she had to wait for nature to fill the holes in her memory every time she had a wipe-out, she would still be waiting. Seeing a mnemonic in writing triggered her memory and filled the holes immediately. She knew that, at some later date, when she had no memory of this morning, she would see the bullet points on her iPad and the whole morning would come flooding back in fine detail, including her need to wee. It would stay there until the next memory wipe-out. When she finished writing, she sent a backup into the cloud and closed her iPad, just as her food and drink arrived.

The waiter looked twice at the old lace glove on her right hand, but tried not to let it show. Harry glanced down at it. She knew she had been wearing it for many years but couldn't remember why. When she was alone, or in company where she didn't feel threatened, she would remove the glove to expose a small anchor tattoo. But she couldn't remember why that was there either. Nothing in her notes had ever triggered any memories. Also, her finger nails were always painted different colours but she knew why she did that: she just found it interesting. It amused her, so why not.

She glanced at her digital watch, 13:44. That was a nice figure. The sum of the numbers was 12, and 12 squared was 144, which was the same time of day if you were wearing a 12 hour watch instead of a 24 hour watch. It was also the number of the building where Yves-Marie's business was located: 144 Rue de la République. As she finished her toasted cheese and ham, she logged on to Google Earth and pulled up the location. The office was on a busy junction of three main roads and three smaller roads about one kilometre away. There was no way she would be able to sit in her car to access his network.

Harry manoeuvred around the laptop screen and spotted a café and bar on the other side of the narrow adjacent road. She hoped it would offer WiFi. If not she carried a high speed USB dongle and could soon piggyback a local service. The challenge she faced was that she was trying to hack a business and businesses often hardwired their internal network. However, with high speed wireless routers now, many were forsaking the miles of cable and were happy to simplify their systems. She would see what faced her when she got there.

Harry packed away her stuff, paid her bill and walked back to the car, then decided to keep walking to get to Yves-Marie's offices. The weather was warm and welcoming, and her rental car was in a zone that required no ticket or resident's permit. She set off, admiring the ancient buildings with their honey-coloured stone, shuttered windows, and impossibly steep roofs. Even the shops were up-market and classy. It struck her that the centre of Saint-Germain was so well-maintained, it must cost a fortune to live here.

When she arrived at the rather complicated staggered road junction, she patted herself on the back for having decided to walk. Though there were a couple of parking places outside Yves-Marie's offices, few other spaces were available. And all of them had a 30 minute waiting limit.

She strained to read the name on the bar-café on the corner just across one of the narrow roads. It wasn't that it was dirty or in bad condition, it was just that the writing was so stylised that she couldn't make any sense of it. She took a photo with her iPad then stepped inside and ordered une noisette - espresso with a dash of milk. She could make it last and French bars and cafés were quite used to customers who took lots of time to read the paper or, in Harry's case, work on her laptop. They didn't mind, except at busy meal times.

Harry logged on and spotted Yves-Marie's router straight away. He was so full of his own self-importance that he had named the router 'Bbox-YvesMarie'. But there was no point in trying to 'brute force' a commercial router, unless you had a couple of years to waste.

The waiter arrived with her noisette and she asked him what the name of the bar was. "Le Thiers," he replied. "It's written on the front of the building." Harry looked down to hide her blush. She'd never developed a hard outer shell, and even the mildest rebuttal bit deep. She used her iPad to look up 'Thiers' and found that it referred to someone called Adolphe Thiers who was once the president of the republic. That resolved, she noted it in her electronic diary, then went back to her laptop.

An 8-figure alpha-numeric security code including all the punctuation, special characters and capital letters gave 64 to the power of 8 possibilities. Which Harry just happened to know was 281,474,976,710,656. If you used a 13 figure code, the number of permutations increased exponentially. So Harry's brute force algorithm was of little use. In a home environment, people tended to code their router with the names of people and places or numbers like birthdays. They limited the possibilities and were much easier to crack.

Harry decided to approach the problem a different way. She sent an email to the admin address listed on Yves-Marie's website. Usually somebody low down the food chain monitored the public email address. They would eliminate the spam then decide who should deal with the query and forward the email to them.

Email viruses were real enough, but Harry knew that computers were no longer infected just by opening emails. On the other hand, attachments could still be dangerous to open. She was relying on the office junior being careless and opening the .xls attachment that she named 'Chiffre d'affaires annuel' - 'annual turnover'. The chances were high that the person involved would open it just to be nosy. The body of the email was simple enough - 'Herewith the figures you requested' - in French of course. Once opened, the macro virus would plant itself on the user's computer then worm its way through the system and give Harry access to their whole office network.

As she waited for a hit, she looked across at Florence's brother's offices on the other side of the road. Saint-Germain was one of the most exclusive dormitory towns for Paris so nothing was below standard. Out of the nine shop units available, Yves-Marie's business took up five. They were the smartest in the row. Blue aluminium shop fronts with subtly tinted plate glass. The signs said, 'De Nussac Assurances' and, if they were to be believed, Yves-Marie was into much more than simple insurance. According to his signage over each of the five frontages, he was also involved in real estate, loans, and even banking services.

Harry noted that on her iPad then looked around the bar. It was, to all intents and purposes a bar, tobacconist, café and it offered tickets for Loto, the popular French lottery. Anywhere else in France, there would be sawdust on the floor, and a dozen men would be standing outside smoking Gauloises. Here, however, in upmarket suburban France, the tone was much more select. The floor was clean, as were the tables, chairs and place settings. Harry wanted to straighten a couple of pictures on the walls because they were out of level. But she resisted the temptation so as not to draw attention to herself.

She glanced at the food menu. All the old favourites that could be found in most city cafés, were there. But there were also some rather more upmarket choices like 'Cassoulet au confit de Canard' and 'Saucisse de Canard aux lentilles et au piment d'Espelette'. These dishes were common in good restaurants but they were not your average café fayre. Harry wondered what the rentals on business premises were in the rarefied air of Saint-Germain.

As she considered, her laptop pinged and she had access to the office network on the other side of the road. Her first target was to download the contents of all the email boxes and for that, she needed to get onto the server. She hit lucky with the girl who had opened her email. The poor young lady knew nothing of security and had a file named 'mots de passe' - passwords - on her desktop of all places. Curious how, despite all the warnings, people could still be so careless about their data being compromised. Harry downloaded the file to her own desktop and found what she was looking for immediately - the username and password to the girl's email client. Once there, she could dig down on the server and get to the mail database, shared by all the employees.

It took her two minutes to segregate Yves-Marie's emails and two hours to download them. Meanwhile, she felt obliged to keep drinking noisettes so that the bar owner wouldn't pay any attention to her. The result was that she had no choice but to visit les toilettes and leave her laptop on the table. She rushed back as quickly as she could and sighed with relief when she saw that nothing had been disturbed.

As the data was downloading, Harry probed around in the accountancy records. One or two items caught her eye. She downloaded the things she felt were relevant. Her visit to Paris was showing signs of being fascinating.

When she had finished, she checked her digital watch 16:23. Interesting, add them up and there was that 12 again. She noted the time on her iPad, paid her bill and stepped out of the café into the late afternoon sunshine. Before leaving, she used her iPad to take a photograph of the front of Yves-Marie's offices. She didn't need it to fill memory gaps. If she had a memory wipe-out, just reading her notes about being here would bring the memories back. And taking a photo could act as a reminder if she needed a visual nudge.

Once she was back at Florence's she would set her search bots running on both sets of data and see what they might find. Meanwhile, she looked up at the blue sky and took a moment to enjoy the late afternoon sun. She decided to take a longer route back to the car, too see a bit more of the town. According to what she had seen on Google Earth, there were some interesting shops on the way.

# CHAPTER FOURTEEN

"How long does a DNA test take?" Florence asked.

"Usually up to about a week," Ken replied, "but Angus said he would get it pushed through as an urgent case, so three days, maybe four. Why?"

"I guess I'm just a bit nervous about it."

"No reason to be nervous. Either the boy is our lost son, or he's not."

"Yes, well—"

The door opened and Harry entered the lounge with her hessian bag over her shoulder, and a green and white shop bag in her hand.

"Hi Harry," Florence said, "Any success?"

Harry rested the hessian bag at the foot of the stairs and rubbed her shoulder. "Ken, turn that cushion round the other way, it's upside down."

Ken grinned, but did what she asked. "So, did you have any success?" he said.

"Quiet, I'm talking to Florence. Yes, I got what I wanted. There's a lot of data so I need to get some search criteria set up and start running them as soon as I can. It's going to take a while. And then I need to work my way through the results. I might need your help there, Florence. My French is reasonable, but not that good on technical things."

"No problem. Do you have to sit and watch things, or can they run on their own?"

"On their own. It could even take days. There was a lot of stuff at both locations." Harry looked at them shyly. "Do you want to eat with me tonight?"

"We never thought otherwise, Harry. The three of us will eat together as long as you are here and as long as you want to eat with us."

"No, I mean, I'm inviting you. You paid last night so I can pay this evening. I thought we might go to Le M64 again."

Ken laughed. "You want to get a good look at Norbert's bum again, don't you?"

"You can be childish." "Stop it." came from Harry and Florence simultaneously.

"Le M64 would be nice," Florence said. "And thank you for inviting us."

"I'll go set up these searches and take a shower," Harry said as she hoisted the hessian bag back onto her shoulder. She left them together. Ken had a beer in his hand: Florence a Martini Bianco. She made a mental note so she could add it to her iPad when she was in her room.

Harry was pleased with progress. Now that she had the downloads from Florence's brother, tomorrow she could help them find the family name of the boy they thought was their son. These were good people who didn't judge her, and she wanted to help if possible. She was sure she could.

In her bedroom, she tutted and moved the alarm clock a few centimetres. Florence had warned her that a cleaner came twice a week, but Harry had been hoping she would give her room a miss. She hated having to put things right again when people had touched them.

It took her less than ten minutes to set a search bot going on the emails from the business location. She found it easier and quicker to run a dozen or so search criteria at a time, then set a second set of searches going with different criteria. She took a long, luxurious shower, enjoying the warmth and the feeling of cleanliness. Amongst the various lotions and scents that were there for guests to use, Harry found a body lotion that suited her. She applied it liberally, luxuriating in its soothing coolness.

When she stepped back into the bedroom, she walked past a long, ornate, gilt mirror fixed to the wall. She stopped and stepped backwards to take a look at herself. She knew she wasn't beautiful, but she also knew that guys fancied her. The trouble was, none of them understood her. She was used to it now, but it could still hurt at times.

Harry was a little shorter than many who had been in her class at school. But she had a sculpted well-proportioned figure to match. Her firm, rounded breasts led down to a gently tapered waist and a rear that Ken called a bubble butt. Her legs were well toned but not muscular. Maybe she should go to a gym, she thought. Then she decided that was a silly idea and immediately forgot it.

She shook loose her coils of caramel-coloured hair

and spools of it plunged around her face and hid a swan's neck, elegant and smooth. She peered closer at her face. Her crescent shaped eyebrows inclined as she watched herself staring at her own reflection. Her eyelashes, which matched her caramel hair colour, blinked once, as if trying to puzzle out who she was. She knew she was complex, but she didn't know what she must do to change. In any case why should she change? She was Harriet Lewis. She was what she was.

Harry practised her bad girl stare in the mirror. It was a look that she saved for anyone who upset her. It was one of the penalties of being different; people felt it was their duty to get in your face for no reason. She creased her forehead into a frown and her eyes glared anger that could freeze another woman's bones. It made them feel like they were nude in the middle of a hailstorm, where every chunk of ice was a frosted dagger cutting into their skin. Whilst it was a little less effective on men, it generally made them back off from taunting her. Anyway, it was usually the women who wanted to pick a fight.

At home on the Isle of Man, Harry often wore Goth clothes in a rebellious way. While she had not come to France equipped for dining out, she had at least toned down to jeans and sweatshirt. But bearing in mind her wish to repay Florence, she had stopped at a clothes shop in Saint Germain and bought herself a green and black dress and a green glass necklace. The French were masters at accessorising and the lady in the shop had gone to great pains to find just the right necklace to go with the dress. Tonight she wanted to be different. And maybe Norbert did have something to do with it if she was honest with herself. Which she usually was.

After dressing, she checked her watch. 18:30. It was a magic figure because if you divided the18 by the 3, you got 6. Add back the minutes and it was 6:30 — the same time on a 12 hour clock. And that 12 was back again. She checked her purse to make sure she had her credit card with her, and then she headed for the door. But something made her stop before even touching the handle. It was just a thought that had niggled at her during the afternoon. From what both Ken and Florence had said, Yves-Marie didn't seem like the sort of person who would take lots of photos of his family. The way they described him, he was way more egotistical than that. "He's a bit precious, isn't he?" Ken had said. "Aptly named, though, don't you think?"

Harry stepped back to her laptop, which she had connected to the external storage drive. She navigated to the 'Pictures' directory on Yves-Marie's private home computer file and clicked it open. There were about a dozen photos which Harry displayed as extra large icons. It allowed her to view them as large thumbnails without opening each image. They were innocent pictures of his family. There was just one sub-directory, which Harry double-clicked, to find ten more sub-directories. She double-clicked the first one and froze. A cold, cold river of ice ran across her face, through her back, and down her legs. It took maybe ten whole seconds for her memory banks to reload, but when they did, she had total recall and collapsed in the chair, screaming like she was on fire.

Ken was first through the door, with Florence right behind. Ken grabbed Harry's shoulders, but she pushed him off, screeching, "Keep away. Just fucking keep away."

Ken glanced at Florence who tried the same thing. This time, Harry looked up, saw who it was, stifled her scream, and burst into tears.

"Harry, what's up? What's the matter?" Florence asked.

Harry nodded towards her laptop. Ken looked at it, then peered closer. "Oh my God," he gasped. "Are these off Yves-Marie computers?"

"His home laptop," Harry sobbed. She looked down at her right hand and drew in a sharp breath. "I know it all now. I know why the anchor is there. I know why I wear a glove when I feel anxious. I remember everything - and I wish to fucking god I didn't."

Her mind felt as if lead were coursing though it instead of blood. Her childhood memories, never particularly good, now felt as if they were tarred. They were disfigured into something grotesque. She kept her gaze off the laptop screen. She couldn't bear to look, because if she saw what she had just seen again she thought she might vomit. Disgust was all she could feel. Disgust for herself and what she had done.

Florence held her tight. She turned to Ken and said, "Go down and pour a large brandy." Then, when Ken was out of the room, she stepped to the computer and gasped. "Oh bloody hell."

"There must be thousands of them," Harry sobbed as Florence scrolled though the images of men with young girls. "There are about 60 Gigabytes of images in that directory."

Florence crouched beside her, holding her hands. She noticed that Harry's foot was jiggling up and down again. "I know it's unpleasant and nasty, Harry."

"It's a lot more than that, Florence. It's squalid filth that defiles innocent children and twists their lives forever. And all for the temporary sexual gratification of a pervert."

"I agree, it's evil, but why has it upset you so much? And what does it have to do with the anchor on your hand?"

Ken came back with a large glass of brandy which he offered to Harry. She grasped it and took a mouthful, then coughed as it bit into her throat and burned its way down to her stomach. She swallowed another mouthful, gulping for air as soon as she had finished.

"Take it easy," he said. "Take some deep breaths and then you can tell us what's on your mind."

She breathed for a moment then said, "Ken, you know about my memory problems?"

"Yes, and so does Florence."

"So you know that I have recurring confabulation and that I fill the gaps in my memory using my notes as triggers."

Ken nodded.

"Well I only started doing that when I was fourteen. So much of my life before I was fourteen has gone and may never come back, unless there's a trigger that helps fill the gaps at some point. Over time, I've filled a lot of holes but by no means all of them." She took another sip of brandy. This time, more cautiously. "I'm shaking and shivering, because seeing those young girls triggered a memory that I had possibly even been burying on purpose. Over the years, I've had momentary flash-backs that have been as elusive as a passing dream. But I've known nothing for certain. Now, in the space of a few minutes, many of my childhood memories of my father have come back."

"I didn't know you had any family."

"My mother lives in Benidorm with her boyfriend. We don't keep in contact. Just a Christmas card and a birthday card each year. I don't have a father. He went missing twelve years ago and a scallop dredger trawled his body up two months later. What was left of him. Someone had strapped an old anchor to his chest and had dropped him into the sea about five miles out from the Isle of Man."

"I'm sorry."

"I'm not. I'm now sure my mother arranged for his 'accident' when she discovered what he had been doing to me." Harry choked back a sob and wiped her eyes. "Whenever I've asked her to fill in the blanks about my early life, she has refused to tell me anything about my father. Because of that, I always used to assume I was illegitimate. Now I know otherwise. Now I know that my father had been abusing me from a very early age."

Florence hugged her and began to sob herself. "Oh Harry, I'm so very, very sorry."

"I remember him coming into my room on my sixth birthday. He got his dick out and made me rub it until it spat stuff on my face and in my hair."

Florence gasped. Ken's face transformed in an

instant from concerned to haggard. He grabbed the arm of a chair for support. "Oh my God."

Now both Florence and Harry were holding each other and crying like they would never stop. Harry sucked in gasps of air as she struggled to hold it together. "And then it happened — again, and again, until — until it became a regular routine. I know now that — that's why I wear that old glove on — on my right hand when I'm feeling stressed. — I used to pretend to be — asleep but he would shake me until — until I 'woke up' and masturbated him again." Harry drew a deep, deep breath and exhaled like a gust of wind. But she couldn't speak. Every nerve in her body seemed like a strained harp-string ready to snap at a touch.

"Take your time," Ken said. "Take another deep breath."

After gulping for more air, Harry looked up at him and continued, "I became a masturbating robot, Ken." She stopped and sobbed again. "That's all I was to my father. A masturbating fucking robot."

"Don't say anything if you don't want to," Ken said. "You can talk about it later if you want."

"No. I have to tell you," Harry said, clenching her fists and relaxing them, over and over. "I have to explain it now while it's fresh in my memory. You see, my father's abuse was responsible for me having difficulty with emotions and with personal relationships."

Ken nodded. He didn't yet understand, but he was beginning to.

Harry continued, "Even though I was young, I soon learned that when a situation is intractable, when every move is a bad move, you have to take yourself out of the equation. Emotions are counter productive in a situation like that. I was too young to understand that what I was doing was wrong and unnatural. But I somehow sensed that there were times for meeting fire with fire, and other times for meeting it with ice. So I became the Ice Maiden. I did what he demanded of me, hoping he would finish quickly. Then he would leave me alone and I could wash my hands, arms and face and go back to bed and pull the covers over my head."

"That's disgusting," Florence said.

"I know it's disgusting, Florence, but I had no choice. I was only six when it began."

"Oh, Harry, I didn't mean you were disgusting. I meant that he was disgusting. The situation was disgusting."

"He would make me take my pyjamas off while we did it. He kept staring at me all the time, and if I tried to cover myself up with my other hand he would shout at me. All I wanted was for my father to love me, so I did what he told me to do because it pleased him. I didn't know any different."

"Where was your mother when this was going on?" Ken asked.

Harry looked up to the ceiling, as if searching for more memories. When she found them, she said, "She worked behind a bar in the evenings. She didn't get home until after 11 o'clock."

"When did it stop?" Florence asked.

"When I was thirteen. He tried to force his penis into my mouth but I gagged and it made me sick on the floor. He made me clear it up. But he came back the following night and upped his game. That was the night he raped me. That was the night when I discovered that the bastard had a PhD in not giving a fuck about me. He raped me then wiped himself on my sheet, pulled his pants on and went downstairs to watch TV."

"What did you do?" Ken asked. "Didn't you say anything? Didn't you tell your mother?"

"I didn't dare tell my mother. I was afraid she would tell me it was normal and that my father could do what he wanted with his daughter. I remember my father telling me so often that what went on in our bedroom had to be our secret. He said that if I ever said anything to anybody, particularly my mother, she would stop loving me and everybody would hate me."

"What about your teachers?"

"I was thirteen Ken and had no friends. I was 'the girl with attitude' and even the teachers didn't want to know me."

"And did you really have attitude at thirteen?"

"Of course I did. Anyone who can't sleep until everything around them is symmetrical and in a perfect order is at a disadvantage. I always knew I was different to other people but I stopped worrying about that a long time ago. I heard one of the teachers say about me once that I had an IQ the same as my shoe size. Well if that was so, I coped well for someone with a size 6 shoe. So they all decided I was autistic. I've read up on autism now and maybe I have social anxiety disorder, but I'm certainly not off the scale. I can't relate to some people because I don't even know who they are. They are strangers to me. So, yes, I already had attitude when I was thirteen.

And, because the teachers shied away from me, nobody had ever talked to me about my virginity. I'd managed to get hold of a book that described what the hymen was. After my father raped me, I was rather hoping that my virginity would grow back."

Harry took another sip of brandy. "Do you want some water?" Ken asked. You've not eaten, and that stuff's going to make you dizzy."

She nodded and Ken went to the bathroom and came back with a glass of water. Harry took it from him and hugged it with both hands. Florence offered her the box of tissues from off the dressing table and Harry spent a moment to tidy up her face. "I'm sorry I shocked you," she whispered. "I didn't mean to scream, but I couldn't help it. It was a reaction to seeing those photos and having huge chunks of missing memory reappear in just seconds after all these years. It was like being hit on the head by a hammer. Like my whole mind was filled by an express train, roaring and flashing and hurtling headlong towards a cliff edge. I'm sorry."

"Don't you dare apologise for your hurt," Florence said. "Don't you dare turn yourself into a victim now. You were a victim then but not any longer." She stroked Harry's cheeks with the palms of her hands. "Relax, Harry. Look at tonight as the beginning of your new chapter. You can't rewrite what's already been written, but, now that you know your past, you can decide where the story goes from here. And you can choose which characters to keep or kill off. Metaphorically speaking of course."

Harry put her head in her hands and let out a noise that was half sigh, half sob. "I can't help myself, Florence. Everything that I can't control makes me anxious. Loud cars make me anxious. People arguing make me anxious. When I was a kid, they pushed me into the regular school system and then acted surprised by the epidemic of anxiety that I displayed. Some folks just aren't built to withstand that kind of chronic stress, and I guess I'm one of them."

"Harry, think of the place in your mind that stores your worries as being like a tea cup. Everything that makes you anxious is like pouring more tea in that cup. If it gets too full, then even the tiniest bump is enough to make it slop over the edges. What you need to do is to work at keeping that cup more empty all the time so that, when a rush of tea comes along, there's still room for it."

Harry made to protest but Florence held her hand and continued. "What happens, Harry, is that if you keep your background stress levels low, you can handle a big problem without doing anything to solve it. It's a form of mental dislocation, a neat trick for those that can do it, an advantage in the right situation. But right now its misuse is your biggest flaw. From now on, when you have a problem, even if it's only a small one, come to me or to Ken. We'll find a solution and then you'll find you can relax more. It's the only way to keep that tea cup empty."

"You're not just blowing smoke up my ass, are you?"

Ken roared laughing. "Jeez, Harry, you do get

straight to the point, don't you?"

Harry allowed herself to smile. "Yeah, I told you I don't do that small talk stuff."

Ken went back to the computer and opened some more directories. "Jesus Christ in a bucket. This is bloody vile. There are babies here, no older than about two. Yves-Marie deserves to be shot."

"We have to hand this over to the police," Harry said.

Florence was thoughtful for a moment and said, "No we don't. Not yet, at least. First of all, how are you going to explain having the contents of my brother's laptop on your disk?"

"We can just tell the police that we suspect Yves-Marie and—"

"—and they'll do nothing. No way can they get a search warrant based on a family member saying they think he is a paedophile."

"Yes, you're right," Harry said, "but you can use what we have to get what you want. And what about his wife, Monique? Does she want to get away from him, or is it better that she knows nothing?"

"She's been dying to escape for a long time," Florence said. "But Yves-Marie has always threatened to throw her out on the street with nothing."

"Can't she go to the courts?"

"That will take forever and he'll make her life hell, just like he's trying to do to me now. It's standard Misogyny 101 - if a man has a healthy bank account it's because he worked for it. If a woman wants to leave him it's because she's sleeping with someone else. They teach it on the first day of the 'Isn't It Awfully Nice to Have a Penis' course."

Harry chuckled. "You're starting to talk more like me now."

"I see where Florence is going," Ken said. "We can't just leave this alone but we can't go to the police with it. On the other hand, I can pay Yves-Marie a little visit, show him what we have, and suggest he settles the matter of your grandfather's estate with no further delays. And also that he settles with Monique for half his net worth after the inheritance issues have been resolved."

"Meantime she can live here with me if necessary," Florence added.

Harry said, "There are some financial things you need to know too. While I was downloading all the emails from his business, I spotted some stuff in his accountancy directories, some letters and spreadsheets and things. I only glanced at them, but I downloaded them just to be sure. I don't know yet exactly what he's up to, but there is skulduggery underfoot."

"Skulduggery?" Florence asked.

"Unscrupulous or dishonest behaviour," Ken explained.

"So best we wait a few days until I have pieced together the whole picture, and then you can go and kick three shades of shit out of the dirty little deviant. And while you're doing so, I'd be obliged if you put the boot in for me personally."

Ken smiled. "I'll make sure he understands the error

of his ways, Harry. And in a few months, when everything is settled, we'll send a selection of files to the gendarmes. No way that perverted piece of human waste is getting away with just a monetary penalty."

"And a kick in the bollocks," Florence added, so Ken wouldn't forget.

# CHAPTER FIFTEEN

As they walked the hundred metres to the Intercontinental Hotel, Florence checked with Harry that she still wanted to go out and eat after the shock of her unpleasant memory recall. Harry was happy to continue. "I want to take my mind off it, and the change of environment will help."

The same tall concierge who had welcomed them the night before met them again at the door. "Good evening Madame de Nussac, shall I ask Norbert to hold a table for you?"

"That would be good, Roger, thank you. We'll take an aperitif in the bar."

"Very good, Madame. I'll let Norbert know you are here."

"You're in luck, Harry," Ken whispered. "Lover boy's on duty again tonight."

"You can be very childish when you want to be, Kenneth Stafford. I wonder now why I bothered to have sex with you fifty-four times."

"Over a period of one hundred and twenty three days."

Florence looked round and frowned. "Maybe this is

a conversation that you two could have somewhere else."

Ken chuckled, but Harry looked suitable chastened. She rolled a strand of caramel-coloured hair back and forth between her fingers. "I'm sorry, Florence. Have I messed up the evening already?"

Florence reached for her hand and smiled. "No, it's me, Harry, I sometimes forget that you have no boundaries. But maybe it would be better to keep discussions about sex for when you are in a private place."

Harry's restless fingers stilled for a moment. "Sorry."

"Don't be. I guess nobody has ever helped you understand that sort of thing, have they?"

Harry shook her head, then said, "Are you going to help me then?"

Florence nodded. "If you want me to."

"Yes, I'd like that."

Florence glanced at Harry's neck, around which was a classic pearl necklace. "That's beautiful," she said. "But you were wearing a green glass necklace earlier when we were in your room. What made you change?"

"Seeing that stuff on your brother's computer has brought back some other memories. I'm going to have another of those Glam64 cocktails with that pale blue Hpnotiq stuff. What are you having?"

Florence took the hint and picked a cocktail from the list.

While the bartender prepared the drinks, Norbert,

the maître d'hôtel, came and wished them all a good evening. He left them with the food menus. This time, Harry was curious about the starter of 'Capuccino de Tourteau, concombre, céleri et épine-vinette'. Crab Cappuccino, cucumber, celery and barberry. "What's a crab cappuccino?" she asked.

Florence didn't know so waved a hand to Norbert who stood at the entrance to the restaurant.

"Oui Madame?"

"Norbert, I know you guys like to dress up lettuce with a name like lactuca sativa on your menu but for heaven's sake, what is a crab cappuccino?"

Norbert smiled. "It's a crab mousse, Madame."

"So why not say so?"

"Tell me, Madame de Nussac. When you create your wonderful descriptions of wines, do you say 'got a fine nose?' or do you say something rather more fanciful?"

Harry laughed. "She's like a wine encyclopaedia. Last night, we had a bottle of 1989 Chasse-Spleen and Florence said, 'It's been ripe for drinking for a few years and has reached a stage where anyone with a nose for wine would say it was sensational. It's graded as a Cru Bourgeois Exceptionnel. Dark bright red wine, meniscus slightly orangey, unclouded. Nose of fresh plum and cocoa. Neat and straightforward attack. Flavours: cocoa beans, leather and black berries. Tight and unctuous structure, mellow tannins. Balance and power. Great persistence'."

Florence looked at Harry with eyes wide open and said, "That was word perfect, and you're not even reading it off your iPad."

"I only need the iPad after a memory wipe-out. Otherwise, my memory is just fine, thank you."

"Better than fine, it seems."

"Will there be anything else?" Norbert asked.

"I think not," Florence replied. "I think I just got put in my place by my friend here."

"I didn't mean to upset you," Harry said, as Norbert went back to his duties in the restaurant.

"You didn't," Florence said with a smile. "I was joking."

"Sort of small talk."

"Probably, Harry. But you'll get used to it."

"Maybe, maybe not. What are you having for the main course?"

"I'm going to go for the 'Croustillant de boudin maison, déclinaison de pommes'."

"Black pudding with a variation of stewed apples."

"Yes, but it's the chef's own homemade black pudding, and he crisps the skin. When I try to do that at home, I always manage to burst the boudin wide open. Your French is pretty good," she added. "Where did you learn it?"

"At school. Like I said, I actually have a pretty good memory when it doesn't wipe itself out. And anyway it only wipes out memories of people and events; it doesn't affect my languages or other basic skills. What about you, Ken, what are you having?"

"I'm going for the thirty day matured beef again. It

was delicious."

"And I'm going to try the black pudding like Florence, so we want a red wine. Can I choose?"

"But of course," Florence answered. "You're treating us tonight, so it's for you to make the decisions."

"Is that how it works?"

"Not always. If Ken was inviting us, he would probably ask me to choose, because he had a limited knowledge of French wines."

"Oh, so I should ask you then?"

"Not at all. Why don't you choose and I'll tell you if it's a good choice."

Harry ran her finger down the list on the wine menu, mouthing each one in turn. After a while, she said, "The 1998 Château la Fleur Pétrus looks good. It's a Pomerol, and I read that the wines from that region are under-rated."

"It's an excellent choice," Florence said, "But are you aware of the price, Harry?"

"Oh yes, they're all here on the wine list. That one is €422."

"That's a lot of money," Ken said. "Is there nothing cheaper?"

Florence said, "It retails at about €200, and the hotel have their mark-up."

"Yes, but surely there's something that doesn't cost €400?"

"Of course there is," Harry said. "But I want to treat my two friends to something nice and I think that will go well with boudin noir and steak."

"Indeed it will," Florence said, "and I appreciate you offering it. I had a few bottles of that in my cellar till yesterday and I can vouch for it being a fabulous wine."

"So how would you describe it?" Harry asked, reaching for her iPad.

"Well in fact, 1998 was one of the best vintages. The normal Château Pétrus is like walking into your neighbourhood flower shop to find an open jar of liquorice and a vat of fresh-squeezed cherries amongst the flower arrangements. When you get some in your glass, just breathe in and savour the scent. Elegant, supple and alluring, the crushed velvet tannins are outstanding when paired with all that ripe, sweet, lush kirsch liqueur in the finish."

"Wow!"

"That would describe your normal Pétrus," Florence continued. "But as I say, the 1998 vintage was quite special. So think of black liquorice, earthy minerals, chocolate covered cherries, and fresh raspberry scents. The silk and velvet, palate-caressing feel in the mouth is pure, sensuous Pomerol at its very best. The '98 Pétrus ends with an elegant, soft, fresh, clean, spicy cherry-filled finish. It's drinking perfectly today, but will age and improve for at least another 15 or more years, so it's also a good investment to lay down for the future. It's one of those outstanding wines where us French would say, c'est comme petite Jésus en culotte de velours."

"Did you get all that?" Ken asked, as Harry tapped away on her iPad.

Harry stopped typing. "Yes, of course I did." Without referring to her iPad, she repeated exactly what Florence had just said, and even translated the part at the end, "It's like baby Jesus in velvet breeches." Then went back to her notes.

Ken looked at Florence and raised his eyes. She smiled and shook her head. This young lady who was delicate and fragile in so many ways, was tougher and more resilient than either of them could have imagined. And she had so many other talents. Her computer skills. Her astounding memory. The fact that she spoke excellent French. And the ease with which she could manipulate complex sets of figures. It all led Florence to believe that, if only Harry could overcome her shyness and her fear of doing or saying the wrong thing, she could build the sort of world that she wanted for herself, despite her memory lapses and her Obsessive Compulsive Disorder.

# CHAPTER SIXTEEN

Ken spent a lazy morning strolling round streets he'd never seen before. His favourite was rue Cavallotti, just off Boulevard de Clichy. During their breakfast together, Florence had suggested he take a look while Harry did her thing at The Sorbonne.

Ken had caught the metro to Place de Clichy and walked the rest of the way. As suggested by Florence, he had timed his arrival for when the shops were closed at midday. It was then that they became interesting. With the metal shutters down, what had been a camera shop became a shop-front-sized Toulouse Lautrec canvas depicting a larger than life copy of his painting, 'Elles: Woman in a Corset'. The wooden surround of the hairdresser's window was Mucha's 'The Arts, Poetry', and on the shutters of the flower shop opposite was Modigliani's 'Chakoska'. Adjacent shops featured Vermeer, Turner, Gaugin and others.

The street was only a few hundred metres long, but the shutters of every shop had been painted to represent a famous work of a great artist. You didn't get to see them when the shops were open but, with the shutters closed, it was a pleasure to see such originality. Talking to one of the shop owners who was just locking up, Ken discovered that it was art students who had undertaken the work as an urban improvement project.

Meanwhile, Harry had marched into the university like she belonged there. A quick check on the floor plan in the main entrance and she was on her way to the study library with her laptop tucked under her arm. When she arrived, she sat on the opposite side of the table to a young man who was working on his own laptop - on Twitter and Facebook, it seemed. She pretended to be working on her computer for a while then tutted. A moment later she tutted again. The young man looked up. "Ça va? - Okay?" he asked.

Harry spoke in French, but made no attempt to cover her accent. "No," she said, almost inaudibly. Then she said it again, in a firmer voice. "No I'm not. It's my emails. I'm a late enroller from England, studying French, and the administration block gave me the SMTP for outgoing mails, but I can't seem to make it work."

The young man said in English, "My name's Vincent. Hang on a moment." He clicked his mouse a couple of times then said, "My university email address runs from this location. My Outlook account is set up with the outgoing SMTP as smtp.e-paris-sorbonne.com using server port 25. You must enable authentication for the outgoing mail configuration, so you'll need the email username and password they gave you."

"Oh damn, that's why it's not working. They said it could take a couple of days before they could let me have it." Harry smiled at him. "Thanks anyway for your help."

"No problem," he said, smiling back. "Do you want

to use my username and password until you get your own? As long as you don't use my email address, nobody will notice."

"Oh, can I? That's really nice of you," Harry said, turning up the wattage on the smile.

Vincent gave her his details and, after Harry had typed them in, she asked, "Can I just test it on you to make sure it works? I'll send you an email so I can check the SPF—"

"Woah, hang on, I'm studying Art and Archaeology. I know basic computing, but SPF is beyond me. What is it?"

"It's Sender Policy Framework and it's a simple email-validation system designed to detect email spoofing. It allows receiving mail exchangers to check that incoming mail from a domain comes from a host authorized by that domain's administrators."

"I'm still no wiser. What do you need to do?"

"I just send you an email and you reply with a short message. Doesn't matter what you say. And if it comes back to me okay, we've succeeded in piggybacking the system."

"Okay, go ahead then."

"I would if I had your email address!"

"Oh right. It's vincent.margaux@e-paris-sorbonne.com."

Harry added this to the email she had already prepared with a rather special Microsoft Word attachment. Within a few moments it had arrived on Vincent's email client. "There's an attachment," he said.

“Yes, it’s just a blank Word document to make sure the system is transmitting them okay. Could you just open it to make sure it works?”

“It’s blank,” he said after a moment.

“Yeah, that’s okay. It’s only to test that I can send people attachments without them being corrupted or blocked. Just hit ‘Reply’ and email me back and I’ll know I’m set to go.”

Seconds later Harry got back Vincent’s reply that said, “I love your hair. It’s gorgeous.”

She blushed and remembered to thank him for his help. After a moment or two of small talk, which Harry was beginning to feel she might one day master, Vincent went back to his studies. Or Twitter or Facebook, whichever caught his attention first.

In the word processing document that he had opened, Harry had included her standard VBA - Visual Basic for Applications - malware. It was the start of the attack. Right at this moment, it was running in the background on Vincent’s computer, downloading and installing an executable file without needing Vincent’s permission.

Three minutes later, Harry had a full-strength .exe installed – a program that had the potential to be malicious. But Harry wasn’t planning anything pernicious. She only needed Vincent’s login details to the university network. Getting that took her less than one minute. Very few people bothered to memorise logins. More often than not, they checked the box on their browser that said, ‘Remember logins for sites’

Another thirty seconds and she was where she had wanted to be all along: logged onto the student network. From there, once she had figured out the server's IP Address it was easy enough for her to hack her way into the database server. Moments later she was downloading the complete contents of the student records in SQL format.

Ten minutes after asking Vincent to help her, she packed away her laptop, thanked him again for his help, and left the building.

# CHAPTER SEVENTEEN

Harry remembered to ask Florence if she could use the printer in her office. Two days ago, she would have just used it. After all, the work she was doing was for Florence and Ken. But now she understood that the office was Florence's private space, so she asked permission first. Then she waited for Ken to return before speaking to him and Florence together. As they gathered in the seating area of the lounge, she placed three photo-size pieces of paper face down on the low table that divided the chairs. She had marked them 'A', 'B', and 'C' on the back and said, "My money's on 'C'."

Ken and Florence looked puzzled but waited for more. And they got more. Harry turned over the sheet marked 'A' and the face of a young man stared at them. Florence and Ken again looked at each other.

Harry said, "There are three people called Tristan registered at The Sorbonne. Is this the person you've seen?"

"You've done it?" Florence asked. "You've cracked the Sorbonne?"

"I told you she was good," Ken said.

"Of course I've done it," came from Harry. "Piece of cake. Wasn't even a proper challenge. Now then, is this the person you think is your son?"

"No," from both of them in unison.

"This one then?" Harry asked, turning over the picture marked 'B'.

Again, an immediate "No," in unison.

"Has to be my favourite then," said Florence, turning over the third picture.

Florence and Ken didn't need to say anything. The looks on their faces said it all. Except to Harry, who had never mastered the art of reading people's expressions. "Well?" she asked.

"Yes that's him," Ken said. "Do you have any more information?"

"Of course I do. I can tell you what grades he got in his last set of tests if you want."

"Could we start with his full name?" Florence asked.

Harry had it all memorised. "His full name is Tristan James Gautier. His parents are Jerome and Sylvie Gautier. They live at 33 rue du Village, Cléry Saint André."

"Tristan James is what we named our son," Florence said. "Do you have a date of birth?"

Harry reeled it off from the top of her head.

"That's spot on," Ken said. "Pity we can't get hold of his birth certificate."

"They don't have birth certificates in France,"

Florence explained. "We all have what they call a 'Livret de Famille' which is a family register rather like a passport that details people's family origins."

"And the university registrar had scanned that," Harry said, "so I have it on my laptop upstairs. It shows that the boy was adopted but it doesn't give his previous name, because they regard that as secret until he reaches majority age."

"Which is eighteen in France," Florence said.

"But it still doesn't get added to the 'Livret de Famille' unless the adopted person wants it to be. I looked it up on the net earlier."

"So we just know that Tristan was adopted by a couple called Gautier, who live in Cléry Saint André."

"Where's that?" Ken asked.

"It's near Orléans," Florence said. "About 150 kilometres south of here. I stopped there once when I was checking out wines in the Loire valley." She brushed aside a tear then reached for Harry's hand. "Thank you so much, Harry. You don't know how much this means to me."

"We'd always thought, our baby boy had gone and that he was never coming back," Ken added.

Florence continued, a smile of true happiness lighting her face. "I had accepted for many years that I'd never get to hold my son in my arms again. I never thought I'd hear his voice, or to watch him grow. I'd given up on the idea that I might see him fall in love, or walk down the aisle with his new wife on his arm."

Harry smiled a little. She was beginning to

understood emotions better now.

"I never imagined that I would get to watch his face light up with love and pride as he held his own baby for the first time," Florence continued. She turned towards Ken, "Just like you did, Ken, when they put Tristan in your arms after he was born." With her free hand, she pointed to the photo on the table. "This boy, this young man, is our baby Ken. He's our child, our son. We were there when he said his first words, and when he learned to walk without our help. We were there to kiss every bruised knee better and to sooth his brow on every restless night. But I wasn't there when he needed me most."

Harry was getting used to emotions but she still wasn't used to seeing so much emotion and she eased away her hand that Florence was still holding. She gave a nervous laugh and pushed a curl of caramel-coloured hair away from her face.

"Don't start blaming yourself," Ken said to Florence. "Somebody snatched him, and before long we'll find out who and why."

"I'm just so glad that we're getting closer, thanks to this young lady." She looked at Harry. "We owe you so much, Harry. Please be sure you add it to your bill."

"No way. You are a nice person and Ken can pay for dinner tonight. Can we go somewhere different?"

"It didn't work out with Norbert then?" Ken asked with a chuckle.

"Stop being stupid." Harry said. "Just for that I'm going to have the most expensive thing on the menu."

Florence laughed. "Serves you right," she said to Ken. Then to Harry she said, "In that case, Harry, as a thank you, before you go back, I'll take you and Ken to one of the best restaurants in Paris. It's called Le Pré Catelan and it's in the Bois de Boulogne, about fifteen minutes from here if the traffic's not too bad. The head chef is a guy called Frédéric Anton who is well known in France. He's often on TV and he's considered to be one of the emblematic figures in French contemporary cuisine. It's a three star Michelin restaurant, so I needn't say any more. He buys all his wine from us, so that makes it our most prestigious account. I like to reciprocate from time to time and eat at his place. It's an experience you'll never forget."

"So maybe Ken can go out and buy himself something decent to wear," Harry said.

Ken stared at her. "Is this a poker face, or for real."

"I think it's for real," Florence said. "You only came over with jeans and sweatshirts and stuff. Maybe spending a few euros on something decent won't break your bank?"

"No it wouldn't, but I only bought a new suit last week for poor old Dinger's funeral."

"So now you'll have two suits. It won't hurt."

"It'll hurt my pocket," he said. "Anyway, changing the subject, how are your searches going, Harry, on Yves-Marie's emails?"

"I've had no chance to look at anything yet. In any case, there's so much stuff and so many search words that it could be quite a while yet before the spider bots get to the end. Anyway, when I got back from The Sorbonne, I went into time warp, I'm afraid."

Ken's look changed to one of concern. "You lost your memory again?"

"Oh no! If that had happened, I would have spent the next two or three days on my iPad, trying to piece it all back together again. No, quite the opposite, in fact. I was just lying on the bed filling in holes from the time before my father disappeared."

"Thank God. I thought you'd had another memory loss."

"I had one about two weeks ago, Ken. That's why I had to check you out at the airport. They don't happen that often. Maybe once a year as a rule. And so far, they have always happened overnight."

"Why not leave those memory holes empty?" Florence asked. "If it's painful to pull back old memories, why not let them rest?"

"Because I want to know. I want to know exactly what life was like in our house. Now that those awful images on your brother's computer triggered the memories of what my father did to me, nature is filling in the rest of the blanks and I'm noting them all on my iPad."

"And are all the memories painful?"

"In different ways, yes. I know for sure now that my mother had my father disposed of because when he didn't come home one day she told me he would never be coming back. She said he was going on a long diving vacation. I didn't understand what she meant at the time and, since my memory was later wiped clean, I didn't even recall her saying it until about one hour ago.

For years, I've thought I was illegitimate because my mother refused to talk about my father when I asked her. I guess that was just her coping mechanism. But now it all makes sense. My father was a bully. He was a control freak who wanted everything done his way, right down to eating meals at specified times each day. My mother had to put the plates on the table in a certain order and within one minute of the time he specified. Otherwise he would throw everything on the floor and storm out of the house."

"Jesus Christ!" from Florence. "You and your mother must have been forever walking on eggshells."

"Every day was like being on a knife-edge," Harry said, "particularly for my mother." She picked at the cuff of her sweatshirt. "My father only agreed to my mother working behind the bar because it allowed him to come into my room and molest me. Otherwise he was possessive to the point of obsession. He told her what she should wear. He told her how she should do her hair. He told her who she was allowed to speak to and who she wasn't. When all those memories came back earlier, my mother seemed to me like a faithful Labrador who took the verbal beatings and abuse then looked at him with sad eyes waiting for a pat on the head. Now, after a little thought, I know that she was biting her tongue through all the criticisms and temper tantrums, trying to make a life for herself and me. My father's attempts at being witty and amusing always involved belittling my mother. I remember now her face as she cringed, but still said nothing. Looking back with my new memories, I can see it all. But at the time, it seemed like that was normal family life. I had no friends, so I didn't know any different."

"You have us now," Florence said. "We're your friends, Harry."

Harry smiled, blushed and nodded, all at the same time.

"And your mother tolerated all this abuse until she found out about what your father was doing to you?" Ken asked.

"Yes. She felt unwell and came home early one night. She saw my father pulling up his pants as he came out of my bedroom. She grabbed a knife from the kitchen and slashed my father's face. He ran away that night and didn't come back. I never saw him again. It was a day or two later when my mother told me he'd gone on a long diving vacation. I can't blame her. She should have left him years earlier."

"So what happened when they dredged up his body?"

"She was shocked. I don't think she ever expected anyone to find him. I remember now that we had the police at the house a lot and they asked me all sorts of questions. But I'd had a memory wipe-out a few weeks before and I didn't know anything. The doctors confirmed my repetitive confabulation and everyone assumed it was another example of my low intellect."

Florence tutted.

"So the police got nowhere?" Ken asked.

"They wrote me off as a simpleton. I'm used to people thinking that now. In fact, I make use of that misconception when I'm digging up information. I use wigs and things to make me look a bit outrageous so no-one expects me to be capable of doing any clever stuff."

"Or remembering facts and manipulating figures like a computer," Florence said.

"So the police never found out what happened to your father then?" Ken asked.

"No. And since there was no evidence against my mother, the case remains unsolved."

"And now you mother lives in Spain."

"Benidorm. She's got a nice fella who treats her right, but it's as though our shared secret keeps us apart. Almost as though we're both guilty of something and don't want to have to face each other and discuss it. So we send each other Christmas and a birthday cards, and that's all."

"Do you miss her?" Florence asked.

"Yes, but I don't want to go and make myself a nuisance and make her uncomfortable, so I just leave things as they are. I've learned to live with it and KBO, as Churchill would say."

"KBO?"

"Keep Buggering On. I am what I am and I can't change."

"It's been a delight to get to know you, Harry," Florence said. "You're a beautiful person, inside and out and I hope that one day you'll feel able to meet up with your mother. I know what it's like to have a child who has no contact with me."

Harry's blush reached her ears. She had no idea how

to respond to a compliment, so she stared at her feet.

# CHAPTER EIGHTEEN

It was late afternoon three days later before Ken got the phone call they'd been waiting for. When he heard the gentle Scottish accent on the other end of the phone, he knew that Detective Chief Inspector Angus Slooth had some news for him about the DNA test.

"I guess you want me to put you out of suspense rather than tell you that the sun is shining and the sea is flat calm." Angus said.

Ken smiled to himself. "That would be nice, Angus. But feel free to do it your way."

"Aye, I shall. You'd better sit down if you're standing up."

"No go ahead Angus. I can take a disappointment, even now."

"Some disappointments outrank others, Ken."

"So the boy isn't my son then?"

"No he isn't. But it's a bit more complicated than that. Whoever it was who you got your DNA sample from is not your son. He is, however, the child who went missing from your home sixteen years ago."

"I don't get it," Ken said, "What do you mean? How can he be Tristan and not be my —. Oh fuck. I see what you're saying. Oh fuck, fuck, fuck."

"I'm sorry Ken. The DNA matches exactly the sample taken from the boy's hairbrush at the time. There's a 95% familial link to your former wife's DNA, but zero to yours."

Ken slumped into the nearby armchair. It was as if his legs had had all the bones removed and his muscles had turned into wet clay. When he found his voice, it was a mere whisper. He asked, "How sure are they, Angus?"

"I asked the same question, Ken, because I knew this was going to be a shock to you."

"Bloody right, it is."

"I had to take notes to understand how it all works. It seems there are two major types of genealogical DNA tests. There's X-chromosome DNA and there's Y-chromosome DNA. X-chromosome tests are for recent ancestry of both males and females. Y-DNA tests a male along his direct paternal line and X-DNA tests a man or woman along their direct maternal line."

"No questions about reasonable doubt, I suppose?"

"I'm informed that Y-chromosome testing is the most powerful DNA testing tool, because the Y-chromosome is transmitted from father to son nearly unchanged. They can compare a man's test results to another man's results to determine the time frame in which the two individuals shared a most recent common ancestor in their direct patrilineal lines. If their test results are very close, they are related within a genealogically useful time frame. A father to son crosscheck would show a very close result indeed."

"And the X-DNA test showed a clear link to Florence but the Y-DNA test showed no similarity to me."

"You've hit the nail right on the head, Ken. I wish it could be different, but the conclusion is certain. Tristan is the youth you've traced there in Paris, but you are not his father."

"Have to go, Angus. I think I'm going to throw up. Appreciate your help. Talk later."

Ken cut the phone connection, rushed from the room, and just made it to the downstairs toilet before being sick. It was ten minutes before he picked up the strength to rinse his mouth, walk back to where he had been sitting, and slump into the chair. In the space of one short phone call, his whole world had flipped upside down. Having built up his hopes, everything had come crashing down round his head. He cast his mind back to the time before Florence had become pregnant. Now, the big elephant in the room that they had never spoken of could be ignored no longer. After a few moments thought, he stood and forced his legs up the wide stone staircase to Florence's study where she was dealing with emails.

She looked up and smiled as he stood in the doorway. Ken just stared at her; this woman whom he had loved enough to ignore her transgression all those years ago, without even telling her he knew.

He shifted his weight so that he was leaning against the door frame, and bowed his head, ever so slightly, finally breaking eye contact with her. "I just got the call from Angus about the test results."

Florence waited for more. Finally she drew a deep breath, "And?"

"He is your son. He is not mine. Your lover, Jean-Luc, impregnated you, not me. Best you go find him and tell him he's a father. Unless, of course, you had other lovers I never knew about."

Florence gasped. "It can't be, Ken. We took precautions. I broke it off with him before—"

"No you didn't, Florence. You broke it off with him when you discovered he was going back to France. Now that we know everything, we might as well clear all the old secrets. You see, I knew about you and Jean-Luc while you were having your affair. My mate Don Thompson was on the same liaison team between the French and British Special Forces that your boyfriend was on. He heard Jean-Luc boasting about his lover. When Don found out who it was, he told me. He felt I needed to know."

"But you said nothing to me at the time?"

"I never challenged you about it, Florence, because I thought you may have chosen to leave me and go and live with Jean-Luc. I didn't want to lose you." He watched indifferently as a tear rolled down Florence's cheek. He continued, "As you carried on with your secret meetings, disappointment set in and I almost stopped loving you."

"So why didn't you leave then?"

"Because you fell pregnant. After that, what kept us together was that I always thought of Tristan as being my son, and I stuck with you because of that. I still loved you, but not with the intensity that we had had before your affair. Three years later, when Tristan disappeared, that old disappointment re-emerged and I drifted away, burying myself in my job."

Florence reached for a tissue and blew her nose. "I never believed Tristan was Jean-Luc's son. When Jean-Luc heard that he was being sent back to his regiment he came to see me several times. He wanted me to leave you and go with him back to France. But I didn't want to leave you, Ken. Anyway, I was so damn certain that Tristan was your son, not Jean-Luc's."

"Well you were wrong. And so was I. I was wrong to have allowed your treachery to continue without challenging you. Looking back, it was never the same after I was tipped off about what was going on."

"Look, Ken, I've said sorry a million times for having that affair. I said it again when you arrived here. I regret it with every fibre of my being, but I can't turn the clock back. I made a big mistake, the biggest mistake of my life, and I've been paying for it for the last sixteen years."

"You've been paying for it? What do you mean, you've been paying for it? It's me that's been paying for it Florence. I still don't know if you would have told me if I hadn't challenged you about it after Tristan disappeared."

"My affair was already over when I became pregnant, and you know it."

"Tristan's DNA says otherwise. Anyway, I only know what you tell me, and that is subject to question. When we got married, I gave you my life and I never take back a gift, because honesty and integrity mean a lot to me. The promise I made at our wedding was my solemn bond. Not because I felt chained but because I honoured you and loved you more than anything else on the planet. So when you took a lover and acted like it was nothing that I gave, it hurt in a way that cut to the core of who I am."

"And then it all fell apart when Tristan disappeared," Florence added in a quiet voice, almost as if she were talking to herself.

"I don't know whether it was because we'd got to that stage in our relationship where we'd begun taking each other for granted, or if it was more serious than that. We clung to each other in the weeks and months after Tristan's disappearance but then the gap between us widened again, didn't it?"

Florence folded her arms and began tapping her fingers on her forearm. "Yes, because you involved yourself in your work again. You left me at home to cope with the stress and an empty life."

Ken's hands clenched tight. "Oh sure, it was my bloody fault, wasn't it?"

"I'm not saying that," Florence replied, her voice harsh and uncompromising.

"Of course you are. Your lies told me two things; the first was that you underestimated what I could forgive. The second was that you underestimated my ability to detect your deceit. Two hurts for the price of one, not bad for a casual indiscretion. Well just remember, it wasn't my fault you decided to sleep around in the first place."

"Well just maybe it was," Florence shouted. "You

and your damn buddies playing army games on the mountains and forgetting you had wives at home," her voice was like iced water now. "You were so wrapped up in 'the regiment' that you forgot you had someone at home, desperate to see you. I needed love. I wanted to feel appreciated, that's all. But after you had showered and changed you would disappear down to the pub to spend even more time with your stupid mates who you had been playing soldiers with all day."

Words had flown from her mouth that she never thought she'd even think, let alone say out loud. She knew from the look in his eyes that they'd hit their mark. In that instant, whatever remained of their relationship shattered into glassy shards. Nothing would ever be the same again.

Ken froze, hands still clenched at his sides, eyes fixed on Florence's, his lips moist with saliva. It was as though someone had pressed the pause button on their argument. Florence couldn't get her words out fast enough, "I'm sorry, Ken. I didn't mean it. I was angry. I'm not saying it was your fault. Ken, Ken!" She continued to shout his name as he wheeled round and strode to his room.

After a moment Florence called out, "Fine, just ignore me, because that makes everything better, doesn't it?" Then she heard his bedroom door slam and Ken stood on the landing with his overnight bag in his hand, staring at her without saying a word.

"Ken please?" Florence said. "You've made mistakes. You've said things you didn't mean in the heat of the moment, and I've always forgiven you. Just talk to me. Let's sort it out this time, okay?

He turned on his heel without a word, pushed past Harry who had emerged from her bedroom, ran down the stairs, crossed the living room in large strides and disappeared into the entrance hallway. When the door slammed shut behind him, there was a sense that some huge surge of energy had dissipated. But what he did leave behind was a foreboding that settled around Florence like a shroud. Up above, she gritted her teeth and dug her nails into the palms of her hands. But there was no holding back the tidal wave of regret that was building inside her. She let loose a howl of anguish. It was a long time before it subsided into sobs. Only Harry was there to comfort her.

# CHAPTER NINETEEN

In the bathroom of his room at the Intercontinental Hotel, Ken tuned out the sound of the television in the bedroom. He'd turned it on to distract him from his emotions. He used his towel to wipe a space in the mirror free from steam. The hot shower had soothed some of his anger but done nothing to reduce his disappointment. As he combed his hair, he glanced at his reflection and saw a man who had been shaped by events in his past that he thought could never be changed. Yet he had discovered today that even those events were never what he had thought they were. The boy whose loss he had mourned had turned out to be somebody else's child. And it seemed possible that the woman he had loved had known all along that the baby wasn't his.

Well screw her. Now she knew the truth she could do whatever she wanted about it. Tomorrow, he would get a flight back to the Isle of Man and carry on his life as before. Only this time it would be different. This time he would have no reason to keep thinking back to the child he had lost, since the child was never his to lose in the first place. And he could wash his mind clean of the memories of the wife who had betrayed his love. She meant nothing to him any longer. She was a footnote in his personal history.

Staring at his reflection in the bathroom mirror, Ken felt shocked. He looked okay, normal even. Inside, the ache for Florence gnawed at the very heart that still beat endlessly for her. He pulled his lips into a smile and let out a frightened gasp when he realised that anyone could mistake this lacklustre grin for real happiness. It amazed him to think he could look so normal when he had crumbled to dust inside.

Someone banged on the door. Room service with the bottle of Scotch he had ordered before getting dressed. He opened the door. A tornado of fury pushed him back into the room. He stumbled and fell backwards, landing in a heap at the foot of the bed. She slammed the door behind her. "I thought I'd find you here, you shameful dimwit. Sulking in the nearest hotel where you could run and hide. I just cancelled your fucking whisky, you miserable oaf. What the hell's the matter with you? I thought you were a man, not a bloody mouse. Jesus, my fucking dead hamster's got more balls than you."

Ken stood up and killed the sound on the television. "Come in and make yourself at home, Harry."

"I bloody have done. Now quit playing at being a loser and grow a pair. I thought you had some brains, Ken Stafford, but I was bloody wrong. You need to start working things out, not whingeing and whining like a baby."

"Okay, Harry, enough. Stop right there. This has nothing to do with you and you don't know what's going on anyway."

"Of course I do. I might have memory problems, Ken, but I'm not stupid, and my hearing is just fine. I heard you and Florence shouting at each other. The arguing came right through the walls as loud as any TV show. The whole bloody street got all the details so I guess everybody pretty much knew what had happened when you stormed off. And since then, Florence and I have had a heart-to-heart. You've discovered that Tristan isn't your child. So now you are just going to wash your hands of it and walk away from the whole thing as though it doesn't concern you."

"It doesn't concern me. He's not my son. He is the son of a man who Florence had an affair with, so it's up to him and Florence to deal with it."

"Oh for God's sake just grow up."

"I just did that Harry. After sixteen years, I just grew up. The past is the past. Let it remain that way."

"The past isn't the past till everybody agrees it's the past. Right at this moment, Florence is lost and bewildered. The past isn't the past at all to her."

"And that's my fault? It wasn't me went off with somebody else. What do you want me to do, wrap her up in a cotton-wool blanket and sprinkle happy dust on her? She made her decision years ago. The result is that her son is not my son."

Harry flopped down into the high-backed armchair and clasped her hands together. "Oh, Ken, for goodness sake get over your self-imposed outrage and get your head on straight. Quit with the drama queen act. You already knew that Florence had had an affair. Did it never cross your mind at the time that Tristan might not have been your child?"

Ken thought for a brief moment. "In honesty, Harry, no. To get rid of Jean-Luc Courtemanche, I reported his affair with Florence to my superiors. They took a dim view of a service member screwing another service member's wife, particularly since he was supposed to be in England as part of a liaison team. They felt it wasn't the sort of liaison that they had intended, so they sent him back to France. I would normally have dealt with my own problems. But reporting him was a last ditch attempt to save my marriage to Florence without letting on that I knew about their affair. So he went back to France and then Florence told me she was pregnant. After that things got better."

"When did you let on that you knew about her infidelity?"

"After Tristan disappeared. Over the ensuing months, our relationship deteriorated due to the stress of the situation. One evening, during a blazing row, I told her that I had known all about Jean-Luc. Shortly after that, we split up."

"So you never loved the boy then?"

"Harry, I don't mean to be rude, but what you sometimes refer to as your borderline social anxiety disorder can display to me as full-blown autism. Through no fault of your own, you struggle to understand human relationships."

"And you, Ken Stafford, can be a complete and utter prick. At least my bloody brain still works, which is more than I can say about you. Sure, one or two males have called me a computer, but I can live with that because I've got my priorities in order. So don't point the finger at me, just because the question makes you uncomfortable. Now, did you, or did you not, love the boy when you thought he was your child?"

"Of course I did."

"But now, you can just switch that off like a light bulb, can you? On, off. On, off. Love him, don't love him."

"That's not what it's like at all."

Harry's eye twitched with a telltale tic. It was one that pre-warned Ken she was about to lose it – big time. Her eyes turned like twin lasers, and for a moment Ken felt himself pinned down, like an insect under a microscope.

"That's not what it's like at all," she mimicked in a loud voice. "So come on then Kenneth bloody Stafford, use your skill with the English language to explain to a poor OCD autistic simpleton with recurring confabulation just what it is like. Because I don't understand how you can love someone one minute and then, through no fault of theirs, have no feelings for them the next minute. But then, what the fuck would I know because, according to you, I struggle to understand human relationships?"

Ken's voice notched up a decibel to match hers, "How can you love another person's child, Harry. Go on, give me a clue if you're so damn smart."

"Oh Jesus H. Christ in a bucket of shit, are you really that stupid? Here's a clue, numbnuts: how do you think parents who adopt kids come to love their children, who they know were conceived by others?"

"Because they often take them on from birth—"

"Duh! Are we getting the message yet, Mr

Stafford?" Harry stood up and pointed her finger in Ken's face. "I'd always thought you were an intelligent guy Ken. I'm well aware of the types of jobs you would have done for Her Majesty's Government as sniper in the SAS. So I know you have a mind that needs to compartmentalise aspects of your life. But I also imagined that somewhere under that cool as a cucumber exterior there beat a heart with just a tiny element of emotion. Seems I was wrong. Not only do you not realise that the love you had for your son never depended on his genes, but even now you don't recognise how much Florence still loves you. And you call me fucking autistic? Jeez, you have no bloody idea!"

"Of course I've no idea, Harry," Ken snarled, matching her anger. "Since you're so good at explaining things, why don't you also explain how my beautiful bride, who told me she loved me, could go off with another man? Come on! You've had sex with me, as you like to remind me, fifty-four times over a period of one hundred and twenty three days. Was I so fucking lousy in bed that you needed to take another lover?"

"Don't be so bloody childish, Ken. It had nothing to do with your sexual abilities. They are just fine, thank you, and I speak from personal experience. It was all to do with self-worth, insecurity, and how she felt about herself. There she was, at age nineteen, married to a guy who had promised to love her from this day forward, for better, for worse, for richer, for poorer, in sickness and in health, until death do us part. Do you remember that bit, Ken?"

"And I kept my half of the bargain."

"Oh yeah, typical male answer that."

"What do you mean, 'typical male answer'? It's a straight answer."

"According to Florence, and you don't seem to want to deny it, you spent all day with your mates on the firing ranges or mending tanks or whatever it was you brave warriors did. And then all evening with the same bunch of blokes in the bar. Real man's man weren't you, mate? And Florence, left alone in a foreign country, was approached by someone she knew, someone she trusted, and he sweet-talked her, and she fell into his trap. And she has regretted it ever since. In fact, no matter what happens now, she will continue to regret it to her dying day.

The man who married her and who she really loved was never there. He was too busy with his fucking mates exchanging stories about who could run up the side of a mountain the quickest. The man who showered her with attention was not her husband, but surely even someone as dim as you can see how easy it would be to fall for his flattery?"

"No I don't Harry. I don't get that at all. Why didn't she just say something to me?"

"Oh sure. 'Excuse me, Ken, when you've got a minute, there's this other guy sniffing round and I'd like you to pay a bit more attention to me.' That would have worked, wouldn't it? And anyway, she was only just out of her teens. She was naïve, and still didn't understand how the world worked."

"And you do?"

"You were four years older. You could have helped her." Harry paused to control her breathing. She lowered her voice. "Tell me something, Ken, before you got me into bed, how long had it been since you had shagged someone?"

"Jesus, Harry, that's not a proper question."

"Yes it is. We've always been straight with each other - as far as I know."

"It was about six months, Harry, okay?"

"Fine, so then when you fucked me, how did you feel?"

"I didn't fuck you, I made love to you."

"No you didn't. First time was just to get rid of some sexual tension. It was the same for me. We made love later. So tell me, how did you feel when you fucked me?"

"Relieved."

"And?"

"I don't know and. What and? And what?"

"For Christ's sake, Ken, you're not a complete bloody zombie. After not having sex for six months, did you feel afterwards that you were still attractive to females? Did you feel that you still had some value? Did you feel that somebody still cared for you? Did it improve your self-esteem?"

Ken looked at Harry but didn't reply.

"Of course it bloody did. You probably shit rainbows and unicorns and fairy dust for a week after. So now you know how Florence felt while you were busy ignoring her and playing boy soldiers with your buddies. She discovered that she did still have a value. The trouble was, it wasn't you who helped her make the discovery. Well grow a pair and get over it asshole. Stop wallowing in self-pity." She strode to the door, opened it, and then looked over her shoulder. "When I feel pressure inside me, it's not like a tangled knot but like a ticking bomb. I need to let it explode somewhere safe where it can't do any lasting damage. So I need to leave before I tell you what I really think of you. Because you wouldn't want to hear that. I shall finish what I came here to do and give Florence the information she needs on her brother's activities. After that, I hope never to see you again. You're not just selfish, you're plain fucking stupid." She slammed the door and left Ken surrounded only by his own whirling thoughts. A moment later, from the far end of the corridor he heard a shout of "Grow the fuck up you big girl." Then the silence was total.

"That's me told." Ken muttered to himself in self-mockery. He let out a long slow sigh, like a tyre with a nail in it. The last time he had suffered a verbal roasting like that was from the drill sergeant who had pushed him into making an effort and building a regular army career.

He paced around, feeling like a big tiger locked in a small cage. And as he paced, a niggling thought, like a light bulb in a dark room, crept into the back of his mind. Since the drill sergeant had been proved right, was it possible that Harry would also be proved right? He pulled open the room bar. Getting drunk on Scotch was not the best option, but he felt in dire need of a drink of something to calm his angry, pounding heart.

He poured himself a Scotch and American and added ice from the freezer compartment. Ken sat in the high backed armchair where Harry had been a few minutes earlier. He smoothed down his fair hair, sticking up at all angles where he'd been pushing his hands through it in an attempt to calm himself while Harry went on the rampage. His mind went back to the time when he and Florence were married. He had loved her more than anything else in the world and would have done anything for her. But then he recalled what Florence had said about him and his army buddies playing soldiers all day, then disappearing down to the pub together every evening.

And she was right. That was the bit that hurt his pride. She was right that he had ignored Florence's needs in order to satisfy his own. And now, as he knocked back the first and poured himself a second Scotch and American, it began to dawn on him why neither he nor Florence had had any meaningful relationships with other people since splitting up. It was because they were still in love.

He reached for his wallet and drew out the old photo that had travelled with him to every part of the globe. It was Florence and him on their wedding day over twenty years ago. And Ken felt something wet trickle down his cheek. Not a sentiment he would want to admit to any of the blokes from The Regiment. He reached deep into the back compartment of his wallet and withdrew a second photo. Florence holding a little boy in her arms, and the little boy was smiling and waving to the man behind the camera.

Ken's thoughts echoed around his head like a moth haunts a light bulb. His mind drifted back to those wonderful few months when Tristan was three – just before he was snatched. He had begun to put words together into short sentences and loved nothing more than a bedtime story. He would always ask for 'The Little Mole Who Knew it Was None of His Business', a scatological masterpiece about a mole who found a pile of poo and set out on a mission to discover who the culprit was. 'Tell it me again,' he would say when Ken tried to convince him to hear another story. 'Tell it me again,' with the velvet soft of his cheek nestled into the pillow and a tired smile on his face.

And if Ken insisted they read another story, Tristan's face would cloud over and his lower lip would stick out. 'No, Daddy, tell it me again. Mister Mole.' And Ken would relent and Tristan's face would break into a beam. He would clutch his teddy close and he would say, 'Love you Daddy.'

For the last sixteen years, Ken had compartmentalised those memories and buried them deep in the back of his mind. He had locked them in a dark place where they could no longer hurt him. Without Tristan in his life, the memories were just too painful to bear. And now, it seemed, he was prepared to bury them forever, like they never existed.

He allowed his head to rest against the high back of the armchair, and he closed his eyes. He had just discovered something about himself that he didn't know existed. Or at least something that he had bottled up in the deepest recesses of his mind for the last sixteen years. He had just discovered the love he had always had for Florence, in all its shapes and forms. And the love that he had for Tristan; the little boy who called him 'Daddy' because he didn't know differently. Ken opened his eyes and looked at the photo again. As he stared at the radiant face of his bride, he realised that the more he acknowledged this love and let it in, the stronger it became. And he was no longer ashamed of the fact that his shoulders shook and tears flowed down his face.

And as he let go of his true emotions for the first time in his adult life, the tears of the past turned into tears for his own stupidity. The past could no longer hurt him but the future could, if he allowed it to. It was not having love that was painful. Sure, Florence's betrayal all those years ago was painful. The betrayal and the loneliness - they hurt. Love doesn't.

Ken knew that if he walked out of her life again now, he would have to face the fact that their relationship would forever be nothing more than a memory. A memory of a wound that had healed over but still left a scar. His stubborn side didn't want to reconcile things and make things up with Florence. But Harry's tirade had forced him to realise that life, love and family were precious and he had to make a choice. The decision was his to make because he was in the driving seat and it was now up to him how the relationship played out. And he knew deep down that he actually did want to make things up with the girl he had loved and lost. But the obstinate Ken Stafford was still clinging onto the old hurt.

As he tried to make sense of the turmoil of his thoughts, he stared down at his hand. It was resting on the arm of the chair but still holding his drink. His hand was shaking enough to make the ice rattle against the glass. He leaned forward, set it down on the nearby table and then leaned back again in the chair. As his mind whirled, he recalled a quotation from Desmond Tutu. 'Forgiveness says you are given another chance to make a new beginning'. And as he finally rested his still full glass on the low table in front of him, he knew that it was time to grab that second chance with both hands.

# CHAPTER TWENTY

When Ken walked back into Florence's apartment, two stern-faced women stared at him. Harry stood and said, "I'm going to check on my data search, Florence. Goodnight." She strode up the staircase without even a glance at Ken.

Ken dropped his overnight bag on the floor. He approached Florence, who stood to greet him, though it was clear that she didn't know what to expect. When she reached out and the tips of her fingers touched his face, he kept his gaze away, unwilling to risk rejection. With her fingers on his cheek she turned his head so he could see that there was no judgement in her eyes, only love. His face buckled and tears rolled unchecked again, washing a path to his chin. They both wanted an embrace that would never end. They both wanted an embrace that would tell them that everything would be alright if they had the will.

"Florence, I'm sorry," Ken said, in a soft, gentle voice. "Really, really sorry. I didn't understand your loneliness. I didn't want to understand. I couldn't deal with it. I couldn't deal with being torn between a steady home life or the thrills and adventure of the Special Forces. Even before my friend Don Thompson told me about it, I had an inkling of what was going on between you and Jean-Luc. But to begin with, I couldn't admit it to myself. That would have meant having to deal with the pain and the recrimination. It would have meant having to deal with which life I wanted to lead the most. I was angry with you, and that was easier. I could deal with anger. I could channel all my feelings into anger."

Florence nodded but said nothing. Her eyes were heavy with unshed tears.

"As time has gone by," Ken continued, "I began to think that I understood your reasons. The more mature I have become and the more life experiences I have had to deal with, the more I have realised that not everything is black or white. There are more than fifty shades of grey. A lot more." The words were tumbling out from Ken now. He kept going, knowing that if he stopped he may not start again. "But I never applied my new philosophies to you, Florence. It was easier to think of you as the villain. It meant I didn't have to think of Tristan's loss." He pulled his handkerchief from his pocket and blew his nose. "I'm sorry," he said again. Please forgive me."

It was almost too much for Florence. A thread of sympathy and she could feel her composure unravelling. It only took one small smile and Ken's strong arms wrapped around her as he pulled her to him. She took in his aftershave, a slightly spicy mixture, and that manly smell of shampoo and warm soap. If she could bottle Ken Stafford's pheromones, she could make a fortune. All part of nature's mating game.

Ken dropped a kiss on top of her head and entwined his fingers in her hair. She pulled away.

Unshed tears stood in her eyes, perilously close to spilling over. She said, "I think I need to sit down, otherwise I may not stay upright very long."

When she sat, perched on the front of her chair, and Ken faced her on a matching chair, Florence said, "Tristan was born early on a cool September morning, Ken, and I watched you bond with him in an instant. When you turned to me with a tiny red-faced bundle in your arms, you said, 'Look, Florence. Look what we made. He's perfect.' And my heart gives a little squeeze even now as I think back to that moment. I can recall like it was yesterday the dark, tired circles under your eyes, the way your hair stood out on end, and the pure love that radiated from every pore in your body.

And I remember too, the anger and pain when Tristan disappeared. I remember you pacing the living room, phoning the police every couple of hours in case there was any news. I remember you going out day after day in all weathers, searching the fields and hedgerows around the house. You loved that boy, Ken, and I loved you for loving him. I really did think he was yours. I honestly and truly thought he was yours. But I can understand how hurt you must be feeling right now."

Ken nodded. "Hurt, angry, disappointed, shocked. Yes, all of that, but Harry sort of put me straight."

"What did she say to you to get you to come back?"

Ken smothered a laugh. "Quite a lot. I didn't get to say much, in fact. She gave me a grade 'A' bollocking."

"So you came back because Harry shouted at you?"

"No, Florence, I'm not that weak-willed. I came

back because what Harry said to me made me stop and think. And I realised that I loved Tristan when I didn't know that he wasn't my son, so why would I not love him now? I would have given my own life to have kept him safe from harm, and he has done nothing that should make me change that view."

Florence glanced towards the top of the stairs and whispered, "Thank you, Harry."

Ken looked up, but there was nobody there. "You're right," he said, "Harry's simplistic view of life was exactly what I needed right at that moment. She took a complex issue and brought it down to one simple question. But you can understand, can't you, why I was upset earlier?"

Florence leaned forwards and took Ken's hands in hers. "Yes, Ken, I do understand. Of course I understand. But I promise you that I never, ever, thought that Tristan was Jean-Luc's child. I always thought he was yours. Even when the doctors said I was three months gone, I didn't believe them; I assumed they had it wrong."

"Which is why you always said he was one month premature?"

"I really did think he was premature. Now, it seems that he was born at the right time, but I was ignoring what was before my eyes. I was in denial. I loved you and I wanted you to be his father."

"You were in a state of confirmatory bias," said a voice from the stairs. Ken and Florence looked up to see Harry descending into the living area. "It's the tendency to search for, interpret, favour, and recall information in a way that confirms one's pre-existing beliefs or hypotheses. And in doing so, you gave disproportionately less consideration to alternative possibilities. Does that wine bottle still have anything interesting in it?"

"Grab your glass," Florence said, "it's still there from when we chatted earlier."

Harry filled her glass, sat down, and continued, "With all my problems, I've had to study psychiatry to some extent. Confirmation bias is well known in the world of psychiatry. It's one of the reasons why I note everything on my iPad. When I have a memory wipe-out, I can refill the holes accurately without needing to interpret how I may have felt. People display confirmation bias when they gather or remember information selectively, or when they interpret it in a biased way. The effect is stronger for emotionally charged issues and for entrenched beliefs. People are biased toward confirming their existing beliefs. Explanations include wishful thinking or that they are weighing up the costs of being wrong, rather than investigating the facts in a neutral, scientific way."

"And how would you interpret Florence's reaction, when she found she was pregnant?" Ken asked.

"I'm not speaking to you."

"Oh well suit yourself— "

"Of course I am, fool. Now that you've acknowledged that I'm right and you're wrong."

Ken chuckled to himself. "Did you just make a joke?" he said. "Bloody hell, Harry, maybe there's hope for you yet!"

"Who said it was a joke. Don't kid yourself, Ken. I'm still mad as a wasp with piles about you, so don't push your luck. As far as Florence's reaction when she discovered she was pregnant: it's easy to accept either interpretation. Either she genuinely believed the child was yours, or she was in a state of confirmatory bias because she wanted the child to be yours. It's irrelevant which it was because her brain told her that you were the father. And she wanted you to be the father. Nothing else mattered. And you thought you were the father, and you wanted the child to be yours. Again, nothing else mattered. So it shouldn't bloody matter now that you've discovered otherwise."

Ken's eyebrows arched up towards his hairline.

"Also," Harry continued, "cognitive dissonance is a well-known and well-researched psychological state. It's the mental stress or discomfort experienced by an individual who holds two or more contradictory beliefs at the same time. Or is confronted by new information that conflicts with existing beliefs. Look it up."

"Ah, the black and white world of Harriet Lewis."

"You can only use my real name when you earn the right," Harry said, "and right now I'm sitting here waiting for you to tell Florence what your next actions are going to be. You know where the young man lives, and Florence wants to get to know her son. So what do you propose, Grey Man?"

"I propose that we go to Cléry Saint André tomorrow and talk to the people who Tristan thinks of as his parents. If they were something to do with his disappearance, we turn them over to the police."

"And if not?" Florence asked.

"I don't know. The least we want from them is that

they tell us how they come to have Tristan living with them as their son. Depending on their answers, we formulate some sort of response."

Florence looked at Harry. "Are you coming with us?"

"No," she said, "You can have Kenneth no-brain Stafford all to yourself. I'm going to stay here and keep picking at the data on my disk. Some threads look as though they may be coming together, and I suspect your brother is responsible for a lot more than just looking at disgusting pictures of young children. I'm hoping I can add some different search terms and get more threads. It's long and complex when you don't know what you are looking for, but when you start to get clues, as I am now, the search becomes easier. It may not be too long now before I have the whole picture. Did you speak to your sister in law?"

"Yes. I told Monique that there were very serious matters that would concern the police. She said to go ahead, whatever it was, because she's leaving Yves-Marie anyway. She was grateful for the offer to live here, but said she had saved up some money and could struggle through on her own. I didn't tell her, but I can help her out if necessary."

Ken smiled at Harry. "Thank you," he said. "Thank you for coming after me and making me come back here. But why did you do that?"

"Because Florence was hurt and you were lost in a world of hatred. I've only ever witnessed one person lost like that, and I've only remembered about it in the last few days. It was my mother after she found out about what my father had done to me. She confessed to me later that she had understood what people meant by the phrase 'pure hatred'. She said she had felt that, not just for my father but for people in general. For the world. And it had felt 'pure'. Not a dirty or evil thing, but a natural free-flowing hatred of everything around her except for me. She took a long time to get over it. I'm not even sure that she's over it now. It was like she was addicted to it and had sunk into the feeling. At one point, she said that if she ventured out of the house, it felt as though she could hurt people just by looking at them."

"And how do your mother's emotions at the time link to you coming and reading me the riot act tonight?"

"Like I said, I only recalled this about my mother in the last few days, and it saddens me that she could be like that. Tonight, I was afraid you were going to do the same. It took my mother a long time to get through the worst of that phase, and I didn't want you to have to suffer the same way she did. You may be stupid, but you're nice stupid."

Ken glanced at Florence who raised her eyebrows. Florence was good at raising her eyebrows. She asked Harry, "Do you still have feelings for Ken?"

Harry looked down at her feet. "I'm not good explaining emotions. I'm more comfortable explaining JavaScript."

"Sorry, I didn't mean to pry."

"You weren't. It's just that it's complicated."

"What is?"

"My feelings for you two. I don't want sex with Ken if that's what you mean. But I've started to think of you both as family. Like older brother and sister. And I didn't want it to end with Ken shouting at you and running away."

Florence reached out to take Harry's hand. "Well thanks to you, Ken's back here and we can work together to solve our problem."

"Good, so now I really am going to check on my data search. Goodnight both of you. I promise not to listen in to your conversations again tonight." As she reached the foot of the stairs, she turned and added, "Unless you're going to talk about something interesting, then you can give me a shout."

"Jeez, Harry, you just made a joke."

"No I didn't," Harry said as she set foot on the staircase. "I was being serious."

# CHAPTER TWENTY-ONE

After Harry had left them together, Florence checked the train times to Orléans out of Austerlitz station. The journey wasn't much above one hour and trains ran about every half hour during the day.

"Shouldn't we check to see that either Monsieur or Madame Gautier will be there before we just turn up on their doorstep?" she asked.

"No," Ken said. "Best we surprise them. That way, they won't have time to concoct a story about Tristan."

"Aren't you nervous?"

"A little, yes. I can't imagine anything that would exonerate these people from a criminal act. I'm nervous about how that is going to affect Tristan. What about you?"

"Same as you. It's going to be a hell of a shock when he finds out. I'm also anxious about whether he is going to accept us. We are total strangers to him and it's possible that we are going to be responsible for putting his 'parents' in jail."

Ken nodded. After a moment, he said, "Remind me what Jean-Luc Courtemanche looked like, Florence.

When I found out about you two, I made a point of eyeballing him, and I've seen him once since, but that was a long time ago."

Florence gave a small smile, though it didn't reach as far as her eyes. After a long pause, she said, "He looked like you, Ken. Fair hair, tall, solid build. Do you remember me telling you when you first got here that I actually married Jean-Luc before I met you?"

"In the school playground."

"We were six years old and he looked completely different then. He was a slightly-built nervous kiddie. I guess army life changed him. When I bumped into him in Hereford, I was struck by just how much he looked like you. Why do you ask?"

"Because when I saw Tristan outside The Sorbonne, I convinced myself that he resembled you and me. He's fair-haired, tall and well built. I tried to morph his face into the face of the three year old who we haven't seen for sixteen years. And it was easily done. It was a near perfect fit."

"Tristan was a lucky boy. He had a wonderful father who adored him. And no matter what the DNA results, I shall never ever think of him as anything other than your son."

Ken nodded and savoured his wine. "So tell me all about your life during our time apart. How did you get to where you are today? We've been so wrapped up in our own thoughts for the past week that we've not really 'talked' have we?"

After an evening of catching up, Ken checked his watch. "We'd best make for bed since we have an early start in the morning." As they stood, he placed both hands on Florence's shoulders. He kissed her full on the lips and one of his hands slipped down to her waist, just like it used to years before. He pulled her against him as the kiss became deeper and she wrapped her arms around his neck and kissed him back. She closed her eyes as weeks of fear, frustration and exhaustion slipped away and she lost herself in the embrace. Ken's hands slid from her waist to the sides of her breasts and down to her bottom. She tipped back her head as his mouth travelled from her lips to her neck and a low groan rumbled from the base of his throat.

Her scent was intoxicating. Florence smelt as he'd always remembered her. She smelt heavenly, like fresh-scented pine and honey. Her aroma was like a drug to him; he couldn't get enough of it. Together they walked up the stairs, Florence leading him past his own room and towards the master bedroom.

Florence wanted more of him. Another small teasing taste was too much to bear. She liked the closeness of him, and the intimacy. Ken's feelings reflected hers. He kissed her again, this time for longer, his lips encouraging hers to open and take up the rhythm. Florence relaxed into him, giving herself permission to respond, not just with her mind, but with her body as well. The lure of the king-size bed through the open doorway was too much to resist. When the kiss ended and they came up for air, she tugged herself away from his embrace, pulled him forwards, led him into the bedroom, and closed the door behind them.

The softness of the nest of pillows enveloped her as she lay back. She placed her arms round Ken's neck, pulling him down with her. A small moan escaped her as Ken's lips travelled down her neck and joined with his fingers that were unbuttoning her blouse. His arm scooped behind her and lifted her enough for him to unclasp her bra. His fingertips, though rough, were tender, delicate and sensual as they explored her body that he had known so well sixteen years before. The past. Such a loaded word, which held so many dark secrets. Ken was both the past and the present and Florence knew right then that she wanted Ken to be a big part of the future too. But right at that moment, she wanted Ken with every part of her body and all of her mind. And Ken obliged.

Afterwards, Ken pulled the duvet over them and they held onto each other with matching needs. Needs that were way more than physical. Needs that were emotional. And they shared an unspoken understanding that they both had demons that they had, at long last, exorcised.

"Are you okay?" Florence asked, lifting her head from the pillow.

Ken didn't answer. The smile on his face and the look in his eyes told her all she needed to know.

"Just checking," she said, snuggling back down. "There's no going back now, is there?"

"I don't plan on going back," Ken said. "I plan moving forwards. Together."

# CHAPTER TWENTY-TWO

The intercity train journey to Orléans was full of nervous tension. Ken and Florence were uncertain of what they were going to find and what sort of reception awaited them in Cléry Saint André.

A driver from the car rental company, which Florence had telephoned the evening before, met them. He took them to the office where Florence signed for a two day hire, just in case they were unable to get back to Paris that evening. She and Ken had shared a small overnight bag for just this possible eventuality.

Finding the small town of Cléry Saint André less than twenty kilometres away was a straightforward task for the satnav. Route d'Orléans, the D951, ran right through Cléry. It went from Orléans to Blois, the beginning of the Loire Valley with its beautiful châteaux. Finding 33 rue du Village was more challenging. The narrow road ran parallel to Route d'Orléans. After considerable head-scratching, it turned out that number 33 was on the junction of two tiny country roads. The satnav showed number 33 about one hundred metres further away, along the side road that met rue du Village.

An old man who was bent double and shuffled up

the street with his mongrel dog at his side, filled them in on the Gautiers. Monsieur and Madame Gautier, he said, were a nice couple who kept themselves to themselves. They lived in the tiny cottage on the corner, but they wouldn't be home until at least seven o'clock because they both worked. The old man seemed anxious to tell Florence and Ken all about how Monsieur Gautier had sold off his smallholding at the back of the cottage to some newcomers. He tutted and wagged a bony finger when he told them that the newcomers had built two large houses that weren't at all in keeping with the other homes in the community.

Florence listened to the old man while Ken strolled down rue Fontaine Grenier to see what the old man had meant. Now he understood why the satnav showed number 33 where it did. Before the new houses were built, the cottage that was number 33 would have had a long garden but now had little other than a scrappy back yard. Ken strolled back and tried to puzzle out how anybody could live in such a small building. The bulk of the cottage was no more than five metres wide and faced onto rue du Village. Attached was a single story lean-to facing onto rue Fontaine Grenier. In the gable end of the main building was a lone window, indicating there was an upstairs of some sort. At the front, at ground level there was a wooden door, but no windows either side. Immediately above the door, a small dormer window presumably allowed light into the living area. It was a curious building that had once been a poor farm worker's cottage.

Ken waited until the old man shuffled away. Florence smiled, "Phew. He wanted to tell me his life story."

"Judging from how quiet it is here, I don't imagine he gets to see many people. I should think he was grateful for the opportunity to exercise his vocal chords." Ken turned and indicated the cottage behind him. "Look at this place, it's tiny."

"According to the old man, Madame and Monsieur Gautier have already sold it." Florence added. "It seems that the owner of the adjacent cottage has bought it so he can increase the size of his own property. The old man said that the Gautiers were moving to an HLM in Cléry." She pronounced it 'ash-el-em'. HLM was the acronym of Habitation à Loyer Modéré or rent-controlled housing, a form of public housing in France, rather like council housing in UK.

"I would imagine they'll be better off in an HLM than here," Ken said. "Shall we knock on the door and test the old man's theory about them both being out?"

Ken did, and they were.

"Okay," Florence said, checking her watch. Let's find somewhere to have lunch and see if we can find a little hotel or auberge nearby. It looks like we'll not be getting back to Paris tonight."

Using an app on Florence's phone, it took them less than ten minutes to reach La Villa des Bordes. When Florence enquired about a room for the night, the owner welcomed them into the elegant 19th century house and showed them to a double room overlooking the open countryside.

"They've upgraded since I was last here," Florence said. "The rooms were pleasant but very old-fashioned a few years ago."

"You didn't say you'd stayed here before," Ken said.

"I didn't realise it was this little hotel until I saw it on the app just now. I was hunting out good Loire valley wines and stayed here a couple of nights." She looked at Ken. "On my own, I would add. I've had very few relationships, casual or otherwise, since we split up."

"Me too," Ken said. "Harry tells me we were together one hundred and twenty three days —"

"— and had sex fifty-four times!"

"So it seems," Ken said, laughing. "I confess I wasn't counting. But that was the longest I've been with anyone in the last fifteen years. Does it bother you that she and I were lovers?"

"Not in the slightest," Florence said. "You were a free agent. Though I am curious how you two got together."

Ken smiled. "We nearly didn't. A day or two after we first met, she blanked me out in the street. Like I was a complete stranger. What I didn't realise at the time was that I was a complete stranger to her. She'd had a wipe-out and, until I told her who I was and she checked it on her iPad she didn't know me from the man in the moon. She did the same when I picked her up at the airport a week ago."

"Yes, but I'm still surprised the two of you hit it off at all. You are exact opposites in many ways."

Ken looked at his watch. "I'll tell you over lunch. I'm starving: let's go down and eat."

After they had ordered, Ken said, "Harry is a

complex character, Florence, as I'm sure you now realise. When you consider what problems she has to overcome she is a remarkable young lady. Sure she's blunt. In fact, she's the least tactful person I've ever met. And for sure she has difficulties with personal relationships. But all of this makes it so much more incredible that she continues to function. When you get below the skin, as you appear to be doing with her, she is a lovely person. She's warm in her own way and she's brave and intelligent."

"Did you love her?" Florence asked.

Ken thought for a moment. "No, I don't think I loved her, though in her own way, she thought she loved me. I liked her a lot and I still do, but I didn't love her. I think more than anything I admire her for having the balls to get on and do well in life. Same as you. You have achieved so much, it's amazing."

Florence smiled. "You know, Ken, you're not such a bad guy yourself."

Ken pretended to ignore her as the waitress served his lunch of Rochefort rice risotto with snails from Chaingy, a small village a few kilometres away on the other side of the Loire river. Florence watched his face and smiled to herself as the waitress place a plate of buckwheat noodles with fried squid and Jerusalem artichokes in front of her.

"You're going to have awful wind if you eat those Jerusalem artichokes," Ken said.

"Not if they're properly cooked. So come on, you were telling me about Harry. How did you get to meet?"

"On the Isle of Man, Dinger, Sparky and I - well, just Sparky and me now - run a personal protection training business. Most people call it bodyguarding, but we treat it seriously. There are plenty of places that claim to train bodyguards, but all that happens is that these people get a diploma in body-guarding, go out to Iraq or wherever and get themselves killed, along with the people they're supposed to be protecting. The majority of training currently on offer is inadequate for that level of work.

We set up a proper PSO - that's Personal Security Officers - training centre on the Isle of Man. There are only about five such centres worldwide, and none of them are in the UK. So it was a big feather in the Isle of Man's cap. It has created jobs and brought revenue to the island."

"So you still handle weapons and stuff like that?"

"The training includes weapons handling, weapon firing, advanced driving skills and similar instruction in advanced protection techniques in all forms of transport - air, road and sea. The Isle of Man is perfectly suited. There are plenty of country roads that we can close off for a day at a time if necessary. There's an old airport in the north of the island that we use for training in and out of helicopters. And we are, of course, surrounded by sea."

"But it doesn't fulfil you, does it?"

"Whatever makes you say that?" Ken asked, taking a break from his risotto and snails.

"We were married long enough for me to sense your moods, Ken, and something is bothering you. You just told me all about your business without a single shred of enthusiasm."

"Ha! Florence the Fortune Teller strikes again. In answer to your question about meeting Harry, we run background checks on all our trainees and, if we don't have a full picture, we get Harry to dig around for us. It's illegal, but she gets to the facts quickly and efficiently."

"You're evading the issue, Ken. What's bugging you?"

Ken finally deserted his half-eaten risotto. It was obvious that Florence wasn't about to give up. He poured himself a glass of sparkling water. "If you want to know, it's because I don't have a Florence in my life. I have no-one to share my life with. If we succeed at something at work, I have no-one to tell about it. If I take a holiday and see or do something interesting, I have no-one to experience it with me. I have lots of friends on the island - good friends - but nobody close like you used to be. We were good together, Florence, even though we both messed up. I spent too much time with my army buddies and you spent too much time with your childhood sweetheart. And then, when Tristan disappeared, we'd lost the base that we had built before."

"You're right," Florence said. She, too, gave up on her lunch, leaving her Jerusalem artichokes untouched. "I'm just the same, Ken. Like you, I've had a few lovers since we separated, but nothing even remotely permanent. And though I've made a success of my businesses, I miss what you miss. I miss the opportunities to share when something goes well, or to look for support when something goes wrong."

"So what are we going to do about it?"

Florence shrugged. "Not much we can do, is there?"

"No, I suppose not."

The waitress approached the table. "Is everything alright with the food?" she asked.

Florence smiled at her. "It's fine," she said. "I guess neither of us were as hungry as we thought. On the other hand," she added, "I could manage your vacherin aux clémentines et marron glacé."

"What's that?" Ken asked.

"Vacherin is a soft, rich, cow's milk cheese from the Jura. They serve it with clementines and glazed chestnuts."

"That'll do for me too," Ken said to the waitress. "What do we do while we wait for the Gautiers to get home?" he asked Florence.

"Two choices, Ken. We can go and take a look at the basilique Notre-Dame de Cléry, which contains the resting place of Louis XI's skull. Or we can stay here and lock ourselves into the bedroom for a little while to see if the bed is comfortable."

"No contest then. Louis XI's skull it is."

Florence kicked him under the table.

# CHAPTER TWENTY-THREE

It was with some trepidation that Ken and Florence tapped on the door of 33 rue du Village at 7:15pm. After a moment, the door opened and a lady of about 50 years of age asked, "Oui?"

"Madame Gautier?" Florence asked.

"Oui. A qui ai-je l'honneur?"

"I am Florence de Nussac and this is Kenneth Stafford. Would it be convenient to talk to you?"

"If you're selling something, you'd be wasting your time since we have no spare money. And if you are from some religious organisation, I will wish you a pleasant evening and send you on your way."

"It is neither thing, Madame Gautier. It is about Tristan. Is Monsieur Gautier at home?"

"He is now," Madame Gautier said, looking over Florence's shoulder.

Florence glanced behind her and saw a man dressed in oily overalls step out of an old Renault that he had pulled off the narrow road and onto the shallow patch of earth in front of the cottage.

Sylvie Gautier called, "Jerome, it's Madame de Nussac and Monsieur—?" She looked questioningly at Ken.

"Monsieur Stafford," Ken said.

"If you're selling something, you'd be wasting your time —" he began.

Sylvie Gautier laughed, "I've done that bit, Jerome. They want to talk to us about Tristan."

"Are you from the university?" Jerome Gautier asked, stepping past his wife and into the gloom of the cottage.

Florence answered. "No, Monsieur Gautier. We are just trying to clarify some matters that relate to Tristan. May we come in."

"If you're not too long, but we're used to having our dinners at 8 o'clock and there is something I have to do first."

Sylvie Gautier stepped aside and let Ken and Florence enter. "So what's this about?" she asked when they were all inside. "Has Tristan done something wrong?"

"Not at all," Florence said. "It's a delicate matter, but we need to get to the bottom of it. She looked at the Gautiers in turn and asked, "Can you tell us if Tristan is adopted?"

Jerome Gautier responded immediately. "That would only concern him and us, Madame. Who are you anyway? Are you from the administration?"

"No, Monsieur, Gautier. I am Florence de Nussac. I was Florence Stafford, and I believe that Tristan is my son."

Jerome Gautier caught hold of his wife as her legs gave way. He guided her to a battered armchair and helped her sit down. After fetching her a glass of water and making sure she was alright, he said in a low, quiet voice, "We always wondered if this day would come. We tried so hard to find you, you know."

Florence looked questioningly at him. He indicated that she should sit in the other armchair. As Jerome Gautier fetched another glass of water for his wife, Ken looked around. The cottage contained two armchairs, a small table with four wooden chairs and a tiny kitchen area. A door led to the lean-to that Ken had spotted earlier and he guessed this would be the bathroom and toilet. A steep narrow staircase occupied one corner of the already cramped quarters. It could hardly be more different to the large, elaborate, living space that Florence enjoyed on Avenue Marceau.

As Ken and Jerome Gautier settled onto two of the dining chairs, Sylvie Gautier found her voice. "We made real efforts to find you. In the end, we adopted Tristan so he could have a proper family."

Florence said, "Perhaps it would be best to start at the beginning. How did you even come into contact with Tristan?"

"Through my brother; his father."

Ken could already sense what was coming, but he allowed Florence to take the lead. Apart from the fact that his French had limitations, it was better that she did things at her own pace.

"Your brother?" Florence asked. "But who was your brother?"

"Jean-Luc, of course."

"Jean-Luc Courtemanche?"

"Well yes. He was Tristan's father wasn't he?"

"It's complicated," Ken said.

"But he had papers," Jerome Gautier said.

"What papers?" Ken asked.

"English birth papers." Jerome stood and reached into a small upright bureau that Ken hadn't noticed. After a moment, he drew out a folded paper and handed it to Ken.

Ken unfolded it and said, "It's a British birth certificate." He screwed his eyes up. "Do you mind if I step to the door with it? It's a bit dark in here." Without waiting for a response, he opened the front door and squinted at the birth certificate. After a while, he said, "It looks like Jean-Luc got a copy of Tristan's birth certificate and had a new one forged, showing him as the father and the birth place as Manchester. You can get false birth certificates for about £450 in lots of London pubs. Good quality passports are only about £800."

"You mean that my brother wasn't Tristan's father?" Sylvie asked.

"That's where it becomes complicated," Ken said. "Until yesterday, we always assumed that I was his father. It is my name that appears on the official birth certificate registered in England. Yesterday, however, we discovered that Jean-Luc is, indeed, Tristan's biological father."

"I don't understand."

Ken did his best to explain and to limit Florence's blushes.

"That would explain a lot," Sylvie said. "Jean-Luc told us that Tristan was the result of an affair of the heart with an Irish girlfriend called Florence Stafford who didn't want an abortion. He told us that he had agreed to take on the boy because Miss Stafford was finding it hard to cope as a single mother because of the stigma in ultra-religious Dublin."

"None of that is true," Florence said, "except for the fact that I did have an affair with Jean-Luc and it now transpires that he was the biological father. Tristan's real father, the man who loved him and raised him until he disappeared, is sitting here in this room. Now it seems that it was Jean-Luc who took the child from us. There was a massive hunt in England, but I guess he must have somehow brought him back here to France."

"But why would he do that? He must have believed he was the father."

Florence glanced at Ken and said 'sorry' with her eyes. To the Gautiers, she said, "After our affair ended, Jean-Luc came back to France. Two years later, he turned up on my doorstep one day while Ken was away. He wanted to renew our old relationship. But I was very firm with him and told him that there was no chance of that ever happening. When he persisted, I told him that I was happy." She reached for Ken's hand. "I told him that I wanted nothing more to do with him. It was just as he was leaving that Tristan woke up and began to cry."

"And Jean-Luc saw him and felt he was the father?" Ken asked, holding tight to Florence's hand.

"Yes. Without thinking, I mentioned Tristan's age.

Jean-Luc and I had a big row, and he stormed off. I never saw him again."

"But why didn't you tell us this when Tristan disappeared?"

"Because it never even crossed my mind. It was a minor event from a year before. Not for one second did I link the two things. He tried to step back into my life and I said no. It was as simple as that."

"But it wasn't, was it?" Jerome Gautier said. "Because it would seem that my brother-in-law took Tristan."

"It seems that way. So how is it that you adopted him?" Florence asked.

"Jean-Luc was away a lot of the time, with the army," Jerome said, "and we looked after Tristan while he was away. He even began calling us Maman and Papa. When Tristan was five Jean-Luc was killed in Afghanistan - it's assumed by The Taliban. Jean-Luc had applied for a livret de famille for Tristan, using the paper you have in your hand from England, which showed him as the father."

Sylvie picked up the story. "When my brother died, we tried to trace a Florence Stafford in Manchester and Ireland but had no luck."

"I was already back in France by then and had reverted to my family name of de Nussac."

"Well Tristan had been with us so long and we'd grown to love the boy so we adopted him and raised him as our own."

"Does Tristan know anything of this?" Florence asked.

"A year and a half ago, when he was eighteen, we told him we were really his aunt and uncle. But he'd thought of us as his parents all his life. He couldn't even remember ever calling us Tati Sylvie or Tonton Jerome. So he was happy to carry on calling is Maman and Papa."

The room was silent for a long minute. "Where do we go from here?" Sylvie asked.

Florence shook her head. "I don't know, Sylvie. I want Tristan to know that I am his mother and that Ken was his father until Jean-Luc took him. But that wouldn't be fair on you and I can see how it might also mess up Tristan's mind, and that's the last thing he needs while he's studying."

"He's at The Sorbonne," Sylvie said. There was pride in her voice and her eyes as she spoke.

"I know," Florence said, "that's where I first saw him. How is he getting on there?"

Sylvie looked at her husband. He shrugged and said, "He's doing well. He's very, very bright, but we may have to terminate his studies soon."

"For heaven's sake why?"

"Money. We have spent everything we have to cover his costs. He's a good lad and doesn't waste money, but we are still finding it very difficult."

"Well that's easy to solve," Florence said. "I can pay whatever you need for him to stay there. He is, after all, my liability too, and you have raised him without any help from me for the past sixteen years. I owe you sixteen years support."

Jerome smiled. "We don't look on Tristan as an expense, Madame de Nussac—"

"Florence."

"We don't look on Tristan as an expense, Florence. We love him as if he were our own son. We couldn't have children ourselves, so in some ways, Tristan was an unexpected gift."

Ken butted in. "Can I make a suggestion - subject, of course, to you and Tristan agreeing."

"Go ahead," from all three.

"Florence has a large apartment on Avenue Marceau. What about if Tristan lives there in term time - coming to see you both at weekends, of course, just as usual. Florence can pay for his studies and his living expenses, and his travel costs at weekends. With her financial help, Tristan can see his way through university. All subject to Tristan's and your agreement of course," Ken repeated.

Sylvie Gautier looked at her husband. "It would be like another gift from the heavens," she said.

Jerome nodded and smiled. He checked his watch. "I don't want to seem rude," he said, "but I'm going to ask you both to leave now. I would love nothing more than to keep discussing this but as I told you when you arrived, I have something I have to do. It's Friday night and Tristan is coming home this weekend. His bus will arrive in the town in a few minutes and I need to be there to meet him."

"Do you have somewhere to stay?" Sylvie asked

"We're at the Villa des Bordes, on the other side of the village" Florence replied.

"I know it. We'll have a long talk with Tristan tonight so that he knows the whole story. Tomorrow morning, perhaps you'd like to come back and meet your son."

To the others, Florence seemed calm, collected, and stoic. She held her head high and smiled in the face of everyone. Yet as soon as she was alone with Ken, she knew that the mask would drop and tears would fall. "Thank you," she replied, "I would love that. I've missed him so much."

Ken stood and wiped away something moist in the corner of his eye.

# CHAPTER TWENTY-FOUR

After Florence had freshened up and phoned Harry to let her know that they wouldn't be home that evening, she and Ken made their way back down to the hotel restaurant for dinner. They both chose the starter of pan-fried foie gras with a celery mousseline. For the main course, Ken ordered slow cooked veal, with artichokes and Florence ordered chicken. Ken poked gentle fun at the ostentatious descriptions on the menu and Florence smiled. It was something he had always done when they were married.

As they sipped their aperitif drinks, Florence said, "What do you make of the Gautiers?"

"Good people, with one exception."

"Which is?"

"They said they had tried to trace Florence Stafford in England and Ireland but had no luck. I don't think they are telling the whole truth. It wouldn't have taken much searching to have found reports of a missing boy whose mother was called Florence Stafford."

"I disagree, Ken. The internet and search engines were in their early days at the time and information was much harder to get hold of. It's particularly difficult if you don't speak the language and have no money to pay for someone to do it for you."

"You might be right, but I'll reserve judgment on that one. I suspect that, by that stage, they had already come to think of Tristan as their own. I don't think they were looking too hard for the mother. Not finding you fitted their agenda better."

"We'll never know," Florence said. "At least they seemed to be fairly calm about us turning up as we did. What's important now is how Tristan reacts when he discovers— "

"What? What is it?" Ken asked as Florence stared over his shoulder. He turned round and he, too, saw Tristan standing at the restaurant entrance, scanning the room.

Both of them stood up at exactly the same moment that Tristan spotted them. He approached them with care and then his face broke into a grin. "You're the crazy woman who chased me up the street," he said. "And you're the English guy who ripped half my hair out."

Ken laughed, "I only took a couple of hairs for a DNA test."

"But you smacked me on the head and said I was being attacked by a wasp."

"So I did," Ken said. "Have you eaten?"

"No, I've just had a long talk with my parents and I decided I didn't want to wait until morning to meet you."

"Will you join us?"

"I'd like that."

Ken summonsed the waitress and asked her to set a third place. He also ordered a bottle of champagne, which came chilled to perfection a moment later. When they moved places and Tristan sat between them, they raised their glasses to each other in a toast.

Tristan placed his glass on the table and smiled at them both. He looked at Florence and said, "So you're my biological mother then?"

"I was your full time mother until you were taken from us."

"And you," Tristan said, looking at Ken, "must be my non-biological father."

"I was your full time father until you were taken from us."

"Fair answer."

"How much do you know?" Florence asked.

"Everything, I think, unless there's something my parents - my adoptive parents - aren't telling me. They told me that my biological father and you had an affair of which I was the result. When my biological father found out that you had had a baby he thought it was his. And now it turns out he was right, though he couldn't have been sure at the time. Anyway, he kidnapped me and brought me here to France. A couple of years later he was killed in Afghanistan and my aunt and uncle adopted me."

"That's about the sum of it," Ken said. "So how do you feel now, after all these years, to discover you have another mother and father?"

"Is that really how you think of me?" Tristan asked. "Do you really think of me as your son?"

Ken smiled at both of them, then addressed Tristan. He said, "Tristan, when you were born, I went home and cried like a little boy. My heart was full of joy and love for you. Yesterday, when I discovered you were not my biological child, I was not very happy. In fact, I was furious. But then a very wise lady who is even crazier than your mother, gave me a sharp reality check."

"Which was?"

"Which was that, if I had never discovered that I wasn't your biological father, I would be sitting here now so full of love that it hurts."

"And how do you feel sitting here now?"

"I feel so full of love that it hurts. You're the baby who I bottle fed, whose nappies I changed, who made me shout with joy when you first said, 'Dadda'. Frankly, Tristan, I'm on the verge of tears, but big men like me don't cry, so I won't."

"Cool. And you Mum?"

Florence's shoulders shook and she had a napkin held to her face so couldn't reply.

"Wow," said Tristan. "I think maybe I'm in a happy place too."

"No problems?" Ken asked.

"Not so far. It's weird, but it's nice. I guess I feel sorry for you guys, losing your son for all these years."

Florence emerged from behind her napkin. She took a few shuddering breaths and struggled to pull herself together. “Can the three of us step outside for a moment?” she stuttered.

“What for?” Tristan asked.

“A private hug.”

“Oh yes. Pretty new mum, handsome new dad, I think I can manage that!”

Some of the other diners peered at them as they left the restaurant. Outside, a few steps away from the building, in the early evening shadows, Ken placed a gentle hand in the small of Tristan’s back and steered him towards his mother. Tristan stepped forward and moved in close, stealing Florence’s breath and the heat from her skin. Suddenly her defences were like a thin tissue, and before she could draw in the air her body needed she melted into his arms. She could feel his firm torso and the heart that beat within. His hands folded around her back, drawing her in closer. Those tiny infant hands embedded in her memory were now the hands of a gentle young man who no longer smelled of baby powder.

Florence could feel her body shake, crying for the missed time they could never get back, crying to release the tension of those sixteen long years without him. Tristan pulled his head back and wiped her tears away with a compassionate finger. Even this smallest of touches brought more relief than Florence’s heart could hold. He was eating her with his eyes, eager to get to know his real mother. Florence looked up into his face and ran her hand through his hair, as if she couldn't quite believe that he still wasn’t just part of a sad memory.

And then Tristan turned and reached out for his

father and Ken was happy to oblige. The three of them stood still for a long minute, holding on to each other and learning who they now were. Understanding that their worlds had just changed and would never again be the same.

Florence wanted to speak but all she could do was croak, "Don't go, Tristan. Not ever again." His mouth painted a soft smile and he nodded once before folding his new parents in his arms once more. No words would come. All three stood still and silent. Then slowly they made their way back into the restaurant, but not before stopping one last time near the door of the hotel for a final silent hug.

Ken looked up at the evening sky on this beautiful summer night. The sky was a shade of pale pink. A sure sign that tomorrow was going to be another good day.

“What are you thinking?” Tristan asked.

“Butterflies.”

“Butterflies?”

“Butterflies. I haven’t felt butterflies since forever. I can’t ignore them. They have been hiding in captivity but are now desperate for my attention.”

“Is he always like this?” he asked Florence.

She smiled. “He’s a big hard Special Services man who has seen action in just about every trouble spot in the world. He’s been shot at, he’s been blown up, and he was nearly killed once by a land mine that shattered his leg. He doesn’t know the meaning of nervous. But now he has butterflies in his tummy. Poor boy!”

Tristan laughed and tugged Ken’s arm. “Come on,

let's go and eat."

Florence wasn't letting go of her son any time soon and held his hand all the way back to their table.

As they were once more seated and were served with their starter course, Ken said, "You're taking all this rather calmly, Tristan."

"I'm a calm person, Ken, er… Papa. Shit, what do I call you?"

"Ken is fine. You call your step-parents Maman and Papa, so no point confusing the issue now."

"And what about you?" Tristan asked Florence.

Florence reverted to speaking in English. "What about calling us Mum and Dad in English?"

"Hey that works." Tristan paused with a fork of foie gras halfway to his mouth. He looked from one to the other and said in a solemn, quiet voice, "You must have loved me a lot to have recognised me sixteen years later, and to have made the effort to trace me."

Florence reached a hand out over the table and placed it on Tristan's wrist. Ken rested his hand on the lad's shoulder. "Oh yes," they said in unison. Tristan stared at the hand lying on his wrist then dropped the fork onto his plate and wiped his eyes with the back of his hand. "It must be contagious. I told myself I wasn't going to do this."

"It's fine to have emotions," Ken said. "Emotions are what make us human. You can have happiness, pride, excitement, relief: every emotion considered good. But what would you be if you didn't feel hurt, or pain, or despair? You can't have the good without the bad. There is no light without darkness.

The trick is to balance them, so the bad doesn't seem so terrible, and you can appreciate the good."

"Yes, but you two have just fulfilled a long-held dream of mine."

"What's that?" Florence asked.

"My parents told me a year or so ago that they were my aunt and uncle. After that, I couldn't get it out of my mind and I wondered who I really was. I don't have a laptop or tablet, but I accessed the university computers and searched for Florence Stafford on the net. It didn't take long to find the story of the little boy who disappeared in Hereford. In one report, it said that my mother's maiden name was de Nussac and that she was French. Another search turned up the whole de Nussac genealogy; it's an old family going back hundreds of years. But I soon discovered a Florence de Nussac living in Paris."

Florence stared open-mouthed. Her voice was high and she spoke with a gasp that could have been surprise or could have been hurt. "And you never made yourself known? Why not?"

"My parents, as you may have noticed, are poor working people. If I went banging on the door of a successful business woman claiming to be her long lost son, they would never have forgiven me. And anyway, after an awful lot of thought and soul-searching, I made my mind up that it was better to let sleeping dogs lie. I never imagined you would find me, Tristan Gautier, living on the outskirts of the tiny town of Cléry Saint André, 150 kilometres from Paris."

"We never would have found you," Florence said,

"if I hadn't just happened to be walking past The Sorbonne at the same time that you were leaving, a few weeks ago."

"Fate plays a hand then," Tristan said. "And I thought you were just a crazy woman. If I'm honest with you, after I found out my parents adopted me, I told myself that if you never found me, you were not looking, so were not bothered about me. It was easier to stifle those emotions that sit brooding about life dealing me a bum hand."

Florence looked Tristan in the eye. "Just for the record, Tristan, I have paid out a fortune on private detectives over the years, but they had no place to start. You disappeared into thin air with no trace and no clues. But I never gave up. I would never have given up looking for you until the day I died."

Tristan nodded. "So now are you going to tell everybody?"

"No, not unless you want us to. I don't think you'll enjoy all the publicity very much."

"My thoughts exactly. So what happens now?"

"Did your parents tell you our proposal about living in my apartment in Paris? That place you are lodging at in Rue Compans doesn't look up to much."

"It's not. It's a flea-infested shit hole. Oops, am I allowed to swear?"

"Just a little, Florence said, otherwise you'll get as bad as your Dad."

"He doesn't — Oh, Jeez, yeah, Dad not Papa! I'll get used to it."

"So will I," Ken said. "Though I must admit, it's nice hearing you calling me Dad again." He chuckled. "As a toddler you were a mouth to stick a bottle in, and a bottom to wipe. I hope we're through that stage?"

"Depends what's in the bottle," Tristan said.

"Come on then. What do you think to the idea of having your own room in my apartment on Avenue Marceau?" Florence asked. "Would that work for you?"

"Is the Pope catholic? What do you think?"

"I guess that means yes," Ken said, smiling at Florence's confusion.

"Okay," Florence said, "here's what I think. It's a big apartment —"

"I know, I've walked past it a few times and wondered what it must be like to live there."

"Well you're about to find out. Subject to your parents agreeing, you can live with me during the university term times and come and see them whenever you want at weekends and during holidays. And before you mention money, it's not an issue. I have sixteen years of catching up to do. And I shall be needing linguists as I expand my business into other countries," Florence added, with a bright smile on her face. "So maybe I can even offer you a job when you've finished your studies."

"Cool again. But you said, 'come and live with me' not 'come and live with us'. Is Ken - Dad - not going to be there."

"That's complicated," Ken said, not for the first time that day. "I have a business and a home on the

Isle of Man, so I guess I need to give some thought to my own future now. Whatever happens, you'll be seeing a lot more of me, that's for sure."

"Okay, I can handle that." Tristan paused briefly, but it was clear he wanted to say more. After a moment, he said, "Stop me if I'm being silly, but do you know a story about a mole?"

Ken's face jumped to attention. "A mole who tried to find out who had left their poo lying around on top of his head?"

"That's it! That's the one!"

"It was called 'The Story of the Little Mole Who Knew it Was None of His Business' and you used to make me read it at bedtime. In fact, I could probably recite it word for word even now. Do you remember it?"

"Not clearly," Tristan said. "It's like a dream somewhere in the back of my mind."

"One day, the little mole poked his head out from underground to see whether the sun had already risen. Then it happened —"

"That's it. That's exactly it," Tristan laughed. "But I don't remember the ending."

"Because you were always asleep before I got that far," Ken said, "clutching your teddy bear."

"Teddy. Yes, I remember Teddy."

Florence laughed. "I've still got that book and I've still got Teddy. The book is amongst my many souvenirs of you, Tristan. You can read the ending for yourself if you want. And I slept with Teddy in my bed for years, convinced I could still smell you on him. He lives on the shelf above my desk now."

"It's strange," Tristan said. "When I started to learn English at school it came quite naturally to me, like it was my own language. I guess that all makes sense now."

"You'll maybe hear it more when you're with us," Ken said. "Your Mum and I tend to talk together in English. When we first met, my French wasn't up to much and the habit of speaking English together doesn't seem to have left us."

"So I have one set of parents who speak French and one set who speak English. Cool!"

"Well talking of your parents, Tristan, I need to talk to you about how we can improve their lives," Florence said. "I don't want to seem like the interfering mother who appeared from nowhere and took their son away. And I guess they are far too proud to accept me buying them a house here in Cléry. But if I bought you a house and furnished it, and you invited your parents to live there, they might not realise what we've done."

"Don't bet on it," Tristan said. "They may not have much money, but they're far from stupid. They would soon understand what you were doing."

"Yes, but would they accept it, since it would be their son who is offering them a nicer home."

Tristan thought for a moment. "Yes," he said, "They would see through it, but they would accept it. They've been offered an HLM, but it isn't up to much."

"Good, so we can get to work on that whenever you want. I gather the house on rue du Village is already sold?"

Tristan nodded.

"So we have to act quickly. Do you want to meet us tomorrow morning and we'll get round the local estate agents. If we can view a decent property, we can do a quick deal for cash."

"You don't mess about do you?"

"No I don't. It's why I've been successful in business. Shall we come and pick you up at, say, ten o'clock tomorrow morning?"

"Wow. I'm never going to be able to keep it a secret, am I?"

"I think you will," Florence said. "You look and sound like your head's on straight."

# CHAPTER TWENTY-FIVE

Florence removed the clip at the back of her head and her shoulder-length hair fell around her wide, generous face. It framed the dimples in both cheeks. One by one she undid the buttons of her pale blue blouse, starting at the top and stopping only when she reached the waistband of her skirt. Her movements were fluid and sensual, her eyes never leaving Ken's. Their smiles and their thoughts were already in a deep embrace, taking pleasure from temporary physical restraint.

Reaching behind her, Florence unzipped the short black skirt she had been wearing and allowed it to fall to her ankles. She brought her hands back to the final two buttons of her blouse, her intentions dancing in Ken's head. And finally she allowed the garment to hang free, exposing her rounded breasts, which were clad only in a tissue-thin white bra. Her matching panties were made from the briefest fragment of cloth, covering only what needed to be covered.

"Well?" she asked.

"Well what?" Ken said. "Seen it before, haven't I?"

Florence picked a pillow off the bed and threw it at him, but Ken caught it with ease and signalled for her to pirouette. She turned as Ken allowed his eyes to detach from her gaze and survey her perfect shape. He stepped back, just enough to study the full length of her silken body. Her skin, though fair as Michelangelo's marble, radiated health and vitality.

The sheer bra covering her firm breasts left little to the imagination. It was scanty and diaphanous, but added to the allure of the wide, brown nipples that peeped from their concealment. The flesh across her stomach was taut, inviting his gaze to wander lower, to the flimsy white cloth that did little to protect her modesty. Her naked, rounded thighs and her slender, stockingless legs were sculpted to perfect proportions - compact, svelte and potent.

"Well?" she asked.

"Perfect." Ken said. "For someone whose next birthday will be her fortieth, you are one beautiful lady, Florence." He stepped towards her and with gentle hands turned her to face away from him. He eased the blouse from her shoulders. Unclipping her bra, he slid his hands around her body to cup her breasts and leaned his head forward, kissing her neck and savouring her scent. As he snuggled in close, a wave of pure elation ran through his body. He turned her to face him again and her perfume electrified him. When he kissed his way up her neck to lips that tasted of cherry, the bedroom disappeared and he lost himself in the moment.

"Perfect," he whispered again.

"Take me, Ken. Do whatever you want with me, because I am yours. No matter what has happened in the past, I have always been yours. I will share my body with you, I will envelop you with my caresses,

I will overwhelm you with ecstasy. I want to spoil you with all the joys you could ever imagine, and those that you can't, so that you can no longer conceive of a life without me."

Florence took his shoulders in her hands and pushed backwards until Ken could go no further and lay on the bed on his back. She moved with unrehearsed grace, removing each item of his clothing with care and skill.

Ken craved her touch. As soon as her moist, plump lips began to kiss his chest and move down to his stomach, he lost all rational thought. He was consumed with the thought of their renewed love for each other, as if it had never gone away. He was amazed at how one touch of her lips could hitch his breath.

Naked, she took him in her mouth, but only for a short minute. After a moment she kneeled on top of him and guided him into her. She was already moist and smooth like velvet and, as Ken began to move in a slow and rhythmical flow, she murmured words he couldn’t make out.

Ken pulled himself closer into her, reaching round to hold her buttocks, experiencing the excruciating joy of every small movement. As Florence leaned down to kiss him, their bodies fit together like two adjacent pieces of a jigsaw puzzle. He wanted to possess her completely. He wanted to touch and feel every part of her body. He wanted to join with her in a totality of emotion and pleasure that he couldn't even start to describe.

Florence’s hand moved around Ken’s waist, warm and soft. She moulded her body to his, sharing her body heat with him as easily as she shared her heart.

There was a purity to her, naivety perhaps, but she was the only flower in the meadow for Ken's eyes.

Under her breath, Florence continued the quiet whispering of encouragement as she moved with him. Ken could hear her, yet it was like indiscernible background music and he didn't need to hear each word to know what she was saying. And though she never increased the quiet intensity of her words, she did increase the pace. And the faster Florence spoke, the faster Ken moved until, without even realising it was happening, they were climaxing together in a long limb-shuddering culmination, until every last ounce of strength and desire was extinguished.

Ken held her tight. He couldn't let her go. He could never let her go. He was in love with her and he had been in love with her since forever. "Oh my god, Flo, what have you done to me?"

She moved from the crook of his neck and kissed him. It was slow and sensuous and sexy. Then she lifted her head and said, "You've not called me Flo for sixteen years. I've missed it."

It was a pet name that Ken only ever used in the bedroom and it dawned on him that he had used it again without even thinking. "I've missed you too, you know. I don't think I've ever made love like that before. I think I was in another reality. It was as though I could read your thoughts."

"And what was I thinking?"

Ken smiled and brushed a stray hair from her face. "You were thinking how it would be perfect if we got back together again."

"And?"

"And I need a little more time, my love. Things have happened so quickly. I've only been in France for a little over a week and now we're talking of a future together. Would you give me a bit longer before I give you an answer?"

Florence said nothing. She untangled herself from Ken's arms and crossed the room. Ken pushed himself up against the padded headboard and watched while Florence took out a bottle of Veuve Clicquot form the minibar.

"I didn't know they had champagne in the minibar," Ken said.

"They don't, but I asked them earlier to put one there for us. I hoped we would have a chance to celebrate something."

"And are we? Are we celebrating something?"

"Thanks to you and Harry, we're celebrating having found our son again, Ken. And I'm celebrating the fact that you haven't said 'no' to me when I wondered if we could get back together."

Ken's gaze followed her as she carried two crystal champagne flutes and wore nothing but a wide smile and a pair of dimples. He could already feel his need stirring again. For a woman of thirty-nine, Florence de Nussac was in great shape. In fact, a woman of twenty-nine would be more than happy to have a body like hers.

He wasn't sure what had just happened. It was sex but it wasn't sex. It was love but it wasn't love. It was desire but it wasn't desire. It was everything all rolled into one. It was as if he knew her thoughts and embraced her pleasure and felt her love. And it was as familiar to him as if the last sixteen years had never happened.

Florence placed the glasses on the carved, mahogany bedside cabinet. She leaned to place a kiss on the end of his nose, and then retraced her steps towards the minibar. Ken glued his eyes to her firm, rounded buttocks. A moment later she returned - this time holding the chilled bottle of champagne, which she threatened to place on his exposed private parts. He sat up and protected himself with his hands.

"What's the matter, Cheri? Is the nasty lady going to hurt the poor little man?"

He laughed. "Not if the poor little man can get out of your way quick enough."

She passed him the bottle, which he uncorked with care. As he filled the glasses, he glanced at her face. "What's going on in that pretty head of yours, Florence de Nussac?"

She leaned forward and kissed him again. "I was just thinking how lucky I was to have seen Tristan outside the Sorbonne and then to have called you for help to trace him."

Ken passed her one of the glasses, taking the other himself and raising it in a toast. "Let's drink to us. All three of us."

As they relaxed on the bed, naked and content, she watched the tiny bubbles rising from the bottom of the amber liquid. "When do you think you'll go back to the Isle of Man?" she asked keeping her gaze on the glass.

"I'm not sure. I have a business to run, but Sparky's quite capable and can manage on his own for a while yet."

"Well, why don't you spend the next few weeks here with me? We could find out what it would be like living together again."

"And what would happen if I didn't say 'yes'?"

She looked thoughtful for a moment, and then smiled. "I'd pour my champagne over you and lick it off until you submitted."

"I think I need to think about it then."

Florence took his full glass off him and placed it at the side of the bed. A moment later, her empty glass joined his as she kept her promised threat.

# CHAPTER TWENTY-SIX

After spending the weekend in Cléry Saint André hunting for a suitable new home for Tristan's parents, Florence, Ken and Tristan returned to Paris together. Jerome and Sylvie Gautier had understood exactly what Florence was doing. But, since she was buying the house in Tristan's name, they made no effort to refuse the offer. Florence transferred money to Tristan's bank account to pay all the fees, and for carpets, curtains and furniture. She suggested that he go with his parents to help them choose. That way, she explained, he could make it look as though it was he who was choosing and that they were helping him make the right decisions. The key to it all was a balance between what the Gautiers could provide and what Florence was capable of providing. Before leaving, she reminded them again that they had paid for everything for sixteen years so it was only right that she should contribute now. They seemed to accept that logic.

Tristan threw what few belongings he had in his shared student accommodation into the back of Florence's car and he spent Monday installing himself in his new room on Avenue Marceau. He was like a boy with a new toy, and his eyes lit up when he met Harry. "Hey."

"Wassoup? Harry asked.

"Just hey."

"Hey is so lame!"

"I didn't say hey, I said wassoup!"

"No, I said wassoup."

"I must have said hey then."

"Well hey back at you," Harry said. "So you're the guy everyone's been looking for? You don't look like much to me."

"Hi moody woman," Tristan said, "The mother unit has just said I should ask you to come with me to the shops and help me pick a laptop and a tablet. Seems you might know how to turn one on."

"You need brains to work one of those, am I right ladies?"

"Ha! You know how to talk the talk."

"And walk the walk," Harry said, glancing at Tristan's open shirt. "Hashtag the gimp has a hairy chest, which is going to make some bondage techniques difficult."

"Hoot!," said Tristan. "Walk gimpette. Let's go."

Ken looked a Florence who raised her eyebrows and asked, "What language are they talking?"

"I think we may be a generation too late to understand it. Maybe Tristan is learning more than English, German and Spanish. Maybe he's learning Harry-talk too?"

"Sounds like it could be fun," Harry said from near the door. "I gather I'm the chapi for the day."

"Chapi?"

"A female who is smarter than her male companion."

"That's rubbish," Tristan said. "It's a girl who only wants to get with a guy for his money or lavish materialistic things. It's urban slang but comes from the word for gold digger in Spanish. It's short for chapiadora."

"He's babbling like a child," Harry said. "Take no notice of him."

"Too much for my poor brain," Florence said, "While you are out, get some new clothes will you? Tomorrow evening, the four of us are having dinner at Le Pré Catelan and jeans and sweatshirt don't cut it."

"Le Pré Catelan?" Tristan demanded. "That's mad awesome. It's like a zillion Michelin stars."

"Just three," Florence said. "That's as far as Michelin go."

"But it's whatsisname off the telly. The Masterchef guy."

"Frédéric Anton."

"Yeah, him. He's like the Holy Grail of modern French cuisine."

Florence laughed. "His dishes can be a little complex, but somehow never complicated, if that makes sense. He manages to hit all the senses in a balanced way, and he has quite an imagination."

"Sounds like your son," Harry said.

"Oh bugger, you're spoiling me too much, Mum."

"Add up all the little spoils I've missed for the last sixteen years, Tristan, and you'll understand why. Anyway, I already promised Harry and your Dad that I would invite them."

Harry said, "Don't worry, Florence, I'll take good care of him."

"That's what I'm worried about," Ken said. "You'll end up turning him into a tearaway."

"I used to be a bit of a tearaway," Tristan said with a hint of shyness. "Not anymore though. After my parents told me I was adopted, I became a lot less arrogant overnight. All of a sudden my best friend was the class introvert, Louise. I'd never given her the time of day before that. I guess everyone has to grow up sometime, but part of me misses the old Tristan."

"Well I like you the way you are," Harry said. "But don't quote me on that: I shall deny I said it. In fact, I've just unsaid it. Kindly delete and empty recycle bin."

Ken looked at Florence and shrugged. "Shall I tell you what my parents did to me when I stepped out of line at school?"

"This should be good," Tristan said.

"Maybe another time, Ken?" Harry said. "We have shopping appointments to keep. Mustn't keep the shopkeepers waiting."

Tristan stood up and ruffled Ken's hair. "I want to hear more, Dad. I want to know all about you and Mum. There's a lot of catching up to do." He turned to Harry. "Come on numbnuts. Rumour has it you're going to dress me like a human being."

"Ha, that's the easy bit. What about trying to act like one, zombie child?"

The pair left the apartment chatting together like washerwomen over a clothes line. Tristan was giddy with excitement.

Some hours later, they arrived back clutching boxes and bags, and still chatting together. It was as if they had never stopped to draw breath. And it was also as though they were talking and thinking on the same wavelength. Seldom had Ken seen Harry so relaxed. She and Tristan were rude to each other in the good-natured way that young people are. No animosity, just gentle name-calling. Even Florence commented to Ken in private that it was like they had been lifelong buddies.

After dinner, Tristan excused himself, to go and play with his new laptop. Harry, Ken and Florence sat around the kitchen table chatting and finishing off the wine. It seemed that Harry was even getting the hang of small-talk.

"How are things going with your traces?" Florence asked her.

"I'm getting there. I've already resolved one puzzle, but I suspect it's connected to something bigger, so I still have a little bit of digging to do."

"What gives?" Ken asked.

"Well here's the thing: a few years ago, there was a company called Bordeaux Fine Wines operating out of Croydon in South London. They went into liquidation following an investigation by the Insolvency Service. Their business was set up on the premise of sourcing fine wines, from France. They conned investors into sinking their money into it, claiming that the wines would go up in value much more than property or shares."

"And how does that involve us or you?" Florence asked.

"Because there was a small life insurance when my father died and my mother was talked into investing in this scheme. First of all, it was just £5,000. Then they pressurized her to add another £5,000. Then more, until she had sunk the whole £42,500 into Bordeaux Fine Wines. And it was all on the say-so of high-pressure salesmen acting on behalf of the owner, investment shark and wannabe toff Sammy Gundlach."

"And what happened to Bordeaux Fine Wines?" Ken asked.

"To date, investors and other creditors such as the tax man have lodged claims with the liquidator coming to almost £58 million. But there's no sign of thousands of cases of fine wine worth £9.3 million that had been bought with investors' money. It was supposed to have been stored in a warehouse in Croydon, but the warehouse was almost empty.

Gundlach drained around £10 million from the firm in dividends to fund his lavish lifestyle. That included a £2.6 million mansion with six bedrooms and a swimming pool. The investigation by the Insolvency Service found that he had spent £626,000 on horses. He spent more than £550,000 on flash cars. Another £170,000 on bespoke jewellery. And £141,000 on private jet hire. But much of what he bought has mysteriously disappeared or been sold on without anyone being able to account for the money. And like the money, he too has disappeared.

He even lashed out on a Christmas party for his telesales reps. These were the unscrupulous individuals who conned potential investors by dramatically inflating wine prices when pitching on the phone to them. The staff party cost £38,500."

"Bloody hell. What a low life. What happened to him?"

"Well that's the annoying bit," Harry said, "For the moment, all that has happened to him is that, in his absence, he has received the maximum directorship ban of fifteen years. Maybe one day criminal charges will follow, but who can tell. The police have been unable to trace him. One thing is for certain; by the time the liquidators have taken their costs, and the secured creditors have taken what they can, there will be nothing left for unsecured creditors like my mother."

"Wine investments are an area where it pays to tread very warily," Florence said. "I recall a company called Vine Capital with a prestigious address in Buckingham Palace Road as its office, but it was just a mail-forwarding service. The owner lived in the Bahamas."

"So these wine scams are well known?" Ken asked.

"I just read of another one yesterday," Harry said. "Some new firm formed by 'a group of experienced and successful wine traders who specialise in rare and prestigious Bordeaux wines'. Their website had an image of a Sauvignon Blanc vineyard in New Zealand. The owners blamed the website developers for the mistake."

"Jeez, what a bag of worms. So your Mum lost all the insurance money after your father's death."

"It goes way deeper than that, Ken. Because of the circumstances of my father's death, it was a couple of years before the insurance company paid out. I was fifteen then and my Mum told me that she was going to invest the money for me, and that I could have it all on my twenty-first birthday. When the scam went tits-up, she was desperately upset and she blamed herself for losing my 'inheritance' as she called it.

I told her it didn't matter, and I meant it. But she wouldn't or couldn't accept that, and she became depressed. She said she could no longer talk to me because she felt ashamed. As soon as I left school, she moved to Benidorm with her new boyfriend. Like I told you, we don't keep in contact much. Just a Christmas card and a birthday card each year."

Harry looked at Florence. "Do you remember that pearl necklace I was wearing a week ago at the Intercontinental Hotel? The night I got my childhood memories back?"

"Yes I do," Florence said. "It was beautiful."

"Well it used to belong to my mum. It was an heirloom. I don't know why I brought it with me because I had no idea we'd be going out posh. But thinking back, I've taken it to a lot of places. Maybe it's because it's my only real connection to my mother now. She gave it me just before she left the Isle of Man for Spain. She said that I deserved it because she had been stupid and thrown away my inheritance."

"Didn't she have friends who could talk to her and explain?" Florence asked.

Harry sat very upright and very still, her hands

gripping one another. Her gaze fell to her clasped hands. "What I know now, which I never knew before, was that when they found my father's body, it was the end of Mum's life in the village. Everybody suspected her and isolated her.

The school was a cesspool of gossip too, so my life wasn't exactly a bowl of cherries either. It wasn't enough for us to fall under suspicion, the community took it upon themselves to find both of us guilty and punish us. They rushed away from us like a human tsunami, holding their breath in collective horror and enjoying it more than reality TV. Everyone except Andy Milner, my only friend since infant school. He told his parents to stick it and cycled round to our place several times a week. He sat next to me in class and never once mentioned the shit storm he was taking for staying loyal. Not one word of complaint, ever. But then his parents moved off the island, and now he and I just have an occasional chat on Facetime."

"So this guy, Sammy Gundlach, was responsible for ruining the relationship between yourself and your mother, and for both of you being shunned by the community." Florence said.

Harry smiled, but it wasn't a happy smile. "As Macbeth said to Hamlet in A Midsummer Night's Dream, 'We were done up like a pair of kippers'."

"You sure that quote's accurate?" Ken asked, with a grin.

"It's close enough. Even the school officials took it out on me. They dreamed up all sorts of untrue stories about my bad behaviour and the doctors dosed me up to the eyeballs with lots of chemical shite. I was off school for a long time and when I returned I was six months behind the others. A few of them said 'Hi' and asked how I was doing, but they were just prying on behalf of their parents. I saw them for what they were, and I hated every one of them. I wanted them to get sick in the head like me—"

"Don't you dare," Florence barked. "You are not—"

"I know that now, Florence, but that's how it felt then, when I was fifteen. I wanted them to know what it was like to be isolated and scared. But I smiled and played along until the day I could leave school and make my own way in the world."

"And you have succeeded," Ken said. "You've shown them all."

Harry looked at Ken. She looked both shy and apprehensive at the same time. Then she looked down at her hands that rested on the table top. "I don't know if I'm meant to say this in front of Florence, so please stop me if I'm out of order. I don't want to offend."

"You won't," Florence said.

Harry reached out and grasped Ken's wrist. Her hands were shaking. She said, "Empathy and understanding is a language that the deaf can hear, the blind can see, and that crazies like me can benefit from. It was your understanding three years ago, Ken, that was the bridge back to some sort of normality. While we were together—"

"For one hundred and twenty three days."

"—I learned for the first time that there were people in the world I could trust. I discovered there were other people like Andy Milner. But I only discovered it three years ago when I got to know you. That's why I was so mad at you when you walked out of here. Florence was hurt and crying and all my assumptions about you collapsed in a heap. I didn't think I could trust you any more. You hurt me too, but I don't really know how to cry, Ken, so I shouted at you instead. I couldn't believe you were so shallow."

"I noticed, and I get that now, Harry."

Harry let go of Ken's wrist. She took the serviette next to her place setting, unfolded it and folded it again. She folded it very exactly, lining up the edges and smoothing it flat with the palm of her hand. Ken and Florence knew there was more to come and waited while Harry composed herself and collected her thoughts.

After a long silence, Harry said, "While we were together, Ken, you extended an open hand to me with no expectations on your behalf. You stayed while I learned I could reveal the scars, the mess, the anxiety that nobody else ever got to see. You let me come close, Ken. You let me hide when I needed to." She looked at Florence. "Do you want me to stop? Have I said too much?"

"Keep going, Harry."

She looked back at Ken. "When you left me, I was heartbroken, but I understood how difficult it must be to live with someone like me. But what was good was that in the time we were together you showed me there was a more considerate world than the one I had known before. For the previous twenty-three years, apart from Andy Milner and my mother, nobody had ever loved me. And for a little while, you loved me, Ken." She looked up. "I'm sorry Florence, I've gone too far now, haven't I?"

"No way, Harry, let it out. I'm so pleased that Ken helped you."

"Well every time I thought Ken had had enough he showed me only patience. I never wanted to be the way I am. I never chose to be like this. I don't need people to see me as strong, but I do need people to see me as normal. And I'm still so far away from achieving that."

"You've made fabulous progress, Harry, just in the short time you've been here."

"Ten days, four hours and," she checked her watch, "thirty seven minutes." Then she laughed. "See, I'm still doing it."

"No harm in knowing the time," Ken said. "It's the bastards who made your life hell who make me angry."

"I don't give a damn about any of them now, Ken. Knowing that there are people like you in the world means I just have to wait. Maybe one day somebody else will come along who is willing to put up with all my faults and limitations."

Florence tutted but said nothing.

"I'd known other men before you, Ken, but none of them ever wanted to stay around. All my former boyfriends, and there weren't many of them, had been like busy little bees. They sampled the nectar, decided they didn't like it, and moved on as fast as their busy little wings would take them."

"You always tasted sweet to me," Ken said, touching Florence's arm without looking at her.

"You've gone too far." Harry said, watching Florence's reaction. She removed her hands from the table and tucked them out of sight on her lap. "Even I know that."

Florence laughed. "Let's agree he's a good kisser and move on, shall we?"

"Yes well I'm fed up kissing frogs and finding they're still just frogs. Ken was my prince, Florence, and in some ways he still is. Oh, I know he's yours, and I'm happy for both of you. And I don't want him back. And I don't give a damn any more about the people who couldn't be bothered to help me when I most needed it. But I do care about Gundlach, because he triggered the gulf between myself and my mother. And it wasn't just Gundlach. He was the front guy, but there was another man involved behind the scenes. There was a French guy who, amongst other things, researched wines. Sometimes, he would find a good wine, and then buy just a few cases so they could distribute a single bottle each amongst some of the hesitant investors."

"I don't understand," Florence said. "Why would they do that?"

"Imagine you are an investor and they are pushing you to invest more, but you're holding out. Then one day, you get a single bottle of quality wine in a wooden box. There's a card inside, 'with our compliments'. You'd be hard pushed to say no to them the next time they rang and told you what a good investment you were making. My Mum got one bottle like that before sending them the last of the insurance money."

"One bottle for £42,500," Florence said. "Hope it was a good wine."

"One day, we'll open it together and find out. But not till Sammy Gundlach and his crooked partner are in jail."

"So what happens if the investor demands that they deliver the wines to their home?" Ken asked.

"In most of these scams, including Bordeaux Fine Wines, you don't have that option. They tell you that the wines in the warehouse represent the joint value of everybody's investments. I doubt that anyone has ever succeeded in getting any money back out, once they have paid it over."

Florence said, "There have also been some incidents of label switching. They decant cheap wine into an empty bottle of the real thing. There was a case recently where a company sold fake bottles of 1787 Château d'Yquem for tens of thousands of pounds a bottle."

"So this whole 'wine investment' scenario is well known then?" Ken asked.

"Yes," Harry replied, pushing her chair back from the table and standing. "But by tomorrow, I will have all the information I need to close this one down for good. I'll need your help with that, Ken."

As she left and headed upstairs, Ken and Florence looked at each other and shrugged. Ken said, "Thanks for your patience and understanding, Florence. You know I wouldn't normally hold a discussion about a former relationship with you."

"I know that, Ken. I sometimes wonder where she finds the strength to carry on."

"She has no choice. She's difficult to work out at times. She can be very frail and susceptible to rebuff in some quarters, but wilfully strong and resilient in others. Do you know what's even stranger? I've thought for a long time that she might be hyperthymesic."

"What the hell is that? She doesn't need any other problems on top of the ones she already has."

"It's a very rare condition. It's when an individual can recall the vast majority of personal experiences and events in his or her life. Very very few people are known to have it. But I suspect it may be responsible for Harry's wipe-outs."

"What do you mean, Ken? You'll have to explain."

"Well when Harry has a full knowledge bank, like now, her recall of events is total. She remembers every last detail. The two defining characteristics of hyperthymesia are spending an excessive amount of time thinking about one's past, and displaying an extraordinary ability to recall specific events from one's past. My non-medical opinion - and it's only a hypothesis, you understand - is that when her brain can no longer hold the mass of memory, it wipes itself clean as a precaution to prevent overload."

"Interesting theory."

"It is only a theory. But maybe it's part of what makes her who she is. It would explain her reaction when she saw those images from Yves-Marie's computer. Most people, if reminded of some awful event like that from the past would certainly be upset, but our brains have the ability to dull our memories. So, while we can recall an event, our brains block out a lot of the unpleasant detail. For Harry, when she saw those images and her memory flooded back, she recalled every single awful detail in glorious technicolour."

"No wonder she was so upset. No wonder she hides in her shell sometimes."

"She has come out of her shell since being here, Florence. Discovering her past history must have been one hell of a shock, but it seems to have answered a lot of unanswered questions for her."

"And maybe she's learning to keep her anxiety levels low so she can cope with any big issue."

"Maybe," Ken said, "and maybe in the last twenty-four hours it also has something to do with Tristan. The pair of them seem to have hit it off."

"You noticed then?"

"Hard to miss. I think our son has the hots for Miss Harry!"

"Oh, and there was me thinking it was Harry who had the hots for Master Tristan. Maybe he'll become her Prince Charming."

"Or another frog!"

# CHAPTER TWENTY-SEVEN

The word 'elegant' did not do Le Pré Catelan justice. There wasn't a single-word explanation that could define the intimate grandeur of the establishment. The building was located in the heart of the Bois de Boulogne - over 2000 acres of wooded parkland on the western outskirts of Paris. This treasure of French gastronomy was also a treasure of architecture and interior design. Harry took photos outside and in the reception area. As the four followed the maître d'hôtel to their table, Tristan stood out. He had the tall, muscular body of a professional athlete and this evening his height and build were emphasised by the perfect cut of an expensive hand-stitched suit.

Harry, too, looked sensational. When she had taken Tristan shopping, she had bought herself a classic understated ensemble. Sticking to the age-old rule that you can never go wrong with black, she cut a chic and stylish figure as she went through the process of shutting down her iPad as they entered the dining room.

Tristan stopped and looked around him in open-mouthed wonder. He'd seen rooms like this in magazines, but could never have imagined the effect it could have on him now. As if his emotions had not passed through enough turmoil in the last few days, this opulent yet welcoming lifestyle was beyond his imagination.

Green, black, white and silver were the dominant colours. Green for a nod to outdoor greenery. Black, white, and silver alternating to highlight spaces, details, and intricate pilasters. The furniture both harmonized or contrasted with the architecture of the building. Classic and modern blended to accentuate the impression of purity and light.

"Come on boy," Harry said, "Hurry up or your jaw will drop off its hinges."

"I'm coming, I'm coming. I think I'm lost in a dream. Don't wake me up."

Harry laughed. "Just be sure you choose something big off the menu. These Michelin three star places have a habit of serving minute portions and presenting humungous bills at the end."

"Have you been to one before?" Tristan asked, as he helped Harry to her seat at the table, and then sat next to her.

"Two star, but never a three star. Your Mum is treating us tonight, so I'm game to try anything."

"Funny hearing you refer to her as my Mum."

"But that's what she is."

"I know, it's just that I've known the same Maman and Papa all my life and I'm not used to having more than one of them yet. How many mothers and fathers do you have, Harry?"

"My father is dead and my mother and I have pretty much lost contact."

"That must be tough," Tristan said, touching Harry's hand and examining the anchor tattoo. "I meant to ask you, what's the tat?"

"An anchor!"

"Yes, I can see that, you nerd. I meant, does it have some sort of relevance?"

"Yes it does, now move on."

"Okay. Moving on, you're pretty and that pearl necklace is something else. You look stunning."

Ken and Florence sat opposite the younger pair. As the waiter flicked open a white linen napkin and offered it to her lap, Florence said to no-one in particular, "He's just like his Dad - chatting up the ladies with his smooth talk."

"Do you chat up the women then?" Tristan asked Ken.

"Only when your Mum isn't listening. Look out, here come the menus."

A second waiter presented a leather-bound menu the size of a newspaper to each of them. Tristan looked at Ken and Harry and said, "Do you two need an English version?"

"Cheeky bugger," Harry said. "My French is as good as your English."

"No way."

"Okay, prove it."

"Christ, it's like having an in-table cabaret," Ken said. "Just get on with it Tristan. I think I know what everything is, but translating it into English will give you some good practice."

Tristan ran down the list like a pro. Speaking in English, he didn't falter once. "Starters are Foie Gras with spices and cream of foie gras with turnip in a broth of duck, aromatised with coriander. Or you can go for crab, cooked in dill with French caviar, crab salad and grapefruit. All lightly peppered to a Thai flavour and a sauce perfumed with fennel. How am I doing so far."

"Very good," Florence said.

"Or you can have the Saint Jacques," Harry said. "Scallops, pan seared at the table in cider with crushed and roasted nuts, lime zest and French caviar. That was just to prove that I know some French."

Ken laughed. "So what's with this French caviar then? I didn't know there was such a thing."

"They raise Siberian sturgeon in huge tanks in the countryside of the Aquitaine region," Florence said. "It's first class caviar. You should try it."

"I intend to," Tristan said. "I've never had caviar. Shall I carry on translating the starters?"

Florence and Ken shook their heads. "I think you've proved the point," Harry said. "So you know a few words of English."

"And you know a few words of French it seems."

The choice of main courses included roast lamb with goat's cheese ravioli, veal sweetbreads with mushroom and caramelised onions, and roast baby pigeon with crusty dates 'embraced with cabbage', as the menu said. As the four of them scanned the choices Tristan whispered to Harry, "Have you seen the prices - €120 just for a starter of scallops?"

"And €145 for a main course of sea bass," Harry whispered back. "And look at the cheese. €45 for a plate of cheese!"

"And I don't care," Florence said in a stern voice. "It's my treat for three people I love. I should have asked the waiter to give you the un-priced menus. For me, the prices are irrelevant. Anyway, Le Pré Catelan spent over one million euros with me last year, so a few hundred spent in return is a good investment. Once you've experienced the service and the food, you may not feel the prices are so extravagant."

"Sorry," Tristan and Harry mumbled in unison.

"That's us told," Harry said sotto voce, doing her best to disguise the smile on her face. "Best we decide what we're going to eat, so we can choose a wine to go with it." As she said it, the sommelier arrived at the table and presented the wine list. Harry made an uncharacteristic grab for it and sat looking smug while Florence raised an eyebrow but said nothing.

After everybody had ordered their meals, the sommelier returned. Harry, who had already scanned the wine list, said, "The1998 Château Yon Figeac would go well with both the starter and the main course. It's a Saint-Émilion so not too heavy. The young vintages need decanting for up to one hour to allow the wine to soften and open its perfume. Older vintages like this one need very little decanting, just enough to remove the sediment."

"Madame knows her wines," said the sommelier,

peering over his glasses at her. He looked at Florence and Ken and added "And Château Yon Figeac is best paired with all types of classic meat dishes, veal, pork, beef, lamb, duck, game, roast chicken, roasted, braised and grilled dishes. So perfect for you all this evening." He nodded and left them to talk.

"I think you upset him," Florence said.

"Why?"

"Because you knew more than him."

"I'm sure he knows his wines way better than I do. I just happen to know that one because you had several dozen bottles before thieves broke into your wine cellar. I read up on all of them afterwards."

"You couldn't have memorised everything," Tristan said. "Mum told me they stole about €200,000 worth of wines."

"I have this weird memory, Tristan. It remembers almost everything I tell it to remember. It's like a well catalogued bookcase."

"I'll vouch for that," Ken said.

"The trouble is, every so often someone goes and throws away all the books and I have to start all over again."

"That's a bummer!"

"It's a real pain in the butt, but it's why I'm always making notes of stuff on my iPad. I can fill in the blanks after a memory wipe-out by reading through my notes. I only need to see a headline, to remind me of a whole event."

"Confabulation," Tristan said.

"How did you know that?"

"I have a friend who suffered a series of seizures and it left him with big memory gaps. He filled them in over time, but I remember him calling it confabulation."

"Unfortunately, Harry's is recurring," Florence said. "And from what she tells us, it's almost total memory loss, not just a few gaps."

"Damn, that's a bit uncool." Tristan took hold of Harry's hand and grinned. "Don't worry; if it happens again, just tell me and I'll remind you how you are my lover."

Harry laughed. "Like I used to be with —"

"Harry! Stop!" from Florence. "I don't think this young man needs to know —"

"—that my Dad shacked up with Harry," Tristan said, "and had nookie fifty-four times over a period of one hundred and twenty three days."

Ken snapped his head round, "How the hell did you —"

"Harry told me earlier."

"Was that not a good thing?" Harry asked. "I don't like secrets."

"Some things don't need to be discussed with my son, Harry."

"I'm nineteen coming up twenty, Dad. I'm a big boy now."

Ken looked at him and smiled. "Yes, you are, and I'm proud of what you've become."

Tristan blushed and stared at the table cloth.

"You've embarrassed him," Harry said. "Let's change the subject. Do you want to hear about what I've found out about things?"

"Yes please," Florence said, with some obvious relief.

"You remember, I told you yesterday about the Bordeaux Fine Wines scam and how my mother lost a load of money, and hasn't forgiven herself?"

Ken and Florence nodded in unison.

"Well the other guy behind Bordeaux Fine Wines, the one in France who was sourcing a few wines so it looked like a proper business, got a bit careless. He left some traces behind, which I have discovered. There are emails between him and Sammy Gundlach that nail them both. I can't hand them over to the police because I can't explain how I came about them. But I have a different plan to revenge my mother and you, Ken, can help me with it."

Ken deciphered her subtly placed eyebrows and realised that Harry wasn't going to take no for an answer, no matter what the situation. He nodded. As he did so, the sommelier appeared resting their chosen wine on his forearm as if it were a baby. He looked from Florence to Harry trying to determine to whom he should show the bottle. Florence indicated Harry, so the wine waiter held the bottle for her to examine.

He looked surprised when, instead of the usual cursory glance at the label, Harry scrutinised it for a moment. "Is there a label on the back?" she asked.

He rolled the bottle in his arm to display a small label that said only 1998 Château Yon Figeac -

Grand Cru Classé - Saint-Émilion -13%vol - 750ml and a bar code. And there, in the bottom corner next to the bar code, a tiny hand-written 'FdN'. Harry reached into her pocket and took out a small torch, no bigger than a ballpoint pen. She passed it to Florence, "Your witness, My Lord."

Florence gasped. She understood immediately what Harry was saying and shone the ultraviolet blacklight torch at the bottle. There, for everybody to see, was Florence's telephone number written across the bottle.

The sommelier was as startled as Florence and almost dropped the bottle. He was well aware of the implications of a marked bottle. "But Madame de Nussac, we bought this wine from your own company a week ago. We are only serving them tonight for the first time because we wanted to rest them before offering them to our clients."

Harry said, "Please don't be concerned, Monsieur. I have a record of all the wines that you bought from Madame de Nussac's company last week and less than 20% are stolen."

"But the scandal will break us. Le Pré Catelan is known right across France for the highest possible standards."

Florence looked at Harry for support. Harry continued, "You and Le Pré Catelan were unaware of the problem, Monsieur. Nobody will ever discover what has happened. Perhaps you can use the ultraviolet torch to make sure that you serve no more stolen bottles tonight. Tomorrow, when you have time, you can separate them and box them up. Somebody will either remove them and give you a credit, or replace them with a similar quality wine that has not been illegally obtained."

Florence nodded her approval. "Thank you, Harry, that's an excellent idea." She turned to the sommelier. "Please tell Chef Anton that I will come and speak with him before we leave. Assure him that all is well. We will resolve the problem without delay and with total discretion. It is in none of our interests to discuss this beyond our small group. Meanwhile, perhaps you would like to open the wine for us."

The wine waiter did so with shaking hands. This was a Tuesday like no other, and his usual quiet calm had deserted him. When he left, Florence looked at Harry and said, "Well?"

"Don't I get a drum roll first?"

Tristan laughed. "Badummmm tish!"

"Is that the best you can do?"

"Yes it bloody well is. I thought it was quite good myself."

Harry smiled at him. "Best drum roll I've ever had."

"Er, when you two have finished with the self-adulation," Ken said, "Florence and I are rather anxious to find out how you knew about that bottle, Harry."

"Emails, Ken. Emails between Florence's brother and the overseas manager of Florence's company, a Monsieur Mercier."

"Anton?" Florence said.

"Well that's not actually his real name, Florence. A few years ago Anton Mercier called himself Sammy Gundlach. Mind you, that's not his real name either."

"What? The guy you were telling us about who ran Bordeaux Fine Wines and who ripped your mother off?"

"And a bunch of other poor investors."

"But how the hell—?"

"He disappeared. The police never traced him because he had help to obtain yet another new identity and also to hide the money he'd taken out of the business."

"Who helped him?"

"Your brother, of course. He was the other man involved behind the scenes. He was the one who researched wines and bought just a few cases so they could distribute a single bottle amongst some of the investors. Your brother and Gundlach or Mercier or whatever his actual name is, have some considerable cash assets stashed away on the Isle of Man of all places."

"Nice little low tax offshore haven, not too far from home," Ken said. "My friend, DCI Angus Slooth will be pleased to hear about this when we are ready. For years, he's been the top man at tracking down illegal money."

"They used some of the money to increase the size of your brother's business," Harry said to Florence. "That would explain why it grew rapidly. But as you know, he deals in more than just insurance. He's involved in real estate, loans, and even banking services. Your brother and Gundlach are planning to asset strip everything and empty all the client accounts. Everything will disappear. They already have false passports, but I think they are still a few months away from making an actual move. Your brother's unwillingness to concede the €400,000 he got from your grandfather is just delaying tactics so he can take as much as he can get away with. He and Gundlach-Mercier will take everything they can and to hell with the consequences. From what I read in their emails, neither of them plan coming back to France."

"Bloody hell," said Florence, "that's outrageous. And Anton Mercier too. I trusted him without condition."

"Enough to tell him what marvellous wines you had stored in your cave at home perhaps?"

"Oh God, yes."

"And for your brother to advise him when you were likely not to be there. He knew you would be at his cocktail party at Saint-Germain-en-Laye."

"He told us he didn't know we were going, but Monique tipped us off otherwise."

"He knew alright," Harry said. "He emailed Mercier-Gundlach to let him know when to hit your wine cellar. He even told them the code for your vigik."

"So mine was just a one-off theft?"

"Yours was one of many. I'm afraid. They've been using your business to sell stolen wines for the past three years."

"But how? How did they cover their tracks?"

"This wine here is a prime example. Last week, they delivered 60 bottles of this rather nice 1998 Château

Yon Figeac to this restaurant at €29.50 a bottle."

"But the restaurant sells it for €118 a bottle," Tristan said.

"High end mark-up," from Florence.

Harry continued, "Sixty times €29.50 is €1,770. There were, of course lots of other wines delivered at the same time, but I'm using this one as an example. The bill that Le Pré Catelan will receive, ostensibly from your company, will show €1,770 for this particular wine. That is the correct figure for sixty bottles. However, the real invoice that will pass through your company's accounts will show only €354. Only twelve of the sixty bottles were from your company's stock. The other forty-eight were stolen from your wine cellar at home."

Florence thought for a moment. "But that means that—"

"—that someone in your accounts team is also in on the scam." Harry finished. "Her name is Valérie Guillot and she is a single mother with an ageing parent at home to look after."

"Oh hell, not Valérie. She's a lovely girl."

"Sorry, but Gundlach - or Anton Mercier - and Valérie Guillot are enabling the scam at your end. When Le Pré Catelan pay their invoice, Valérie Guillot pays the money into a separate bank account that you know nothing about. She then writes out a cheque from that account to pay your company the correct amount for the genuine stock delivered. She puts a proper invoice through your sales ledger for the correct amount. One debit, one matching credit, the stock all nicely balanced, and nobody is any the wiser"

"And how did you discover all this?" Tristan asked

"Because I'm a genius, gimp boy. Pay close attention and you can learn something useful other than a few languages." Harry reached a hand towards him, but seemed to change her mind at the last moment, dropping it back into her lap.

Tristan bopped her on the shoulder. "Don't get too cocky Mrs Amnesia. I can handle you any day."

"Tristan! That's not very nice."

"I'm only joking Dad."

"He was only joking Ken. Your son is nicer than you. I might adopt him."

“You’re too old for him.”

“Tristan will soon be twenty and I’m twenty-six.” Harry said.

Ken held her gaze for a moment, the little grin now a broad smile. He didn’t miss the small flush of colour on her cheeks before she turned away.

“And I like older chicks,” Tristan added with a laugh. “Older chicks are cool. Particularly this old bird next to me.”

Ken looked at Florence and shrugged. "Youngsters!"

“What do we do now?” Florence asked. “First of all, the reputation of my business is going to take a hammering once this goes public. My own overseas manager part of a wine scam. It takes years to build a good reputation, and only minutes to destroy it. But we do have to take this to the police somehow. We can’t just leave it to rest.”

"Not until we have your €400,000 back." Ken said.

"But how are we going to let the police know about all those images? And about the money from the Bordeaux Fine Wines scam? And about who stole the wine from my wine cellar? We can't say anything without letting them know that we hacked Yves-Marie's computers. And that could wreck any case they have against him. The court could deem the evidence inadmissible"

"Leave it to me," Ken said. "It's time for me to call in a couple of favours with the police on the Isle of Man."

"What's the plan, Pop?" Tristan asked.

Ken laughed. "Can we just stick to Dad? Too many alternatives will confuse an old man like me."

"Go on then. What's the plan, Dad?"

"As I already mentioned, my chief inspector friend, Angus Slooth, is renowned for tracking illicit funds passing through the Isle of Man. Also, I've helped the chief constable, David Pownall, a few times, so they'll work with us on this. We can tell them which accounts to look at on the island and they'll then contact Scotland Yard. They'll tell Scotland Yard that they have traced illegal funds on the island and that the trace goes back to the Bordeaux Fine Wines scam. Scotland Yard will contact the guys at 36 Quai des Orfèvres, Paris's criminal investigation force, fingering Yves-Marie and his accomplice, Sammy Gundlach or Anton Mercier. The French police will storm in and snatch Yves-Marie and his computers and discover everything we already know."

"Including the images," Harry added.

"Everything," Ken said. "I'll make sure of that. Meanwhile the Manx police will get the credit for a major bust and I'll get another brownie point with the chief constable."

"But what about the €400,000?" Florence asked. "The investigators wouldn't deem it illegal, but it's all tied up and mixed up in his bag of worms."

"It won't be by this time tomorrow. I'll go and have a quiet word with Yves-Marie before the shit hits the fan. Maybe Harry would like to come with me."

"Nothing I'd like better," Harry said, aligning her place setting with the edge of the table. "What's he like?"

"He's a smug, sanctimonious git. When he speaks, he has this look on his face, like he has something nasty stuck underneath his little piggy nose. I met him first at our wedding and I didn't much like him then. But that didn't matter. I was marrying Florence, not him. Unlike a good wine, he doesn't improve with age."

"Then I'm your woman. You can play the good guy, and I'll play the bad guy, only I won't be playing."

"I'd like to be a fly on the wall for that one," Florence said, with a wicked smile.

"It needs to be a well-co-ordinated approach," Ken said. "I'll ring Angus first thing in the morning. If it's properly timed, Harry and I will be able to pay your brother a visit tomorrow afternoon. International law enforcement can work quickly when it wants to, and child pornography is a mighty good catalyst.

# CHAPTER TWENTY-EIGHT

"I suppose you had better come in. I hope this is good because I've left the business to be here this afternoon. It would have been easier if you had told me what you want over the phone, Kenneth,."

"I'm sure your business will manage without you for an hour, Yves."

"Like I told you last time you were here, my name's Yves-Marie."

"And my name is Ken, not Kenneth. And this is Harry."

"Harriet, I presume?"

Harry looked the man up and down with a disdain that matched her feelings. She disliked him. She would have disliked him even if he were not a pervert. Always one to test her feelings, she acknowledged the emotion and held it up for examination. Why? Why did she feel disdain? Easy answer there. He was a fake, that was why. Working class origins hidden under a false accent and middle-class trappings. She couldn't have said how she knew, but she did.

"Harry," Yves-Marie repeated. "Short for Harriet, I

presume? Or do you have one of these strange New Age names like Harrison or a nouveau-snob name like Henrietta?"

"Madame Lewis to you," Harry snarled. "Only close friends can use my first name, and you don't fit into that group. You never will."

"Oh dear, how tiring. It's going to be one of those sorts of meetings is it? I suppose you're here to argue on behalf of my sister for the return of my grandfather's investment in the business?"

Harry stared at this repulsive man. His heavy eyelids hanging at half mast, giving him a sleepy, bored look and the rest of his fleshy face sagging in the same general pattern. Grey suit, grey hair, grey lips and grey eyes. His face was expressionless, the eyes behind the square, gunmetal spectacles, completely empty. "Why are you wearing a pony tail?" she asked. "You're almost bald on top and you've got this stupid pony tail. You look like a real twat."

Yves-Marie wheeled round. "Madame, I don't know who the hell you are, but you can leave right now. I don't need English people coming here to insult me."

"You're fat too, and your breathe smells. I wouldn't trust a reptile like you with my pocket money."

"Out! Out!" Yves-Marie screamed, pushing past Harry and opening the apartment door.

"Best you close the door," Ken said quietly, "unless you want all the neighbours to know about your penchant for young children."

"What? What do you mean? I don't know what you are talking about."

"No, of course you don't, you bloody pervert," Harry snarled. "Pervert!" she screamed at the top of her voice. "Filthy bloody pervert!"

Yves-Marie slammed the door shut. "What the hell is this?" he shouted, adding menace to his voice. But both Ken and Harry could now detect his uncertainty.

"This is a visit from two people who want to help you stay out of jail," Ken said. "And before you start denying everything, I should warn you that we have all the evidence documented and ready to go to the police. Unless you co-operate, of course."

Yves-Marie's voice was still loud, "I have no idea what you are talking about, and it's time you left."

"If you were half as angry as you pretend to be I'd have a black eye and broken ribs; so shut up Yves-Marie. Get a grip and listen. I don't need you verbally pissing all over me because we've caught you out in your perversions."

"Why do you have a litre of sweat on your top lip?" Harry demanded. "I bet you break into a sweat just chewing your lunch. Do you always sweat that much? Can't be very nice for your wife. Ah, but she's already left, hasn't she? What's the matter? Couldn't you get it up without a bit of help from a little boy or little girl?"

"Madame —"

"Don't waste your breathe," Ken said. "Harry has a particular dislike for filthy deviants like you. The more you protest your innocence, the more she will bait you with the truth. Now why don't we all sit down and discuss this like adults?"

After a long pause while he eyeballed Ken and Harry, Yves-Marie led them into the kitchen. He was reluctant but knew he had no choice, so indicated for them to sit round a laminated table. "Say whatever it is you have to say, then get out," he snarled. But the bravado was hardly even skin deep now and a sheen of sweat on his face reflected the light from the window. His bluff was thin as a cigarette paper.

"First of all," Ken said, "you will go online to your bank right now and transfer €400,000 to Florence. She will pass it on to the administrator of you grandfather's inheritance and he will deal with it according to all the proper rules and regulations."

"And why would I do that?"

"Because you don't want the police coming here with a search warrant and taking your laptop as evidence."

"Don't threaten me Ken." Yves-Marie's voice had menace in it. But they were only words, and Ken was not an easy pushover particularly when he had the facts on his side. "Evidence of what?" Yves-Marie demanded. "What is it you claim to have evidence of?"

Harry held up her iPad. "This," she said, showing him a photo of a naked young girl fellating an old man. She swiped the screen, "Or this," she swiped again, "Or this," another swipe. The next photo was a naked man having sex with a girl who was no older than seven. "That's a nice one isn't it, you scum? I have another 4,187 just like them, all from your laptop. Are you sure you wouldn't prefer that we call the police, because I don't want you to get away with this. Calling in the police right now would be my preference." She swiped the iPad again to display another image.

Yves-Marie stared at the picture of two men double-penetrating a youngster. He said nothing.

Ken said, "I assure you, Yves-Marie, you won't like prison one little bit. I speak from personal experience. If you go to prison for having all those illegal images on your laptop - and you will go to prison, make no mistake about that - you are likely to be sharing a cell with some bubba."

"You know what a bubba is, Yves-Marie?" Harry asked, swiping forward to another sick image and showing it to him.

He shook his head.

"A bubba is 150 kilo of black muscle with a cock the size of a well-endowed stallion. A bubba rules his prison block by ass-raping all men smaller than him – which is just about everybody. He has a lot of prison bitches and ass-fucks them until their sphincters have either ripped apart or reach the same diameter as a softball. Are you getting my drift, Yves-fucking-Marie?"

"He's sweating like a blind lesbian in a fish market," Ken said. "I think he's beginning to understand."

"I guess having a bubba rip your ass apart must be a similar sensation to a grown man pushing his prick inside a seven year old girl," Harry said as she swiped forward to another image and pushed it in Yves-Marie's face. "A bubba is extremely horny and has a permanent hard-on," she continued. "Do not drop the prison soap when Bubba is near. Bubba likes nothing better than fucking white trash in the ass while in the shower. Never piss off Bubba.

Never become Bubba's cellmate. Oh, of course, they won't give you any choice about that, will they? Bubba loves nothing more than to de-virginize prison newbies. So Bubba is sure to request the pleasure of your company. The only way to avoid Bubba raping you is to make him your friend. But Bubba still ass rapes his friends. You are still an ass-virgin aren't you, Yves-Marie?"

Ken laughed and imitated an American accent, "Ha-Ha. Bubba has his eye on you fat boy. He's gonna make your ass bleeeeed!"

Yves-Marie looked down at his hands. He spoke quietly. "I think you've made your point. Put your tablet away." His eyes flicked up from the table. He glared at Ken until he noticed Harry's hatred pouring across the void between them. He lowered his eyes again. "What's the deal?" he asked. "How do I know you will stick to your word?"

"You don't," Ken said. "But when we leave, you will want to delete all that filth from your laptop. I recommend you put it through a digital shredder if I was you. Computers have a habit of leaving traces behind, and you wouldn't want that, would you."

Yves-Marie was quiet for a moment. "I'll need to get some funds released to be able to transfer that much money," he said. "It might take a couple of days."

"Liar!" Harry shouted. "You whinging whimpering weasel. Ten minutes ago, your business high interest account had a balance of €1,623,421.96"

"How the hell—"

"Don't waste your breath," Ken said, "and don't try to stall us again or we'll turn you over to Bubba.

Make the transfer right now, dog's breath. Get online and do it while we watch."

"This is outrageous."

"So are dirty old bastards like you ogling over other dirty old bastards having sex with children," Harry spat.

Yves-Marie stared daggers of hatred towards her. He stood up and went into the room that he used as a home office, dragging his feet as he went. Ken winked at Harry and the two of them followed him. Ken gave him the details of Florence's bank account and watched over his shoulder as he made an electronic transfer for €400,000.

"Right. It's done. Now leave."

"Not quite," Ken said. "You also need to transfer the euro equivalent of £42,500 into this account."

Yves-Marie took the paper off Ken and started to read. "Harriet Lewis?" He looked up at Harry. "That's you, isn't it?"

Harry nodded, but the expression on her face said that she hadn't been expecting it. "Why didn't I think of that?" she asked Ken.

"You'd have got there in the end."

"Why should I give you £42,500?" Yves-Marie asked.

Ken answered. "Because you and your partner Sammy Gundlach conned Harry's mother for that amount."

"I don't know what you—"

Ken slammed his hand flat on the desk. "Quit with

the denials and prevarication," he shouted. "We have details of everything. We know all about your involvement in the Bordeaux Fine Wines scam. Do it now, Yves-Marie. And for arguing, you can round it up to £75,000 and we'll call it quits."

"But that's—"

"—the price you pay for being an asshole."

"Double it." Harry said.

Ken and Yves-Marie both looked at her.

"Double it," she said again. "£150,000 and not a cent less."

"That's bloody robbery," Yves-Marie snarled.

"Something you'd know about. Now transfer "£150,000 or these images go straight to the police."

"It will take a few days to arrive in your bank." Yves-Marie said, his voice filled with defeat.

A Cheshire cat grin lit up Ken's face. It made Yves-Marie wish he could take a step backward. "No it won't," Ken said. "You can transfer it from your account at Island Bank on the Isle of Man. Harry banks there too, so it will be instantaneous."

"But—"

"No! Stop! There were no laughter lines around Ken's eyes now. I thought you might have understood by now that we know everything and we are holding all the aces. You don't even have a pair of two's. So just do it, and then we'll leave you to enjoy the rest of your day with your filthy photos."

Yves-Marie sulked like a spoiled child. After a

moment's hesitation, he logged on to his account at Island Bank and made the transfer."

Harry smiled. Ken stared at Yves-Marie. "One more bank transfer and we're done."

"What do you mean, one more? Enough is enough!"

Ken kept his face neutral, but he was feeling good. His lips twisted into a half smile at the thought about what was still to come. Seeing someone as evil as Yves-Marie getting his come-uppance could make you feel so many things. The world was full of happiness this afternoon. "Enough will be enough when I say so. There's the matter of giving your wife some money while you sort out your affairs. You know she's not coming back, don't you?"

"Thanks to you and that fucking sister of mine, yes."

"Good, so now you can transfer €500,000 to her bank account. She banks at the same place you do, but then you already know that. Oh, and don't even think about reversing the transfer after we have gone, otherwise, the police will be knocking on your door quicker than you can blink. They'll probably bring Bubba with them."

"You bastard."

"You're right there, little man. I am indeed a bastard - a real thoroughbred pig's-arsed son of a bitch. On the other hand," he indicated Harry, "my friend and I are also owners of all the data that is currently on your hard drive. Now, can I suggest you make that transfer and leave your good lady wife with enough money to be comfortable while she sues your ass off for every penny you have. Then you can start cleaning up your laptop as quickly as you can. As I see it, you can either take the easy route, make this final transfer and learn not to be a dirty little pervert in future. Or you can try being the wise guy again and find yourself serving a very long sentence in La Santé Prison. If you end up there, I don't fancy your chances of survival beyond one year. Prison lags hate nonces. Many paedophiles commit suicide after a few weeks inside. It's your choice."

"You two are the most hateful pair of—"

"Shut up!" Harry shouted in his face. "Your hatred of us is nothing but a transformation of your own shame and insecurities. It is everything that you hate about yourself but you don't have the bloody courage to face up to. It is easier to lose yourself in the theatricals of your pathetic twisted mind, casting yourself as victim, than it is to swallow even an ounce of truth. In pointing the finger at me, you are blaming someone who's already had more than their soul can take several times over. Ken knows the real me, but you'll never see me for who I really am. You hide from the truth with the ever-changing illusions conjured up by your own filthy mind. You are the most despicable pervert I have ever met in my life - bar one, and he died an unpleasant death."

Yves-Marie's shoulders drooped. He'd never let any woman speak to him like that before, but he knew he had no answers for Harry's barbs. He was defeated. Without a word, he went back to his laptop and made the transfer to Monique's account.

"Is that it now?" he said, looking at Ken. "You've damaged me enough."

"Two more things," Ken said. "First what is Sammy Gundlach's real name? And don't say, Anton

Mercier, because we know that's false too."

"I'm not going to grass him out," Yves-Marie snarled. "You've had enough from me already."

"Harry, phone the police will you. Tell them we have—"

"Alright, alright. His name is Matheo Rousseau."

"He's French?"

"Yes. He comes from Marseille. Why do you need to know?"

"Because we need to tell the police about him. He stole a load of wine from Florence, and we just need to tie down who he is so he doesn't do another runner."

"Erm - What wine? - Florence, you say?"

"Not that you would know anything about that, would you Yves-Marie?"

Yves-Marie didn't answer.

"Ah, but of course you do. So here's the $64,000 question. Where is the stolen wine?"

"No really, I—"

"Police, Harry. Let's hand the bastard over to Bubba."

"Oh for fuck's sake," Yves-Marie whispered. "Will that be the end of it?"

"Tell me where you store all the stolen wine and Harry and I will walk out of here and you will never see us again."

"It's all in a small commercial unit in a town called Achères. It's about five kilometres up the road, towards Cergy."

"Address?"

"Unit 1, Allée des Souches. It's an unmarked industrial unit."

"Thank you, Yves-Marie. You see how easy life can be when you co-operate?"

"And now you'll leave me alone?"

"We're on the way. Come on Harry, let's leave the nice kiddie-fiddler in peace."

Harry turned as if to leave the room then changed her mind and strode back to where Yves-Marie still sat at his desk looking haggard. She drew back her fist and unleashed it onto the pudgy nose in front of her. Yves-Marie's blood spurted over both of them and, as Harry stepped back, Yves-Marie collapsed on the floor with an ear-piercing wail.

Harry clasped her right hand inside her left. She turned to Ken who now stood behind her. "Clumsy bastard, isn't he?"

"Never seen anyone fall over so easily in my life," Ken said.

They stepped from the office, into the entrance hall and opened the door to the communal landing beyond. Standing there were four men in suits. Ken glanced at the man at the front. "Commissaire Leroy?"

"C'est moi."

"He's all yours Commissaire. Everything is there, just as promised."

"Thank you Monsieur Stafford. I'm glad you sorted

it out. Any change to the information you gave us earlier?"

"Just that Anton Mercier's real name is Matheo Rousseau."

"And that all the stolen wines are at Unit 1, Allée des Souches, Achères," Harry added. "It may take a bit of sorting out, but all those belonging to Madame de Nussac have her telephone number on them in ultraviolet. Easy to identify."

"I'm glad somebody has taken precautions," Commissaire Leroy said. "Can we claim the credit for that too?"

"Of course," Ken said. "But please don't forget our little agreement. You charge Matheo Rousseau under his real name and make no mention of which company he was working for. That way, we protect the company's reputation. The company is a victim, not a perpetrator."

"Understood and respected, Monsieur. And I assume you two have never been here?"

"Never, although Monsieur de Nussac appears to have fallen over and had a nose bleed."

"Oh dear. These things happen though. Images of young children, you say? Don't worry, we'll help him to his feet."

"We may have to help him to his feet several times," one of the other officers said.

Ken and Harry watched and smiled as the four officers entered Yves-Marie's apartment and closed the door behind them.

"You lied in there," Harry said, still holding her

hand. "You told him we weren't going to report him to the police."

"I told him we weren't going to. We already had, so I wasn't lying. It was just a little slip of the tongue."

"You also said you'd been in prison. Have you been in prison, or was that another little slip of the tongue?"

Ken nodded. "I did spend a few weeks in prison, so that was true."

"What happened?"

"It's a long story."

"Did you share a cell with a bubba?"

Ken laughed. "I was in a military prison. A bubba wouldn't have survived there; he would have had his face ripped off. How's your hand?"

"Sore, but it was worth it." Harry looked up at Ken, stood on tiptoes and planted a kiss on his cheek. "Thanks for that money, Ken. I'll make sure my Mum gets it. Maybe it will help us mend some broken bridges."

Ken gave her a long hug. "I hope so, my dear friend. You deserve some good things in your life."

"I've got you and Florence and Tristan now. I'm sure it will all work out for the best."

"Not going back to the Isle of Man then?"

"I'll decide that when you do! Let's get out of here. I'm done with this crap."

As they reached the car, Ken asked, "By the way, what was the idea of making Yves-Marie cough up €150,000? Was that just a bit of token revenge?"

"No. When I was here in Saint Germain the other day, downloading stuff off Yves-Marie's business server, I had a little stroll to get back to the car. I saw something nice in a shop. I came back here when you and Florence were in Cléry, meeting Tristan's parents, and I bought it. I paid for it with my own money, but since we are making Yves-Marie pay for being a pervert, I thought I would add it to his bill instead. Your former brother-in-law has just reimbursed me."

"What was it?"

"Something for Florence."

"Something for Florence costing €75,000?"

"Not quite that much. They should have delivered it this afternoon."

Ken looked at her puzzled. "Harry, what have you done?"

She smiled. "I've never had any real friends in my life, who just accept me for who I am, Ken. You and Florence, and now Tristan too, don't criticise my faults. You try and help me deal with stuff without ordering me around and telling me what to do and how to do it. At school, the teachers used to just tell me to 'shut up.' Same thing for all my adult life. People either ignore me, look embarrassed or tell me to go away. But with you and Florence, it's like you tell my anxiety to shut up instead. I don't know how you do it, and I don't need to. That you can do it, and so effortlessly, is enough."

Ken nodded his acknowledgement. "It's all about liking people without wanting to change them, Harry."

“So I thought it would be nice to say thank you to Florence. Two weeks ago, she never knew me, now it’s like we’re best buddies — or have I imagined all that Ken? You must tell me, if I’ve imagined it.”

“No, Harry, you didn’t imagine it. Florence has huge admiration for the way you handle your difficulties, and so do I. Plus we’re both very fond of you. When you’re not shouting at me, or punching perverts in the face, you can be a nice person.”

Harry smiled again. “I think I will mark today on my iPad as a good day. Do you think Florence will like her surprise?”

“You haven’t told me what it is. What is it?”

No answer.

Three quarters of an hour later, as they walked through the door of Florence’s apartment, they came face to face with Tristan and Florence sitting side-by-side. Tristan had an arm around his mother’s shoulder. He smiled and held one finger in front of his lips. “Shhhhh, my Mum’s having a bit of a ‘moment’.”

Ken and Harry took in Florence. She was looking empty, like a vacuum had sucked out all her thoughts. Her face was washed blank with confusion. It was as if her reasoning couldn't turn fast enough to take in some information or other. Every muscle in her body had frozen. Amazement didn't adequately describe her features. It looked like someone had taken her spark of wonder and poured gasoline on it, turning it into a roaring flame. But the look of confusion couldn’t reflect what she was feeling inside. And when she saw Harry, there was a delicious moment when, little by little, a smile crept onto her face. As it spread, it stretched from one side to the other. She looked up at Harry and said, "It was you, wasn't it, Arree Laywiz?"

"Don't know what you're talking about," Harry said.

"This!" said Florence, jumping up and taking Harry by the hand. "This is what I'm talking about, Harriet Lewis." She dragged Harry, with Ken and Tristan following behind, into the dining room. Either side of the fireplace stood a pair of matching Louis XV bomb-fronted commodes.

Harry glanced to where the original commode had stood between the windows. The space was now empty. "Oh, you found a matching one, did you?"

Behind her, Ken whispered, "Poker face," to Tristan, who grinned.

Florence said, "Don't you 'oh, you found a matching one' me. If it was Ken's idea, he would have bought one from Ikea. If it was Tristan's idea, he would have searched his pocket for small change and found he didn't have enough. But, when Ken told me a bit about you, before you came here, he told me you were quite a wealthy young lady. So who else could have shelled out enough to buy the matching commode? It must have cost a small fortune."

"Are they a pair?" Ken asked.

"They are the originals, without a doubt. You've only got to examine the grain of the wood to see they came from the same veneer and those gilt bronze mounts are also original and made by the same craftsmen. And then you've got the Breche Violette marble top, extracted from Serravezza, in the Carrara region in Italy. The tops are two 'slices' of the same piece of marble. Everything about them says that these commodes are a perfect original pair, and have just been reunited."

"Nice, aren't they?" Tristan said, with a wide grin.

"Pack it in, you lot. Come on, Harry, it could have only been you."

"No way, Florence. I'm not very good with objects. I can have difficulty identifying things that look similar in shape."

Florence looked stumped for a moment. Then she smiled again. "But you took photos with your iPad, you crafty cow. If I got a Bible, would you swear on it that it wasn't you?"

"Yes, sure. I'm an atheist, so the Bible doesn't mean a thing to me."

Florence looked at Ken, who was mirroring Tristan's smile. "Tell me the truth, Ken, did Harry buy this?"

"The truth, Florence?"

"The truth."

"No she didn't. So far as I know, Harry has spent no money buying that piece of furniture."

"Well now I know you're lying because one of the men from the antique shop in St Germain who delivered it a little while ago said something about Arree Laywiz. I didn't understand what he meant, but was too shocked to ask him. It's how a non-English-speaking French person would pronounce Harry Lewis. Arree Laywiz – Harry Lewis."

"Vivid imagination."

"Vivid imagination, my arse."

"Doesn't mean she paid for it."

"Of course it does."

"Doesn't."

"Well who else could it have been?"

"Maybe your brother. Oh by the way, while I think about it, that €400,000 is in your account. You can transfer it to the executor of your grandparent's estate whenever you want."

"And your wine is in a commercial unit in Achères," Harry added. "The police are aware that you marked yours with your phone number, so you should get most of them back when they've finished their investigations."

Florence stroked the front of the commode and left her hand there, not wanting to let go. After one more look at it, she said, "Are you going to tell Tristan and me how it went down then?"

"With pleasure," Harry said. "We introduced Yves-Marie to Bubba!"

"And then you can tell me where this commode came from," Florence added, "because it's certain my brother didn't buy it for me."

# CHAPTER TWENTY-NINE

"This movie is dumb," Tristan said for the fifth time. "Can't we watch something different?"

"Don't be such a girl," Harry retorted. She wrapped her arms around his torso and hugged him close. "It's getting late. Are you tired?" she asked as his arms encircle her waist and his head lolled onto her shoulder.

"Just a little," he murmured with a tiny sigh. "I'm just so content with the way the day turned out. Buying Mum that commode was mega-generous, you know. Maybe it did end up with my uncle paying for it, but to begin with you bought it from the kindness of your heart. You're a nice lady."

Harry smiled a happy smile but said nothing. A few minutes later she felt Tristan's body relaxing and his soft regular breathing stirred the hair on her shoulder. According to him, it was all in the eyes, and Tristan had looked deep into her soul earlier in the day.

"I see it in your eyes," he had said. "The person you really are. There are times it gets lost, when you feel threatened. But despite your problems, there is something in your spirit that dances when you relax, like a fire giving just the right amount of warmth. Dad tells me that the flames can die too, when you are angry or uncertain. But he knows, and I know, that that isn't the real you. That's why I love to look into your eyes, to see the real Harriet Lewis. When I look at you, I see a brave lady who dares to embrace life despite almost insurmountable difficulties. And I know who you are."

That was earlier today, but Harry would never forget. This evening he had said even nicer things, which had made her blush. She looked down at his face. So much like his mother yet, curiously, so much of Ken in him too.

Tristan nudged closer, opened one eye and said, "Hey, it's me. What are you thinking? No, hang on, don't tell me, let me guess. You were thinking of me!"

Harry said, "Ha! You obviously don't know me if you think I care about you."

"I do know you, Harry. You're a cheeky mung and cheeky is good. Cheeky lets you be yourself. We laughed so much the other day when we were out at the shops. And I loved that. You make me happy and we seem to connect. Don't you feel that we connect? That's all we ever need to connect, you and me - just laughter and eyes, no words. If we were struck dumb our feelings would be just the same, you know."

"I admit, you do make me smile," Harry said. "That is why my suspicious nature trusted you before my mind had time to weigh you up. In time, maybe I will heal because trusting me to just be myself is therapeutic and you, your Mum, and your Dad are performing miracles."

"Harry, you are irreverent, funny, real as hell and

perfect with your idiosyncrasies. I can't explain my feelings for you because they're all confused. They're confused because I've never met anyone like you before. And I'm loving it. Maybe it's you who performs the miracles, not us."

"You're talking crap, little boy. It's your bed time isn't it?"

"Are you coming with me?"

Her breathing became softer, the pensive look melting into a smile as soft as the morning light. She had the feeling that she might at last be able to begin the task of putting the past behind her. Her body squirmed just a little as her muscles relaxed. Harry's heart thumped so hard that she swore it was audible. Their eyes met and Tristan smiled back. It was only a small smile, but it was enough to make her go weak in anticipation. There was something about that gaze of his that she thought she would never find in another man, as if in that moment their souls had made a bridge. "Sure," she whispered, "I'm coming with you. It's time we got to know each other a bit better. I'll show you my Dara Knot if you're really good."

# CHAPTER THIRTY

Florence pulled the duvet over their nakedness. "What happens when you leave?" she asked. "If my toes get cold, I won't be able to warm them on your back."

Ken turned and with a cheeky grin, followed by an even cheekier wink, said, "Maybe we could come to some arrangement."

Florence sat up. "Yes please Ken. Go on, I'm listening."

He paused. Then he said quietly, "But first we have to clear something up."

Florence hesitated. "Go on."

Ken's smile disappeared. "You may not want to see me again when I tell you what I have to say."

"That will never happen, Ken. I want you in my life, always."

Ken drew a deep gulp of air. A lump made a bid to establish itself in his throat. The elephant still wasn't dead. In fact, the grandfather of all elephants still loomed over him. Now it was either going to stamp all over him or lay down and die, and Ken didn't know which it would be. But he had to find out.

"We all have secrets," he said. "Most are guilty, a few are unpleasant and some are far too wretched and personal to share. But during the past two weeks, you and I have exposed almost every secret we ever had between us."

"Not almost, Ken; we've come out with all our secrets. There's nothing more to know."

"Oh but there is, Florence."

She looked at him with a puzzled expression. "There isn't, Ken, honestly. I have no more secrets. The elephants in the room have all gone."

"All except one. And it's a big one. In fact, it's bloody huge."

"What? What's the secret that's so big and bad?"

Ken gave a deep sigh. He rolled onto his back and stared at the ceiling. He watched it for a long time until it became obvious that he had stopped talking. When Florence prompted him to go on, he did so, still staring at the ceiling as he spoke. "I arranged the death of your lover, Jean-Luc."

"You what?"

"I arranged for the father of our son to be killed, Florence. A close friend of mine slit his throat and left him to die on a dusty road in a rural Pushtun village in eastern Afghanistan."

Florence grasped Ken's hand tight. Her mouth fell open, but no words came out.

"I'm not going to apologise for it, Florence. I hated Jean-Luc more than I ever hated anybody in my life. He was destroying my relationship with the woman

I loved."

"It takes two to tango," Florence whispered, finding her voice.

"I'm aware. And, looking back, I'm also aware that I was partly to blame, for spending too much time away from home. But I still saw Jean-Luc as the anti-Christ. I demonised him in my mind to such an extent that it obsessed me. That's why I reported him to my superiors. It's not the normal course of action in the armed forces. Normally, you sort out your own problems. And normally, I would have done. But I was uncertain what your reaction would be if I kicked the shit out of your lover. I was scared, Florence. Scared that you would leave with him."

"I would never have done that."

"But I didn't know that, did I?"

"No you didn't. We were going through a bad patch, you and me."

"I went through hell, not just a bad patch. You said you loved me and I took you at your word. You said I was your soul mate and you became part of the bedrock of my personality. Then one sunny day, under a cloudless sky, I discovered you were in love with someone else. It would have been kinder to have killed me."

"I didn't love him, Ken."

"That's not how it seemed to me at the time. I was filled with a bitterness I couldn't control. I would have seen him six feet under and walked away without shedding a single solitary tear, not one. But I never, ever stopped loving you. The girl I met in that bar, the one with the big eyes and the bigger heart, was infatuated by somebody else, And I was afraid, Florence. I was afraid that your infatuation would take root. But there it was. I was yesterday's news and he was the new beau. You held him close and made love to him. And all the while forcing me to smile and make small talk like I didn't know what was going on behind my back. In a situation like that, the hate doesn't ebb, Florence, it multiplies."

"Ken, we've been through this. I know I hurt you. I understand how much I —"

"I fantasised about what I would do if ever I got my hands on Jean-Luc alone. Not about reporting him to my superiors. It wasn't that kind of justice I wanted. My fantasies were always about what I would do to him. An eye for an eye, a tooth for a tooth, and a bullet in the head for a stolen wife. But that was never going to be practical. If I had killed him like that, the police would have started asking questions. It wouldn't have taken them long to find out that I had the best motive. All it would have done would have been to land me in prison and I'd lose again. So I began to think about having him removed while I was elsewhere with a perfect alibi." Again, Ken's voice quietened and he stopped talking.

"I'm so very sorry, Ken, for the hurt I have done to you."

"Shhhh. It's okay. It's over and I have no more anger or hatred left in me. I'm only telling you this so that you'll maybe understand why, even years after the two of you stopped seeing each other, I still hated Jean-Luc with every fibre in my body."

"I understand that Ken, I do."

"After they shipped Jean-Luc back to France, I made love to you with a renewed passion. It was almost as if I was reclaiming my territory. But I also carried on hating him. That, too, with a renewed passion because I loved you to the very fibre of my being and he had defiled that love. My only relief was the joy I felt when Tristan was born. And then, for three years, my life revolved around you and Tristan, until that day that he disappeared."

"That's when it all fell apart, wasn't it?"

"It is, Florence. The stress, for both of us, was too much to bear and, as you know, we drifted apart."

"But we're good now Ken, aren't we?"

"Let me finish my story and then you can decide."

Florence nodded.

"After you and I split up and you came back here to France, my mind started blaming everything on Jean-Luc. I even imagined he had been responsible for Tristan's abduction."

"As if," Florence whispered through tight lips.

"He became an obsession, Florence. I found myself with no wife, no son and I didn't have the compulsion or the will to start again. For the past sixteen years, I have jumped from one short-term relationship to another, not caring whether they lasted. Because the only people who ever mattered to me were you and Tristan."

Florence reached for a tissue from the night stand and wiped her eyes with a shaking hand. "Me too," she whispered, "Me too."

"Anyway, one June day in Afghanistan, I saw Jean-

Luc with a small French contingent. I hid behind a Warrior tank so he wouldn't see me. My mates, Dinger and Sparky were just behind me and asked me what the hell I was doing. I pointed Jean-Luc out to them and told them that I wanted him dead. They asked why, but I didn't tell them. We had only recently met up and they knew nothing at all of my past."

"So they killed him?"

"Yes, but not quite yes. That's not the whole story. That night at the bar, I had too much to drink. I suppose it was a reaction to seeing my nemesis. Dinger and Sparky pushed me to say why I wanted Jean-Luc dead, but I wouldn't tell them. I just told them that it was very important to me. In the end they left it alone, and they never did find out why. But the next morning, when we were all sober, they asked if I meant it. I could see that they intended to do it if I said yes."

"So you said yes?"

"I told them that something had gone on between Jean-Luc and me a few years before. I told them that if they were going to do anything, they would need to do it when I was somewhere else, just in case anybody decided to ask questions. But above all, I wanted Jean-Luc to know it was coming, and I wanted to see the fear in his eyes, and I needed to deliver that message myself."

"How did you do that?"

"I cornered him behind the barracks one night. He was strong, but my hatred was stronger. I told him that I wasn't a hero until he came after my wife; then it was war. I let him know in no uncertain terms that he had crossed the line and I wouldn't forget. To this day, I can tell you exactly what I said to him. 'I won't rest,' I said, 'until you're beaten. And I don't mean just beaten down, I mean dead. There isn't a place you can hide where I won't find you and destroy you. I don't care how it happens, I don't need you to suffer, I just need you extinguished from this planet.'

He laughed, even though I had him in a headlock and could have broken his neck with one twist. In a cold, calm voice, I said, 'You may think I am overreacting, but you underestimated how much I love Florence.' He laughed again. He knew that, by that stage, we had separated. 'Don't think I'll play by the rules,' I said. 'Love allows us to exterminate vermin that take our wives. I'm coming for you, Jean-Luc Courtemanche. Just know it.' Then I let him go and I walked away."

"So when did he die?"

"A few days later, the chance arose when I had to escort the bodies of some dead colleagues back to Brize Norton in Oxfordshire. I was going to be away for four days."

"And that's when they killed him?"

"They found his body with a stab wound in the back and his throat slit. That was a typical Taliban method. Nobody ever questioned that it wasn't the Taliban. Jean-Luc was bringing up the rear of a small patrol near a little village where they had urgent intel that a group of Taliban fighters were hiding. They went in to flush out the insurgents. It was a textbook operation. Single file, spaced well apart, scanning the side streets, rooftops, windows. Some shots rang out and everybody on the patrol took cover. Some dived into the nearest mud-brick house, some sheltered behind anything that would give them cover. Jean-Luc stepped behind the wall of an adobe house and never stepped out again."

"These two friends of yours killed him?"

"Dinger gave him the good news while Sparky was on the rooftop keeping the rest of the patrol's heads down by firing random shots in the air. The village was in the French area of control and it was Dinger and Sparky who had called in the false intel. They waited for the patrol to arrive and fired shots just as Jean-Luc was close to where Dinger was hiding. Dinger grabbed him, told him, 'This is from Ken,' and slashed his throat. Jean-Luc never saw it coming, but it took him a minute to bleed out while Dinger kept his foot on his back and held him face down in the dust. Dinger and Sparky were dressed as rag-head farmers so, when he was dead, they just walked away and merged with the goats. During the minute that the life was draining out of him, Jean-Luc knew exactly why he had been killed. Honour satisfied."

"Dinger is the man who just died, isn't he?"

"We put him to rest three weeks ago."

"Then the matter is closed."

"Is it, Florence? Is it closed?"

"What do you mean? Of course it's closed."

"But how do you feel about the fact that I ordered the execution of your lover?"

"I don't have to live with it, Ken; you do. But from my point of view, if I had known that he kidnapped our son, I would have killed him myself. I have no sympathy whatsoever for him. He stole sixteen years of our son's life from us. In doing so, he also stole our marriage from us - a marriage that we were rebuilding after my mistake. He deserved to die."

"So do you think you could learn to live with a killer?"

"When you were on assignment, you killed on behalf of the British government and I never questioned it. I knew that you were able to compartmentalise these things so they didn't affect our daily lives. That day, you killed on behalf of us and it isn't going to affect the way I feel for you now. I love you Ken Stafford. Always have and always will."

Ken rolled over so his face was above Florence's. He kissed her long and deep, with great tenderness.

When they came up for air, Florence asked, "Will it ever come back to bite you, Ken?"

"In what way?"

"Dinger is dead, but Sparky still knows what happened. Might he ever say anything?"

Ken laughed. "Never in a million years, Florence. Anyway, if he did, I would deny everything and he would condemn himself as an accessory to murder."

"And you never told him the truth about Jean-Luc? You never told him why you wanted Jean-Luc dead?"

"On the day we cremated Dinger, I told Sparky that I had once been married. Until then, he had no idea. I have never discussed Jean-Luc with him since the day I got back from Brize Norton and he and Dinger told me I owed them each a pint of beer. No drama. We keep our own secrets in Special Services. But this was one secret I had to tell you about if we are to make a fresh start."

"And are we, Ken? Are we going to make a fresh start?"

"Is that last elephant truly dead?"

"Deader than a dodo."

"So what do you think? Shall we make a fresh start?"

A tear of happiness rolled down Florence's cheek. "I think we should test out your stamina first. Come here, lover."

When he kissed her it was sweet and gentle, and it tasted of her tears. She wanted to speak but all she could do was whisper, "Don't go, not again." His mouth painted a soft smile and he nodded before folding her in his arms. One moment they were apart and the next they morphed into a single being. The warmth of his body met her nakedness, giving her hope. One of his hands clasped around her lower back, the other stroked her hair. With each soft touch more tears fell; tears that neither of them wiped away. After so many years they had the chance to make new memories, and wasting time wasn't on the agenda.

# ABOUT THE AUTHOR

Graham Hamer was born a few years before Queen Elizabeth came to the British throne (the second Queen Elizabeth, that is). One event was televised, one wasn't. His own event happened somewhere between England, Scotland, Ireland and Wales on a funny little island where the cats have no tails and the occasional witch still gets rolled down a steep hill in a spiked barrel. He left the Isle of Man to get a life. He got one. Then he went back. You'll find him there now if you know where to look.

Accountant, pig-herder (briefly), businessman, business analyst, web site builder – hell, writing's more fun

**Did you enjoy**

**WEB OF TANGLED BLOOD?**

**Leave a review!**

**THANK YOU** for choosing to read Web of Tangled Blood.

If you have enjoyed Web of Tangled Blood, it would be great if you could post a review on Amazon (and if you are addicted to Goodreads, a review there would also be fantastic). We may not judge a book by its cover, but we do judge a book by its reviews. Spreading the word by leaving a review inspires others to choose Web of Tangled Blood as their next read. I would love to hear what you think of the book. Thank you so much for your support.

All the best

Graham

**What next for Florence, Ken, Tristan and Harry?**

If you have enjoyed Web of Tangled Blood, you might like to follow up on our characters when many of them become part of another episode in our 'French Collection' series.

**Cenotaph for the Living** is next book in the series

The following books by Graham Hamer are also available or will be published shortly

**THE CHARACTERS COMPILATION**
**Chasing Paper** – Characters Compilation 1
**Walking on Water** – Characters Compilation 2
**Tommy Gee** – Characters Compilation 3
**The Zone** – Characters Compilation 4

**THE ISLAND CONNECTION**
**Under the Rock** - Island Connection 1
**Out of the Window** - Island Connection 2
**On Whom the Axe Falls** - Island Connection 3
**China in Her Hand** - Island Connection 4
**Devil's Helmet** - Island Connection 5
**The Vicar's Lot** - Island Connection 6
**Chicken Rock** - Island Connection 7
**The Platinum Pirate** - Island Connection 8
**Picasso's Secret** – Island Connection 9
**Travellers** – Island Connection 10
**Flint** - Island Connection 11

**THE FRENCH COLLECTION**
**Web of Tangled Blood** – French Collection 1
**Cenotaph for the Living** - French Collection 2
**Jasmine's Journey** - French Collection 3
**Taken on Face Value** - French Collection 4

**THE ODDBALL ODYSSEY**
**A Little Bit Odd** – Oddball Odyssey 1
**Odd Gets Even** – Oddball Odyssey 2
**A Little Bit Odder** – Oddball Odyssey 3

You can find out more about the author and his books at
**http://www.graham-hamer.com**

Printed in Poland
by Amazon Fulfillment
Poland Sp. z o.o., Wrocław

64192345R00192